ALL
THINGS
LEFT
WILD

ALL THINGS LEFT WILD

A NOVEL

JAMES WADE

**BLACK
STONE**
PUBLISHING

Copyright © 2020 by James Wade

Published in 2020 by Blackstone Publishing

Cover and book design by Kathryn Galloway English

Printed in the United States of America

First edition: 2020

ISBN 978-1-982601-05-8

Fiction / Literary

1 3 5 7 9 10 8 6 4 2

CIP data for this book is available
from the Library of Congress

Blackstone Publishing

31 Mistletoe Rd.

Ashland, OR 97520

www.BlackstonePublishing.com

For Jordan

PROLOGUE

Two barn swallows hopped and danced between thin branches in a grove of tangled salt cedar, never getting too close or too far from one another. It was as if their movements were circumscribed by some choreography they were born knowing, and should either decide to quit the routine, the other would surely die of incertitude, and the world would become in an instant a less balanced place.

I watched them, turning away from the sad scene in front of me. The cemetery wasn't much to look at, unless you were needing to look at wood crosses and chewed-up dirt. There were a few rocks. Somebody had tried to set up a little fence around the graves and their markers, but it didn't take and now there were old posts lying about on the ground like bodies waiting to be buried themselves.

Fall was late in coming, but the morning air was crisp, and the baked brown grass held onto the dew as long as it could, fighting the rising sun over water rights. The land sloped down into town and the trail up the hill was covered in greasewood and flowered yucca, and the preacher had spoken of the beauty of the morning and the wonder of eternity and all that it held. Beyond the plots the trail gave out, like some woebegone spirit too tired to continue, and there the sumac grew thick and would oftentimes mantle the valley with its perfumed scent. Higher still, the earth pitched itself toward the sky and borne upon it were the juniper and pine of the high country and out from amongst them he rode, atop the old bay horse he'd given to her when they married.

I saw him there on the ridge. He sat his horse like a drunk, slightly slumped and tilting off to one side. He was a drunk. The preacher spoke to the part about life everlasting, but he was too far away to hear. He was too far away for anything.

He had on a black coat and he'd taken off his hat and there he sat in reverence and in sobriety. I turned back to the preacher, and when he was finished I scanned the ridge again and there was nothing and no one and the service had ended.

I smoothed my hair back and pulled my hat down firm over top it and the few dozen people shrouded in black began to all move as one, trudging toward the cheap pine coffin in a manner withdrawn, sending up muffled prayers, wondering about rain and war and if it was too late for breakfast. They nodded at us or gave half-hearted smiles or both. There were hands on our shoulders and pats on our backs. Some offered kind words. Others offered food. We watched them go.

"He was settin' up there on that ridge," Shelby said. "Just past the tree line."

"I know," I told him.

"You seen him?"

"I did."

"Well?" he asked.

"Well what?"

"What do you think?"

"What do I think about what?"

"Nothing, I guess." Shelby walked toward the line of mourners as they filed down the hill, and he stopped midway and turned and stared for a while at the tree line, then walked on.

I stood and watched as the gravediggers lowered her down and filled in the dirt, and when they were finished I stood some more. I didn't want to go back to the house yet, not even to change clothes.

I walked out from the graveyard and followed a well-trod deer path to Red Creek and sat in the grass. The morning sky glowed golden behind a bank of blue-gray clouds, a quiet caution to the world's awakening.

The sun was distancing itself from the horizon line, but the clouds had yet to burn off, leaving the eastern half of the world to be filtered through an orange tint. The creek moved slowly, matching the pace of the morning, the water shining pale pink, and on its surface, a bleeding reflection of the world.

A cat-squirrel duo on the far side of the creek were hard at play with some game I could not follow. They barked at one another or at me or at nothing, then in fits and starts they hopped from one tree to the next, clinging to the bark with their arms and legs splayed in an almost sacrificial manner.

A siege of herons passed overhead. The long-legged shorebirds flew beneath the lowest clouds and I saw them and they me and it would be months before they returned north, passing again along the same sky.

I watched them glide across the morning, unencumbered by the changing of the times, following the flight of their fathers and their fathers' fathers, all the while unburdened by such things as doubt and desire. Participating by blood. Born into decisions made long ago and born knowing, but not knowing why. I envied the certitude of their existence. I longed for the conviction of those like my mother who, despite all to the contrary, could maintain a faith in the way of things, holding tight to a structured and resolute reading of every breath until her last.

Instead, at a moment I couldn't recall, or perhaps in a series of built-upon moments, I accepted ambivalence and unease, and there inside of me they did remain in some dogged cellar of the soul, determined that I should never know peace or certainty again.

* * *

I walked into Longpine and into the Tanglefoot and sat at the bar while a table of men in the corner played cards.

"You ain't old enough to drink," the bartender said. I knew his face.

"I hadn't even asked yet."

"I'm sorry about your momma and all, but I ain't gonna serve no kid."

"Alright, well I reckon I'm old enough to just set for a while."

The man took a swipe at the countertop with an old rag, then flung it across his shoulder. It rested there as natural as if it had been born of the man and so cradled its entire life.

"I won't kick you out, if that's what you're asking."

"I'm not asking anything," I said, and then I stood and walked out.

I walked around back to the livery and leaned with both hands on the top of the gate and a boot raised up against the low post. I watched the horses and talked to them and called them by names that weren't their own, but they answered anyway.

An old dog was laid up in the shade of the stable roof, his feet kicked out in front of him from on his side and he made yipping noises, and as he got closer to whatever he was chasing he started to growl and the whole time I stood there he never opened his eyes.

My mother talked in her sleep, toward the end. She whispered things. Called out names I knew and names I didn't. Sometimes she talked so clearly, and maybe she was even awake, but she never remembered later. I wondered if my mother found the people she was looking for, or would she wake up like the dog and find herself covered in dirt and the whole chase just a dream.

"Figured I'd find you here," Shelby said. "Anything good?"

"Shep's got his paint horse yonder. Mustang or two I hadn't seen before."

"Probably goes with them boys in there dealing cards."

"You been inside?"

"Old Moss told me you come in wanting a drink."

I shook my head.

"Hell, I can get you a drink, little brother, just let me know," he said.

"I didn't want a drink then, and I don't want one now."

"Suit yourself."

Shelby spit and slipped a flask from his boot and took a pull and stretched his mouth out.

"How come it is folks wear black at a funeral?" I asked, still watching the horses mill about the stable inspecting one another and their surroundings.

"Couldn't say."

"Well, why do you think?"

"Shit, son, I got no idea. It's just what you do."

"I think it's to hide the fear," I told him.

"What fear? What are you even talking about?"

"I think folks are afraid of dying."

"At a funeral?"

"All the time. I think they're always afraid of dying and a funeral makes them think about it more than they might otherwise."

"What's that got anything to do with wearing black?"

"I been thinking about that—"

"Aw hell, he's been thinking," Shelby said and rolled his eyes.

"I have. I been thinking everybody says there's a big white light when you die. And everybody says Heaven is a bright, pretty place."

Shelby drank again from his flask and screwed the cap back on and let it drop back into his boot.

"Alright, I'm with you."

"Well, what if they ain't so sure about all that? And so when somebody dies, they all dress up in black, thinking if they can make this world look darker, the next one might seem brighter no matter what."

"Christ Almighty, Caleb, are you sure you ain't had nothing to drink?"

"I haven't."

"Maybe you ought to," he said.

"I figure a bunch of them people today were crying, and how come? They didn't even hardly know her. But they was crying."

"Folks can't cry?"

"I think they were crying 'cause they know they're gonna die."

"Hell, we're all gonna die."

"That's what I'm saying."

"What?"

"Never mind."

"You're wearing me out, little brother. This ain't what I came to talk to you about."

"Why'd you come?"

Shelby looked around and we were alone, and about that time the dog raised up his head and double-checked.

"I got a plan," he said, unable to contain his grin.

I stood watching the dog struggle to its feet, shaking off sleep and disappointment.

"Well," Shelby said.

"Well what?"

"Goddamn, ain't you gonna ask me what it is?"

"I figured you was about to tell me."

"I am."

"Go on then. If you're waiting on me, you're already behind."

"We're gonna rob Randall Dawson."

I nodded. The dog trotted off, his tongue falling from the side of his mouth.

"What do you say?" Shelby asked, grinning again.

"I say you need to slow down on that whiskey."

He tossed his head, dramatic, and put his hands on his hips.

"C'mon, Caleb, that rich sumbitch ain't gonna miss a few horses."

"Oh, horse thieves is it?"

"He cost Daddy his job."

"Daddy cost himself his job, and please don't tell me this is about him. He ain't coming back."

"He was there today. We seen him."

"And by God, where is he now?"

"We could do it, little brother," Shelby said, ignoring my question. "I got it all planned."

"I'll just bet you do."

* * *

That night my brother went to work at the bar, tending to the needs and whims of cutthroats, gamblers, and local drunkards. He'd worked at the Tanglefoot since our father decided it was too burdensome to be both a lawman and an alcoholic, him choosing the latter.

With Momma sick, Shelby was left to grow up at the feet of society's worst, and maybe it was a sad situation or maybe he was always destined to find the shadowed figures no matter what path he walked.

It was his eighteenth birthday the day we buried her. I'm not sure he even knew.

I walked into the empty house for the first time, or at least the first time I could recall. The door swung shut behind me with the help of the wind, and I stood there in the dark, unsure of what to think, let alone what to do. My heart quickened for no reason I could place. I took a step back and leaned against the door and put my hand to my chest. My throat was closing and I was dying—I was sure of it. I steadied myself and walked to the cupboard and felt in the dark for the water jug. I drank and took a deep breath and drank again. I took off my hat and leaned into the wash sink and emptied the jug over my head. I stayed there, dripping and breathing, until I figured I wasn't dying anymore.

I wiped my face and hair with a dish towel and crossed through the kitchen and gave a look into the living room like maybe somebody would be there, but they weren't. I paused at the foot of the hallway and looked again, just to be sure. Her room was across from the back porch, and I could feel the cool of the night coming in through the wire screen. I went into the room and sat on the edge of the bed and folded my hands into my lap, and the mattress was indented on her side and I looked down at it and put my hat back on.

There were rolled cigarettes on the low-set table by the bed. I leaned over and picked one up and examined it, then set it back in the same place, as if anyone would notice otherwise. I rose and moved to the closet and opened the door and stared into the dark and took a step forward, then backed out and closed it again and walked and stood in the hall with the whistling wind. I felt my own pulse, then regarded again the room as it stood, untouched by all but death. Through the frame I saw it and tried my best to commit it to memory, and also her, knowing I would never see either again.

I

The boy was dead and the winds came up out of Mexico angry-like, pushing north over the mountains, sweeping into the desert below, picking up the dirt and moving it across the plain with the ease of a brush stroke on canvas. They howled and sang and the prickly pear and yucca clung to the earth, where their stunted limbs danced in motions aberrant.

The winds spilled into the dry, rocky arroyo, where even our shadows were covered in dust. I pulled my shirt up over my mouth and nose, and Shelby fussed with tying his bedroll and in it the sand and sentiment of the storm.

We put our stolen horses and our backs against the bank of the ditch and pieces of dead cholla and cactus came down with the dust and peppered our hats like a mutant rain. The horses sneezed and stomped, and I loosened the bridle bits and talked to them and made promises I planned to keep but we'd seen, the horses and me, what happens to plans.

"This ain't good cover," Shelby said, and it wasn't.

He pulled his shirt over his face, and we turned the horses up the draw and out into the mess. Shelby pointed and I saw the canyon and nodded. We led the animals across the plain and the wind seemed to blow harder, as if it had seen us.

We pressed forward over the cracked earth with the wind at our back, sweeping past us and flattening our clothes to our skin on its way east into the San Rafael Valley. We circled the ravine until we found a passable trail.

There was a creek bed without much water but the horses drank anyway, and we waited until the winds died with the sun before moving on.

Things were different at night, cold and still and dark, and when the clouds burned off, the stars were still there as they'd been since before we began shining lights back at them. They scalded the night sky in their dying, and when they fell we whispered wishes to ourselves for things only the stars might understand.

We bore south and east and followed a path beaten by cattle, letting the horses decide their steps. They knew better than us, the horses, in the dark and in general. When the ride was too long we ate fruit from a tin and Shelby made the fire while I tied and tended the animals. I loosened the straps of the saddles and ran my hand along the sides of their bellies, and their breathing was strong and slow. I told them they had done well and I touched their faces and said I was sorry for everything that happened. I fed them without rationing, as if extra oats could right the world's wrongs. I carried both saddles, one atop the other, and along with them the blankets from the horses' backs, and the stirrups drug in the dirt as I came upon the fire.

I looked at my brother and wondered what he was thinking, now and always, and this time I asked him. He looked at me with the load of gear in my arms and laughed and said he was thinking about how much money I could make as a pack mule.

"Keep laughing," I told him. "Maybe you can joke your way out of that noose they're getting ready for us."

After things had gone sideways at the Dawson Ranch, we'd made south through the territory, expecting someone to follow, but no one did. We had no plan save what Shelby would decide each morning and mostly it was the same.

"Let's keep heading south," he'd say, and we'd bury the fire while our stomachs grumbled.

We followed the earth's shelf down from the rim country and into the desert valley below. We passed Phoenix, staying to the east, and chanced a stop in Tucson for supplies. We had only the money we'd set out with before the robbery. And for the boy's life we had only the two horses we rode. Things had not gone in accordance with Shelby's plan.

We left Tucson with a sack full of tinned fruit and some dried beef and headed further into the desert.

* * *

"You sure ain't said much," Shelby told me, our horses trotting through the waxy candelilla of the lowlands the day after the windstorm.

"What am I supposed to say?"

"Hell, I don't know, anything. Something about the weather, maybe."

"It's hot."

"Yessir, it is that."

We rode on, but silence was not much of a strength for Shelby, no matter the circumstance.

"You reckon Philadelphia stands a chance against Chicago in the World Series?" he asked. "I saw in the paper in Tucson where they'll be matching up."

"I don't care."

"It ought to be a good one."

"Alright."

"What are you so sore at, little brother?"

I pulled up on the horse and Shelby made a circle and did the same and there we set in the middle of the desert in the middle of the day, sweat pouring from our bodies and with it any righteousness we'd ever known.

"He's dead," I said.

"Who's dead?"

"That boy is dead, and you want to talk about baseball?"

"Well it ain't gotta be baseball. We could talk about boxing, but I didn't really want to get started on that nigger Johnson. I promise you if they give ol' Jeffries a rematch—"

"Stop. Just quit opening your mouth." I spit into the dirt and put the horse forward and Shelby scowled and followed.

"You better watch how you talk to me, son," he said. "Outlaws turn on their partners all the time. That's a fact."

"We ain't outlaws."

"Sure we are," he said. "We're the Bentley Brothers, known far and wide as the most dangerous guns west of the Mississippi. Hell-bent on living a life full of adventure, stealing horses and the hearts of women, and riding them both as long as it suits us."

"And you'd like that life?" I asked.

"I might even steal me one of them Ford motor buggies."

"You wouldn't even know how to go about it."

"I bet I could I figure it out."

"You realize Dawson probably has every marshal in the territory hunting us? We're gonna hang. You understand that, don't you?"

Shelby shrugged.

"I ain't got no problem killing a marshal," he said. "But if it makes you feel better, how 'bout we just make it into Mexico, find us a little ranch to work on. Piquito ranchero, I believe they call it. Then we can be real vaqueros instead of outlaws. How 'bout that?"

"Look yonder," I said, pointing.

Dust drifted up from an old wagon road crossing east to west below us. Men on horses moved past like miniature figurines, the dust trailing them as they rode. There was no sound.

"What?" Shelby asked.

"Might be a posse. Might be hunting us."

Shelby laughed.

"You read one too many of them dime novels, little brother."

We set and watched the riders as they dismounted and moved into the brush along the road and then were back on the horses and moving down the trail and dismounting again, searching for something.

"Still," Shelby said, "I guess it's best we steer clear."

* * *

We rode past the Papago Indian Reservation and into the Coronado Forest. We wound our way through Santa Cruz, watering the horses at stock tanks and creek beds. We passed only game hunters and tree dwellers, gruff folks who eyed us with suspicion and madness.

There was no rain. The days fell hard upon my skin, which burned and peeled and burned again. I imagined it a precursor to Hell, and during the long rides with little water I became convinced whatever god controlled the sky was surely showing me my future eternal.

Whether Shelby felt remorse, I could not say, but in the end it was not him who'd murdered the child. And so it was my soul, beyond saving, that was bound to navigate the everlasting flames of the underworld. Never seeing my mother again.

We made no fires at night, and the heat from the day was chased away by an urgent cold that sank into my bones, and I shivered in and out of dreams. I saw her face and the face of my father and the face of the boy. They were each one set against dark clouds and a rolling thunder. When lightning struck, the faces were illuminated and I could see they weren't all the way human. They were ever-changing, like portraits with dripping paint, and their mouths were open wide like they were screaming, but I heard only the storm.

2

The sky darkened and there were naught but bones and Randall felt them and saw them—his own bones aching and Harry's resting in the box—and the rain was like a crawling shadow on the mountains beyond. The site was slanted and covered in desert spoons, which were Harry's favorite, likely because of their name, and the gathering storm sent ahead its wind so that the tall plants might bow before it. Randall's body mimicked their contortions. With the shovel he lurched toward the dirt, the blade piercing the earth again and again, and the wind carrying the sounds of his mother's whimpers. He swore he heard the pounding of hooves, but when he looked up all was still and bracing. His mother's head was lowered in grief and tears, but his wife stared straight ahead with no emotion to be discerned. Randall watched her until her eyes found his, and he saw there a hollowness to rival any canyon, and she turned away as the first drops of rain turned dark brown on the dust before him.

Some of the ranchmen had come, and others had stayed behind at the barracks. Randall had not required attendance, though he doubted the difference that would have made. As the rain began to fall in earnest, the men replaced their hats and started a staggered and premature dispersion. None offered their help, and Randall hated them all and drove the shovel down with a violence he was not accustomed to. His hands bled against the wooden end and his back and shoulders were afire. He saw in the distance several head of cattle making for a mesquite grove to wait out the storm. Above them the sky fractured and cracked and the herd called out to him or to one another or to God as the dirt went to mud, slick and unbalanced.

Among those gathered stood a boy Randall recognized. A boy, inexplicably called Tadpole, who had been a friend to Harry during the lonesome days on the ranch. He still held his hat across his chest and was the only one to do so, and his lips trembled so that he might not cry and show weakness to the older men around him.

The preacher had been delayed on account of the weather and so it was Randall, covered in mud and rain, who spoke the words of the Lord to the few souls who yet remained.

"In the sweat of thy face shalt thou eat bread, till thou return unto the ground; for out of it wast thou taken: for dust thou art, and unto dust shalt thou return. Amen."

"Amen," whispered a few.

"Harry was a good boy," Randall said, then paused. "A good boy who loved horses—" His voice cracked and so too did the thunder. ". . . horses and his family and . . . he was only trying to do what was right. Trying to protect us."

Randall began to sob. "I should have protected him," he cried, and with a muted lurching the coffin came unsettled from the stunted hill.

It slid into the hole and Randall, falling backward, narrowly avoided its path. The wood crashed below and Randall's mother screamed and the lid splintered and snapped, and Harry's body spilled out into the mud and pooling water. Randall dove, splashing into the grave, and picked up his son and held him close and rocked and cried. His wife stood straight and stern and unchanged.

* * *

The storm since passed, Randall was on the great porch and looking out at the land, his land, where always his father claimed the future of their family lay. And how right he had been, Randall thought, and a rainbow came and the cattle returned across the mesa and he felt his wife by his side.

Joanna was the daughter of a highly regarded doctor in the bustling metropolis of Philadelphia, and he a budding poet—so said those who cared of such things. He used the words of his father and his grandfather before him to speak of a West he could barely remember. As a boy he'd ridden a horse, he knew, and once stalked a great elk with his grandfather, but he'd grown up in academies along the East Coast and had learned table manners instead of survival skills. Still, his inexperience did not dilute his romanticism of the wild spaces that lay beyond the setting sun and with his words he entertained and entranced the young girl. He promised a life of adventurous splendor and did so with all the confidence and naivety of the soldier yet to see battle, and in the end his tenderfoot notions had betrayed them both.

His grandfather, the esteemed commander Lieutenant Travis Dawson, hero of the Mexican War, had been given land in the new territories of the Southwest as a grant from the United States. His grandfather would often say the government hoped the Apaches would kill him off, so as it could take back the lands once they proved fertile for cattle. Instead of only his own fresh scalp, the lieutenant brought to the Southwest a group of renegade soldiers who wanted no part in the coming conflict between the states. In exchange for parcels of his land, they helped Dawson drive back the Apaches and established several ranches in parts of the Arizona and New Mexico Territories—the greatest being Longpine, which soon became a boomtown of sorts.

When the Civil War did come, covering the country in a dark ritual of familial bloodletting, Dawson and his comrades had no qualms enriching themselves through cattle trade to both the Union and Confederate armies. The territories followed the violent example of their creator and divided themselves during the war. Dawson, being perhaps the most well known of the pioneers at the time, was asked by a newspaperman from Taos which side he supported.

"I will take no side save that which furthers my fortune," his quote read. "And should there be a man obliged to point out my sin and greed, I would say to him: I have served the United States in its wars, now I will let its wars serve me."

The lieutenant's son, Randall's father, had been raised in a boys' school in Baltimore but was summoned West before the war in an attempt to keep him away from the fighting. During his first five years in the territory Edmund Dawson had taken a wife, lost an arm to a poisoned Apache arrow, and been appointed as a delegate to the newly reunited states. Despite having a wife who had fallen into depression after losing two children before birth, Edmund was a successful statesman and made the harrowing trip to and from Washington, DC, with growing regularity. Randall was born while his father was away in the spring of 1878 and by the time he was of schooling age the two switched places, Randall taking up residence at Mormont Boys Academy in Philadelphia and his father returning to the territory with a dream of statehood.

He wrote Randall frequently, describing the majesty of the West and the unbridled opportunity of expansion and wealth. It was poetic and it called to Randall, and so he read and wrote of these spectral visions in his mind. Whether they were memory or fantasy or some crude conjunction of the two, he could not say. He knew only that his destiny, like that of his country's, would be found among the red rock and deep canyons of the storied frontier.

* * *

"You brought this upon me." Joanna's words were glazed in a frost, and when he turned to her she would not face him. "You gave me nothing save death and hardship and then at long last there he was and he was mine and you let them take him away."

"Joanna, we must not—"

"You let them take him," she cried and there was a craze in her voice, and Randall thought of the child that was never born as they'd first journeyed west, and the girl taken by fever only days after entering a world that wouldn't keep her. They'd tried many times and nothing would take, and then there was Harry and he brought back a light once lost and now lost again, perhaps forever.

"I am sorry, Joanna, truly," he said, and his own grief burrowed inward as his nature was to tend to hers instead.

"I don't want your apologies. I don't want your ranch or your cows or your goddamn poems. I don't belong here," she wept and looked to be on the verge of collapse, but before Randall could move to embrace her she stiffened again.

"You don't belong here," she said, flat. "This is a cold, wild place, and for better or worse you are neither."

"What do you want?" he asked and there was an urgency in his asking and she heard it and she looked at him and answered.

"I want you to kill them. I want you to find those boys and I want you to kill them for killing your son. My son."

"What?" he asked, having expected a plea to go back east for a visit or even for good. Though he knew it to be inappropriate he was close to laughter at the thought. "I've already sent word to Sanford in Texas."

Joanna turned away again and folded her arms and was silent and this caused him to continue. "The brothers Bentley were seen headed south and with the political upheaval along the borderlands they will surely turn east. There are two marshals, very fine lawmen, in New Mexico who are no stranger to our family, and Sanford's Rangers are camped just a few days' ride into the Texas plains. They will have nowhere to go."

Still there was silence and again Randall attempted to talk the shadows away from his wife's soul.

"Darling, you can't possibly believe I'm better equipped to hunt these men than a trained officer of the law."

There was movement and Randall hoped it was a spark of reason and she turned to him once more.

"I do not believe you better equipped," she told him. "I do not believe you remotely equipped for this or any other action outside of scribbling falsities on parchment, but I do believe—I know—that it was your son they killed. Your son. Not Sanford's or his Rangers' or any other man's. Yours. And I also know that I cannot bear to live another day with a man who would not seek to avenge his own son. That is what I know with God as my witness, Randall. Your line has been broken, and though it pains me greatly I will try again to give you another son but not until you have set this right, do you understand? You set it right, Randall. You set it right for our Harry."

And then the tears came and again he moved to embrace her but she pushed him away and retreated into the house, and he was left alone with a soft wind and the faraway howling of a single coyote calling out for anyone to answer.

3

We were two days through Santa Cruz, keeping the river as a barrier to our west, when we came to the border. We crossed a few miles east of the Sonoran city of Zorrilla. The river was shallow, its current weak. The land on either side mirrored the other, two halves of an equal world.

We rested the horses, then led them up the southern bank and onto a ridge overlooking the new country. We stayed on the ridge, bearing west until we chanced across a bygone path too narrowly trodden for cattle and followed it away from the river and across the salt flats and into the wastelands.

When one trail gave out another started up, and even in this remote and uncultivated landscape there were signs of those who'd come before, those who'd carved out from the desert their own bearing and set forward across the plains and lived in ways followed and ways abandoned, all the while a reminder that no course is left uncharted, no lesson learned of its own accord but rather taught. Always taught. And in these observations, be they fruitful or sterile, we can see only what we're shown. The world builds of itself, knowledge carried and stacked like bricks and with such heights, such illimitable reaches before us. And so we are forever engaged in the quest for the greater, our ambitious eyes blinded to the footprints of our ancestors and the bones and dust left behind and also ahead, and so on in rhythm, in pounding percussion.

Still we forge onward, as if ours were the first world, as if we alone by our very existence are inimitable across the vastness of the universe, and in doing so we elevate our own creations to undeserving positions of power and importance. And for all that is ennobled there are those left lowly, those who are bound to carry upon their bent spines the worries of a burning world—a world which will rise again from the ashes and bury its transgressions shallow, in graves overflowing, and set about the search for a new fire, so all might burn once more.

The matrix of intersecting game trails and old Indian bridle paths and the decisions made therein brought us at last to the prominence overlooking Zorrilla. The outskirts of the town lay desolate and depraved upon the desert, and were it not for the crude homesteads, the scene could have easily belonged to some lost world, some fallen kingdom.

I put the horse forward and we navigated the unstructured placement of a half-dozen hovels and lean-tos, each shack more tumbledown than the last. From one such structure came a three-legged dog, not much larger than a newborn kid, and the small creature commenced to yapping and bouncing about. My horse, none too impressed, studied it as we moved on. Two women, one old and one not, crouched over stained buckets and shucked corn. They looked up as I passed, and I stopped my horse and touched my hat. The old woman paid me no mind, but the younger one rose and walked out to meet me. Her hands on her hips, she looked up at me as if I were some oddity to behold.

"Hola," I said.

She nodded.

"Hola."

"Dónde es saloon?" Shelby shouted and the girl backed away.

* * *

We moved through the shanties and back onto the plains.

"We're Mexicanos now, bud," Shelby said, taking off his hat and waving it in celebration. His shouts and yips carried across the Sonoran Desert and died before reaching the horizon.

I stayed quiet.

Dark clouds moved in, robbing the world of light. Within minutes the rains were falling, and Shelby and I moved the horses into a thick canebrake near some offshoot of the big river.

"Think it'll flood?" he asked.

I shook my head.

"River was too low to start with."

He nodded.

The rain came and would that it could wash away our sins. Instead it only turned the dirt to mud and sent all manner of creatures, good and evil, seeking whatever shelter might be had. Water pooled at the rim of my hat and hesitated there, as if unsure what to make of this newfound freedom, then continued on to the ground, where it was lost to the silt and slush of a saturated truth.

We slid off the horses and held blankets over our heads. The horses shifted in the thicket and searched for some comfort that wasn't there.

"Did you hear that?" Shelby hollered at me through the drumming of the rain.

I turned my eyes out toward the plain and listened.

The storm crawled along overhead en route to the places we'd come from, and through the sheets of water it dumped upon the land I heard first one faint cry and then another.

"You hear it?" Shelby asked again and I held up my hand.

The dull bass of a drum permeated the air around us. We squinted from under our blankets but saw only a faded country masked by rain.

The drumming grew closer and less muted and soon shapes began to move through the curtains of water. Men appeared, maybe seven or eight. They marched in a single column with the drummer at one end and a man carrying a small, crudely sewn Mexican flag at the other. They stood straight, their drenched uniforms sticking to their bodies. They slogged through the mud and the rain as if neither were there, as if they were spirits upon the land, answerable to nothing and no one save the phantom force which commanded them only to march, as if they had been called down by the old gods of this country to turn back these gringos, these intruders who already took too much of the land belonging to their ancestors.

Shelby and I looked at one another and back at the men. They halted, facing the river, fifty yards from where we stood. One of the men stepped forward from the others and turned and shouted something at them. He then spun and again faced the river.

"Rendirse, rebeldes!" the man cried.

There was no answer.

"Rendirse!" he repeated, the men behind him standing motionless, rifles shouldered and faces forward.

"What in the hell do you reckon is happening?" Shelby asked.

"Couldn't say."

"What's he saying?"

"Hush."

Then from out of the brake more ghosts emerged, these even less human than the last. Three of them, wearing tattered clothing and no hats. Only one had both shoes. They trudged forward, defeated, with their hands in the air.

The shouting man beckoned them to come closer, and they did and he spoke to them at some length and a few times patted them on the shoulder and the back. Then the man lowered his head and shook it in a slow, dramatic fashion, as if some grave disappointment had befallen him. The man returned to the column and stood nearest the drummer and raised his arm in the air. The soldiers brought their guns to the ready and the ragged men stood facing them, their chins in the air.

"Madero!" one of the men screamed into the falling rain.

"Madero!" the other two called.

"Díaz!" answered the leader of the soldiers, and he brought down his arm and the soldiers fired and the three men jerked and twitched and collapsed into the mud and onto one another, and we held tight to our spooked horses as they stomped and tore at the tall canes surrounding us.

The soldiers reloaded, approached the dead men, and fired another round into them. The leader then went about stripping them of what little belongings they had. When it was over, the soldiers marched back out across the plain and east toward La Morita. The flag flapped in the wind and the rain and pulled at the stick it was fastened to. As the soldiers began to fade from our sight, the cloth came loose and whipped into the air and hung there for one stolen moment before it was beaten down into the mud by the relentless rain.

* * *

When at last the storm moved on, I walked out from the river and to the bodies left lying there. I stared down at them. They had fallen in positions unnatural, or at least unnatural to the living.

"Bring me a plate," I called to Shelby, and while the ground was still soft I dug shallow graves and the digging was slow and, in the humidity, torturous.

"You ain't making much headway, son," Shelby said. He was chewing on the last of our dried meat.

"Go quicker if you grabbed that other plate and helped."

"Shit, we just bought them plates in Tucson," he replied. "I ain't as eager as you to go ruining mine on account of some dead Mexicans."

"They ought to be buried."

"They ought not have pissed them soldiers off, I reckon."

"This from the outlaw," I said.

"Well, then they ought not have got caught. That sit better?"

"I hope that boy got a good burial."

"It sure as hell wasn't no open casket," Shelby said, laughing.

"You're a real sumbitch, you know that?"

I went back to my work. When I was through, I rolled the bodies into the holes and apologized to the men for not having dug deeper and then I filled in the mud and stacked stones from the river to mark each man. Perhaps I should have spoken some words or a prayer, but I doubted God was listening so instead I just said, "I'm sorry," and I was.

* * *

We rode out that evening, cutting through the old disputed lands along the border, headed for the San Pedro River and then Agua Prieta. Shelby said he knew some gambler there who could help us get settled. I was forever hesitant but always agreeing in the end.

We rode past the sun as it set behind us and we listened to the coyotes call, and as night began to fall the jackrabbits would dart from one mesquite bush to the next, never quite assured in their own safety, never finished running.

We put the horses into the San Pedro at noon the next day and the cold water was a welcome relief to all involved as the sun continued to tear through October with no sign of slowing. The third day after the river we came to a mature paloverde tree. It grew on a short hill, shading cacti and scrub brush scattered beneath it. Its green bark split near the roots to allow for multiple trunks which rose up and out and splintered into smaller branches. The tree itself was not twenty feet, and any sturdy limbs were much lower still. Yet from one of the branches hung a naked man, his bare feet only inches from the ground. His neck did not look broken, but the rope had strangled him, and in case it hadn't, he was full of bullet holes, the half-dried blood running down his exposed legs. His face was swollen and his eyes bulged and across his chest hung a slapdash sign written in blood onto a slab of mesquite bark and fastened with a thin string: Viva Madero. Viva México.

Shelby looked around and we saw no one approaching nor anyone fleeing.

"That old boy look familiar to you?" he asked, spitting into the blood which had pooled just below the man's feet.

"Looks different without his uniform," I said.

"Wonder where the rest of 'em are at."

The answer came to us slowly, one rope at a time. The Sonoran Desert was not conducive to hanging trees, but the men who'd killed the soldiers made do. Each tree we passed held a new body and each body held a sign.

"Lord have mercy, son, these boys mean business," Shelby said as we rode past the seventh tree. The man swung and the branch bent and creaked and then snapped and came crashing down alongside the body.

"You gonna bury all these fellas, too?" he asked.

I didn't answer.

"Something's going on. And whatever it is, it ain't good."

Later in the day we came perpendicular to a road running north and south and upon it a caravan of cart mules and women and children. Pots and pans were nailed to the wooden carts or slung over the mules on long ropes and they rattled and clanged against one another like some distorted wind chime.

There were a few men with the group and one of them rode toward us and unleashed a string of Spanish we couldn't follow. When we didn't answer he scowled at us and pointed south and started yelling.

"We're American," Shelby said, loud and slow. "Ah-mare-ih-cun."

A second man rode up and spoke to the first and the first man threw up his hands and rode away.

"Apologies, my friends," the second man said. "Rodrigo is, uh . . . angry. His brother is killed on yesterday. He is very angry."

"Well, shit, I'd be angry, too," Shelby said.

"What's goin' on here?" I asked. "Where's everybody going?"

The man turned to look at the people passing by as if he hadn't noticed them, or perhaps to confirm they were still there.

"It's very, uh, danger. Dangerous. These people have family who fight for Madero."

"What's the Madero?" Shelby asked.

The man seemed to think about this. He turned again and looked back at his people.

"Madero," he said finally. "He is the leader of the, eh, revolución."

"Revolution?"

"Sí. Yes."

"Well, hell."

"We take these people to Estados Unidos. They are safe there. Díaz, the government, cannot reach them."

"We done rode into a goddamn war, son," Shelby said, ignoring the man.

"Is it a war?" I asked the man. "Are they fighting everywhere?"

The man shrugged and then nodded his head uncertain.

"What about Chihuahua?" Shelby said.

"Sí," the man said. "Eh, Chihuahua is, uh, more bad than here. Worse."

"Well," Shelby said again. "Hell."

"What do you want to do?" I asked him.

He spit.

"I'll tell you this much. I'd sure rather die in America than down here in this shithole," he said. "No offense, there, compadre."

* * *

We decided to cross back into our own country but agreed it wise to not venture too far from the border until we made it to Texas. We'd always heard a man could get lost in Texas and we aimed to do just that. New names, new lives, Shelby told me. I did my best to believe him.

We rode alongside the caravan for a while. The sun faded over the Sonoran plains and with its setting the world was cast in colors magnificent: blood orange in the west and all manner of purple and pink projected over the hills in the fading east.

The children chased one another with sticks and the dogs ran with them, not knowing the game but happy to be playing. The older girls watched the two gringos, Shelby flashing them a crooked grin. There were campfires aplenty once the night was irrefutable, and the makeshift village gave me a strange solace. We were all running from something, and there was a certain comfort in that.

An old man sat near us, and three old women and the man who spoke broken English. When the children had quieted and the stars were high overhead, the old man began to speak. No one had inquired but no one interrupted and, as he spoke, the flames seemed to rise in front of us.

Shelby and I were quiet, but the English-speaking man, perhaps not wanting to be rude or perhaps taking upon himself the responsibility to impart an elder wisdom, began to give a somber translation of the old man's words.

"He says this war will be a good and a bad thing for his people," the man relayed. "He says many people will die, but perhaps it is for a greater purpose, eh, reasoning."

"The rebels," I asked, "are they some sort of freedom fighters?"

The translator paused, thought, then expressed my question. The old man shook his head and threw his hand to the side as if to dismiss my comment. He spoke at length.

"He says all men are free. He says since the great American war, there are no slaves, only free men. Free men, he says, are more dangerous because they are more, eh, fuerte, es, uh, strong."

"So what then? Why the fighting?" I asked.

The old man heard my question relayed to him and he looked at me and nodded and held both hands to the sky and then to his chest as he spoke.

"He says only free men choose violence because only free men have a choice."

"No comprende. I don't understand."

"Mexican gibberish," Shelby said. "You ain't 'sposed to understand."

The translator smiled, "Is no gibberish. Is meaning, a country cannot exist without its people. The land, sí, yes, the land is only land. The people, they are who makes the country."

"And Madero is for the people?" I asked.

"Sí. Madero is maybe for the people."

"Maybe?"

"Madero is picked by the people, but Díaz is not give up his power. Madero is maybe for the people, but that is no matter. The matter is the people choose Madero, yes? The people, maybe they are right or maybe no, but they must be heard."

"I understand."

"Sí?"

"Yes."

4

The hound, its lineage tracked to some of the finest-bred litters in Great Britain, was on its right side, so fat its left feet did not touch the floor. There was a fire in the stove, though the nights had not yet turned cold and bitter, and Randall liked the way it made the house smell. He sat in the great room and looked at the piano and squeezed his hand so hard against his glass of brandy he thought surely it would shatter.

"You don't have to go," his mother said. "She will not leave you. It's only the grief. It will pass."

Randall rose from his chair and walked to the stove and opened the door. He crouched down and poked at the fire with a long, sharp rod and stared at the wood as it became overwhelmed by flame, and the hound raised its head and grunted. Randall watched the fire until too much of the smoke was escaping and he shut the door to the stove.

He rose, and so too the dog, and both walked past his mother onto the porch and there took stock of the night and its sounds. More than one thousand head of cattle had once belonged to this land, and wild horses roamed the hills above the ranch. He had land and mineral rights, timber too. When he returned from Pennsylvania those many years past there were oil men and miners, cowboys and grifters, all vying for his father's claim.

He was classically trained in piano and had a deep appreciation for the arts. He studied philosophy, could not hold his whiskey, and still felt uncomfortable atop a horse. His build was slight, his features small, and he knew nothing of cattle or horses or working the land. Such things he left to his hired men, who took advantage of his ignorance and drank and gambled and told false tales to their curious employer.

His father was the smooth talker that Randall was not. Edmund Dawson would have convinced the hired men to work harder, tell no lies, and be loyal to his family. He would have achieved this feat through a modest conversation that held such a warmth and air of sincerity the men would have worked against gravity itself to not let him down. Whereas Randall much preferred the written word, seeing as it gave him time to think and sort out his thoughts, his father needed no tools save his tongue. Though it was not his tongue which was cut off after he was shot in the back by the husband of one of his many lovers. A true statesman, his father once wrote, is willing to please as many people as possible.

So it was that Randall returned to the territory, seeing himself as a prodigal son come back to conquer, and with him his new bride and a hope eternal.

But the West, as it turned out, was indeed wild and the weather ranged from drought to flood and back again. With unreliable men and a lack of the resources made plenty in the East, Randall found this place to be a much harsher reality than the visions in his head. Having never failed before, Randall ignored his wife's pleas to return to Philadelphia and instead began trying to reshape the world as he wished it to be. It is this curse of irrational confidence that leads a few men to great achievements in history while leading most to the sorrowful understanding that the world cannot be remade by men, as the world is of men.

Nevertheless, Randall made his attempt to modernize Longpine. In the end he succeeded only in replacing the local sheriff, a drunkard, and his inexperienced young deputy who had shot the town dentist by accident while cleaning his gun.

As he and Joanna failed to produce a living child, Randall turned more to his library and spent even less time on the ranch. The estate was losing money, and the town was being overrun with gamblers and gunslingers and the like.

"And so it is to this end," he spoke to the dog, and he was at once awash with anger at the murder of his son, the uncivilized nature of the land, and most of all his own failings as a man. The celebrated heroes of history were men of both thinking and action, and he found himself wanting greatly in the latter.

"There is a world removed from the one that birthed me. It is a world unlike the one in which I grew and was molded. It is the real world," he told the dog, who twitched its ears. "And it is full only of ignorance and evil."

His brandy gone, Randall felt himself drunk and he cursed his education and societal upbringing and he vowed to harden his heart against evil and become a man and not a dandy, which he knew they called him and he knew they were not wrong.

In a state unfamiliar Randall ascended the staircase clumsily and without manner. Through the darkness he moved to the bed and found Joanna's sleeping figure and began to grope her and pull at her nightgown. She jerked away and he continued his pursuit and they began to struggle against one another without speaking, and finally Joanna pulled free an arm with which to slap him and she did so with the force of a wasted life and she wept as he pulled up his trousers.

"You think me not a man. I will prove otherwise," he said and his words were slurred and his body swayed as he stood.

She screamed and laughed and said he knew nothing of life on the trail and would surely die, just as their son had, and leave her alone in this miserable and forsaken land. She heard him in the kitchen and in the stable and then he was gone. The hound followed for a time, but turned back panting and again Joanna wept. And without anyone to tend it, the fire began to die.

* * *

Randall rode a white Arabian called Mara and took with him five canteens of water, one pound of tobacco, a cherrywood pipe, enough dried meats and berries to last several weeks, and two gold-handled .41 caliber Colt Thunderers, neither of which had ever been fired by his hand. He left in charge a man name Roscoe who had once worked for his father and seemed the least likely to mutiny against the family.

He set out at midmorning and rode the length of the ranch. It was a crawling sky, the blue heavens outstretched and pulled thin over the forgotten world below. The clouds sat heavy and white like pale mountains in the distance, and the San Pedro flowed clear and steady, urged on by some unseen hand. Pronghorn deer moved into the river valley and took turns lifting their heads and watching for danger as the herd grazed. An exaltation of horned larks fluttered amid the twisting limbs of a lone cypress tree, streaks of yellow and black appearing and vanishing and appearing again.

Randall was a long time in the saddle as Mara climbed up above the valley, picking her way over the slip rock and gneiss. The vegetation thinned and what trees there were became shrunken, and by noon he'd reached the top of Wolf Mountain. Randall watered Mara from his hat and staked her to graze and when he put his hat back on the cool of the water dripped down his neck and made him shiver.

He walked to the far ridge and squatted and looked out across the hill country, the craters and cliffsides rising and falling and fading in the west to squinted-at lines upon dark horizons. His eyes strained to see further, yet still the land eventually gave out, blending into the gray and blue sky as if the earth itself ceased at such a point, and there was no one and nothing to tell him otherwise.

Horse and rider followed the ridgeline south until late afternoon when they came to the edge of the ranch. There they sat in the relative warmth of the autumn sun. Below them the San Pedro looked like a great river of rocks, the water navigating each boulder, flowing and unbroken despite the masses of granite and limestone and gneiss. To see it from the Wolf Mountain mesa, the river appeared snakelike, winding and bending through the cypress and mesquite as though its determination alone would always and forever outweigh the changing landscape and evolving world.

At the last planked bridge before the ranch gave way to the wild rimland of the territories Randall saw the boy sitting on a horse of muted orange, a rifle in his hand.

"Tadpole?" Randall called to him.

"Just Tad," the boy replied. "I'm coming with you."

"I'm sorry, son, but you have to stay."

"The hell I do. Harry was my best friend. I want to kill them sorry suckers who done that to him."

"Let me handle all that," Randall said. "You stay here with your father and help work the ranch while I'm gone."

The boy spit.

"Daddy don't care what I do one way or the other. And no offense, Mr. Dawson, but you ain't exactly no Texas Ranger or nothing."

Randall grimaced but kept calm.

"You're a good boy. A tough boy, I'm sure. So stay here in case the Bentleys double back. They may try to come back for the rest of the horses."

The boy studied him, weighing his words and looking for what was truth and what was not.

"Alright then," he said at last. "I'll stay and guard the ranch."

"I'll see you when I get back," Randall told him.

"Whatever you say," the boy replied as he rode back toward the main spread.

* * *

Randall rode hard for two days, hoping to put enough distance between himself and the ranch so as to not change his mind and turn back, revealing himself a coward.

In each town he inquired after the boys and in Tucson a man said he'd seen them. He said two men on the horses Randall described had passed through, headed south. Randall paid the man and hoped his information was truth and then rode on.

Only one day later he crossed paths with a caravan of Mexicans who were escaping north so as to avoid the bloody business of revolutions. Randall flashed his posters around, asking if anyone had seen these *hermanos gringos*. An old man called to him.

"Yes?" Randall asked excitedly. "You've seen these men?"

The old man nodded and began to speak Spanish.

"No," Randall waved his hands in front of the man. "No habla español. Inglés?"

"I speak English," a younger man said and came and stood near his elder.

"He says he has seen these men. He has seen them in Mexico first and then in America. He says they go to uh . . . Tejas."

"Texas, yes," Randall encouraged the man.

"He says these are men who . . . uh . . . he says they are black and white."

"No, no, they are both white," Randall said, pointing to the likeness. "Both white. Dos gringos."

The old man waved him off and continued speaking.

"He says souls are black and white," the translator said. "Eh . . . one good and one bad."

"I'm sorry," Randall said. "I don't . . . I don't understand."

"He says they go east. Tejas."

* * *

Randall kept south for another half day, then turned east not far from what he believed to be the Mexican border. At night he built small fires and hoped any banditos or revolutionaries would leave him be.

The eastward hills outlined a disturbance in the distant curve of the earth's plane, rising and falling in metered sequence like the breath of a newborn. The sun paused at its highest point, the apogee of the world observed, and even at its most distant positioning the warmth of its being enveloped all before it, some drinking in its energy, others seeking shelter from the harshness of its rays. And into such heat Randall walked, leading the horse behind him, unsure of what deliverance or disaster might be met on the road ahead.

In the late afternoon he ventured from the road to search for water and was quickly lost. He heard his wife's words and saw now the truth in them. He could see the sun in the west but could discern nothing else, and the road was nowhere to be found.

Randall sat in the failing light like some desperado of old. He sat and there was nothing to be done. There may have been a time but such time had long passed and these things in motion were so set in a world far away and yet the same.

Mara stirred behind him and what colors did appear, and they were drawn fleeting across the makeshift sky in hues of purple and pink. The dusk is provisional, always, but no more so than the day or even the life. And when a life ends, there is still the changing sky. As when the dusk turns to night there are still the living, and neither depending on the other yet both existing and both unsure of how to do anything save carry on.

As he sat he thought of the nature of man and questioned it and wondered aloud if he actually hoped to find the men who murdered his son. He hated them, and that he knew, and he wanted them to suffer, but he had assumed it would be at the hands of other, more violent men.

"Is it my inexperience in the art of combat that stymies my courage," he spoke to the night. "Or have I no courage to begin with?"

Perhaps, he thought, I am a coward and a dandy, as they say, and I rode out only because I know I will neither find nor face them.

"In fact," he spoke again. "I'm certain I will encounter only myself on this quest and at such time will appease my own guilt with the notion that I at least tried."

He thought of his grandfather, the great warrior and conqueror, and of his father, who spoke of the wildness of the territories as if it were the only way to truly measure a man's soul. He was ashamed when he thought of their strength and vision and him having neither. But he shook away the thought and decided the future of the world would be crafted by civilized men and he then felt foolish for having agreed to such a primal and unsavory mission as he found himself on.

And if I do find them, he thought, and I somehow gain the upper hand and take my revenge, what then? What am I but a killer, all the same. No, I will put an end to this folly in the morning and Joanna will understand because she is a civilized woman of society and I am her husband and these violent means are not our way.

There is strength in knowledge and compassion, he told himself. There is honor in such things.

Still, sleep was slow coming and the coyotes were quiet and something moved in the dark and Randall tried to remember if he'd loaded his guns.

* * *

That night Randall dreamed his son was eaten by a black bear. They were in the Rim Country south of Longpine, deep in the forests that sloped up from Christopher Creek and the fall leaves had turned and the trees were tired and ready to be rid of the extra weight. The bear opened wide its mouth and began to swallow Harry whole and Randall's guns would not fire and so he spoke to the beast as if it were a man.

"Let him go," he begged the bear, and to Randall's surprise the bear spit the boy out and he saw that it was not his son but himself, and his grandfather was close behind and he knew they were hunting.

"Run," Randall told the bear, but it would not.

"Run, please, there are men with guns coming. They want to hurt you."

Around him the pine trees shed their needles and Randall heard his grandfather approach and he turned to look and saw instead Caleb Bentley on charging horseback.

The fool thinks he can ride down a bear, Randall thought. But the bear was gone and Harry in its place, scared and alone and unable to move.

"No!" Randall cried as the horse bore down on his son, and his voice came out as a great roar and he felt a thick black fur on his back and long claws on his hands and feet.

He awoke from this uneasy slumber and stared at his hands and the veins within them. He thought again of his father and grandfather. Of his son. He felt a growing violence within himself. He would not turn back.

He rode out and into the cool of the morning and the sun crested the horizon line and left backlit the uneven hills and mesas. The awakening world was aglow with orange and red and layered pink light, while to the west the sky was a deep dark blue, and all below it looked to the day's coming. They gave what blessings they may and hoped for one thing or another and hoped for peace and hoped for rain; if all the hopes of all the world were drowned in a great sea, still the dark sky would brighten.

* * *

He regained the road, crossing into New Mexico on the third day. He vowed to keep to the main trails and in doing so he passed many travelers with wooden carts of peppers and oils and herbs, and the wheels rattled and bounced along the dry, rutted roads. They led mules loaded with garments and fabrics and waved at Randall and his fine horse, and he tipped his hat as he passed. At night he made camp not far from the trail and the coyotes yipped and cried and the stars shone in a way he'd never noticed and the fire reminded him of the stove and it all seemed like some dream. Randall Dawson the hunter, he thought to himself, and what a strange dream it is.

5

We left the caravan near Naco as they sought asylum in the new world. Outlaws as we were, Shelby and I slunk along the border, crossing back and forth like hunted prey. We saw no more of the revolution until we reached Agua Prieta.

The city was afire with unrest, unlike anything I'd ever seen. I'd heard tell of the savagery of the War between the States but never had I witnessed such atrocity as corpses piled in the streets and burned—or worse, left to rot.

We rode into town on a Tuesday and found the village beset at every turn by chaos and violence. Mobs, soldiers, assassins—it was like a childhood dream of heroism gone wrong. There seemed to be no boundaries nor reasoning to half the killings, and as the rebels began to don soldier garb the confusion only grew.

We inquired after the gambler named Calhoun but heard he'd fled or been killed or was leading a group of revolutionaries—depending on who was to be believed. Amid the growing carnage we escaped back into Arizona and then New Mexico.

We stayed out of the towns and moved east and kept watch at night for the things we feared. Shelby would stay quiet most mornings and then when the sun was well overhead he'd open his flask and laugh and imagine himself running a ranch in Texas like folks talked about or going all the way to Florida and growing oranges, and he repeated to me how things would be just fine and each time he said the words he grew more desperate himself to believe them.

Shelby had long imagined a life different than his own. He raised me up at least for the most part and took to working in the saloons and learning from men older and harder than him. Longpine was a rough place in a country full of them, and Shelby thought himself rough, and maybe he was. He idolized the gamblers and gunslingers and the way they drank whiskey and bedded whores and talked tough like there was nothing in the world to fear. Shelby clung to these men as our father clung to whiskey, both escaping the pain of their losses and working toward a future different than the past. But salvation, if that's what they were searching for, was slow in coming, and the sins of this life will surely follow us all into the next.

* * *

"Reckon it's about time we named these horses?" Shelby called to me and for a while I ignored him and so he called again. "Bad luck to be riding a horse ain't got no name, even if it is stolen."

I said I wasn't going to name my horse and said I didn't believe in luck, and he told me to suit myself and that his was called Bullet.

In truth, I did want to name my horse and call it by its name and call it mine. But it didn't sit well with me to do so because of everything that came with me sitting on back of it. I closed my eyes hard and tried to shake the memory away but it just made things worse, and now the dying feeling was on me again and I put my hand on the horse's neck and breathed with him and it soothed us both.

He was a Missouri Fox Trotter, like my father used to ride when he was sheriff—seemed like all the lawmen back then rode Trotters. This one had a smooth chocolate coat with jet-black hair and a white splash just above his eyes. He was smaller than the quarter horse Shelby rode, but I could see he was surefooted and even across the rocky mesa-scattered plains he gave a comfortable seat.

We rode rogue through the High Pinos and spent hours a day

searching arroyos and canyon draws for water, shooting rabbit and squirrel to stay fed. We crossed the Animas Plain and navigated the elevated passes between the Organ and Franklin Mountains and found ourselves at long last near the base of the pie-shaped Guadalupe peaks just north of Texas. The wind stalked us across the landscape, harassing our movements until we were forced to take shelter in the Carlsbad hills near the entrance of a forgotten cavern.

The sun set slowly, a shimmering red ball sinking to the bottom of some invisible sea, leaving a darkness that is always there, always waiting for the light to be snuffed out so that the world might return to its natural state.

That night the glow of our fire descended into the Chihuahuan Desert and across the once untamed Apache lands. To the south the long-stretching salt flats eventually gave way to the sloping deserts along the feet of the Franklin Mountains, wherein the wind had first manifested as if being called down by some ancient force set on blowing the world back to the way it once was.

"Brother," Shelby said, as we lay beneath the mouth of the cave, looking out at the rotation of the night sky, "you reckon there's only the one god?"

"You think there might be more?"

"I don't know. The Indians got them a god, and Mexicans go on about the Virgin and whatnot. Tom Meechum said he met a Chinaman who had his own thoughts on the matter and they didn't sound nothing like ours."

"Well."

"Just curious what you thought about it."

"I don't think too much about any of it."

"But you believe in God, don't you? The Christian God?"

"I'm not sure what it is I believe."

"That's dangerous talk, little brother. Whether there's one god or twenty, ain't none of 'em as powerful as the Lord, I can promise you that."

"Alright then."

"I can promise you."

"Okay."

Cassiopeia moved overhead and below the cavern coyotes wailed and snapped at one another concerning the rights to some fresh carcass and in the end the one who'd made the kill had the spoils stolen, as is the nature of such things.

"You know, there was an old boy come in the bar one night. Think he was from down in Louisiana somewheres. Lake Charles, maybe. Anyhow, he was drunk enough to shoot turtles. I mean he'd got himself good and liquored up. Started talking about how God was gonna bring a great storm and cover the world in water. Like how he did with Noah."

"Maybe he ought to."

"He said everything used to be one big ocean."

"You believe that?" I asked.

"Naw."

"That desert out there was the bottom floor of a sea once."

"Where'd you hear that?"

"Momma told me."

"Bullshit."

"I swear. Her people was descended from the Mescalero."

"So?"

"So this was their country back before everything."

"Don't mean it was no ocean."

"It wasn't an ocean then. It was back before there was people. That's what Momma said."

Shelby stayed quiet for a time, staring out. Then he rolled onto his side and pulled his blanket up over his shoulders.

"Ain't no way," he muttered and minutes later he was snoring.

* * *

The light broke the plain and we set out, starting through the Guadalupe Mountains just after dawn. The northwest side of the peaks were hidden from the rising sun and the cold winds cut through the dark morning as we climbed. The rising elevation turned the desert first to forest then to grassland and eventually gave way to the rock-covered summits, where we saw at once the sun and the plains and the days ahead of us.

We ate the last of our food and agreed it was not satisfying, and I apologized to the horses because there was no water. The coming down was slower than the climb and the horses shied and took cautious steps and we dismounted and led them so they might see it was safe, and when even then they did not trust us we took off our shirts and covered their eyes and led them anyway. The arid east side of the Guadalupes held no conifers or mountain grasses, and the descent back into desert seemed rapid and unnatural. Near the base of the mountains, where the hills and caverns sloped down into flat, dry terrain we found what I thought could be the last stream in all the world and there the horses took their water as it flowed down from greater heights.

We crossed into Texas ahead of the dusk and followed an old Indian game trail down into the lowlands and through the salt flats, and I thought about the Mescalero and whether or not they'd all been cleaned out and I imagined them hiding in their caves even now and waiting until the new world collapsed in on itself and the old ways of living returned.

The wind had left scattered a collage of dried junipers upon the desert floor and there they appeared as a collection of bones, brittle and rotting, and a graveyard to navigate without disturbing those who came before us.

The light fading, we topped a ridge of rock and chamisa and sat our horses for a while and looked out over the terrain both new and familiar.

"Texas don't look all that different," Shelby said.

"They got Rangers here. Folks say they're the best lawmen in the country. That's different."

"You still think old dandy Dawson is gonna come a-huntin' us?"

"I would. If it had been my boy."

"Well, it whatn't your boy, it was his, and I'm telling you that sumbitch ain't gonna do nothing. He was hoping the marshals would get us and they didn't, and sometimes folks just get away."

"And you reckon we're them folks, huh?"

"Hell, why not? So long as we stick to the plan. No more using the name Bentley. We're the Crawfords. Just a couple good old boys looking for some work."

"What happens they get 'em a poster with our likeness?"

"You know, you're starting to aggravate the shit out of me. There ain't gonna be no poster."

"And if there is?"

"If there is," Shelby spit his words through gritted teeth, "them Rangers are busy settling rich folks' disputes over cattle land. Damn, little brother, it's like you're hoping to get caught."

"Maybe I am. Maybe that's what we deserve."

"To hell with that. What happened was an accident," he said, then grinned. "If anybody got what they deserved it was that spoiled little shit."

I looked at Shelby's face, long and thin and his nose hooked. He had deep-set purple scars from pimples past and wore his hat tilted back just enough to push down on his ears and let his curly blond hair come creeping out onto his forehead. Like my mother, his eyes were burning amber. His grin stretched into a smile and showed his crooked yellow teeth and he laughed until he coughed, and I knew my brother was a bad man but I knew I couldn't leave him. He was all I had left.

6

He came to the trading town of Mesilla just before dark and found the square alive and festive with Mexican comerciantes and men playing music and the smell of smoking meats, which brought spit to his lips.

A young boy came and took Mara's reins and Randall protested. The boy looked up and said nothing and pointed to a stable. At the stable an old man eyed first the boy, then the big Arabian, and only after filling a bucket with water and pulling out a large brush did he look at Randall and spit onto the straw-covered ground.

"One dollar," he said and Randall obliged and the man scratched his bald head and pointed to a feed trough.

"One dollar," he said again and Randall said he had his own oats and the man scoffed and waved his hand.

"You'll take good care of her, I assume?" Randall asked and the man waved his hand again without looking up, and the boy grabbed Randall's arm and pulled him back toward the square.

"Best food is there," he said, pointing to an auburn pueblo near the stagecoach line.

He continued to point and show Randall the best clothes, best knives, and best girls.

"What about the sheriff?" Randall asked. "Law man?"

"Sheriff is there," the boy pointed and Randall followed his direction to a short, paunchy Mexican man with a thick mustache and tin-plated badge. He held a cigar and leaned in closely to a señorita selling oranges and grapefruit by the bag, and the girl laughed at his words uncomfortably and shied away. The sheriff seemed pleased enough to put the cigar back into his mouth.

"Sheriff," Randall said, approaching, and the man appeared immediately vexed and bade the girl give him a moment to deal with official business.

"I'm on the trail of two murderous men, brothers, who killed my son and a man who worked on my ranch."

The sheriff waited and when nothing more came he puffed his cigar and laughed.

"Two brothers?"

"Yes, have you seen them?"

The sheriff looked around in an exaggerated fashion, then removed the cigar from his mouth.

"My friend, there are many brothers in this very square."

"I have a likeness," Randall said and produced the papers from his pocket.

"Oh, yes," the sheriff said and Randall saw the recognition on his face.

"You've seen them," he said, but the sheriff shook his head.

"No, but I have seen these drawings. They sit with many other drawings of faces that come to this place from people who want me to solve their problems. But why should I care about these faces?"

The sheriff turned back but the girl had been replaced by her grandmother, and his shoulders slumped and he said that Randall should visit with him inside of his office.

Firecrackers popped nearby though Randall could think of no occasion, and a man hammered away at the piano inside a cantina. Along the wooden storefronts there were candles set into small sacks filled with dirt and overhead from roofs and trees flapped streamers of blue and red and green. The sheriff said nothing as he walked. Randall followed. The music stopped and a man tumbled out of the cantina clutching a stab wound in his belly, and the sheriff turned to watch and still did not speak, and the music began again. Randall moved to help, but the injured man cursed at him in Spanish and pushed him away with a bloody hand. The sheriff laughed and beckoned Randall keep up; they were almost there.

The office was at the end of the square and it was filled with electric light and the smell of mescal and tobacco. The sheriff gestured for Randall to sit in a wooden chair, but he instead stood by the only cell and wondered how often it was without occupancy. The sheriff seemed not to mind and sat behind a plain oak desk and relit his cigar and the two men lived in the silence of the moment until the sheriff spoke.

"Who are these men, these brothers you are looking for?" he asked and studied Randall closely, as if he were more interested in the man than the answer.

"Grifters, from Arizona, around the Payson area," Randall said, then hesitated. "They tried to rob me of horses—and cattle too, I'd imagine. Killed my son, my only son. I tracked them south through the territory. Folks at the border said they headed east from there, which would bring them through your area."

"You tracked them?"

"Yes."

"You are a tracker?"

Randall didn't answer.

The sheriff nodded as if he was remembering something long forgotten. "And these brothers," he said, "why is it that they came to rob you?"

"Sir?"

"I have seen many robbers and bandits. They steal from stages and banks, mostly, and trains. So why is it these brothers stole from you?"

"Well, I don't know what you want me to say. I own a lot of land, a lot of cattle. I expect that makes me a target."

"A target."

"Yes, sir, a target."

"And you are not knowing these brothers before they come to rob you?"

Randall hesitated.

"I knew their father. He was the sheriff, but he was a drunk so I had him replaced."

The man nodded as if he understood something no one else could.

"I'll ask you another question, señor," he said and ashed his cigar onto the stone floor. "If you had to shoot at a bird, you would choose a sparrow or a vulture?"

"What?"

"Which bird are you choosing to shoot at? The sparrow or the vulture."

"The vulture, I suppose."

"Why is this?"

"What?"

The sheriff rolled his eyes and outside there were more firecrackers and the music was part of the night as much as the air and the stars and the stench of the cigar.

"Why shoot the vulture?"

"Well, it's larger, easier to hit. I suppose it's also an unsightly bird. I doubt it would bring me the same guilt as if I shot a sparrow."

"I agree," the sheriff said. "It is a bastard bird. It preys on the dead and dying. It makes a much better target, yes?"

"Yes, fine."

"Men like these brothers who did this bad thing to you, they also choose which bird to shoot at. Are you understanding me?"

"You're saying I'm a vulture? That it's my fault?"

"There is no fault, señor, only targets and choices. You'll drink with me, yes?"

The sheriff ignored Randall's declination and pulled an amber bottle from somewhere in his desk and took a long drink of it and closed his eyes. He extended the bottle to Randall who again refused and again the sheriff seemed not to mind and turned the bottle to his lips once more.

Randall saw wanted posters by the dozens crammed into a wire basket near a small stove. The sheriff saw him looking and shrugged.

"Like I say, why should I care about these faces?"

"These are bad men," Randall protested. "They should be brought to justice."

"Whose justice? Yours? God's?"

"The justice of the law."

"Ah, yes, the law. The law that is made against my people and my family who have lived in these lands for two hundred years. The law that is made against the red men who are here longer than us all. This is your law?"

"Fine, then the justice of the Lord God who said thou shalt not kill."

"Ah, a divine punishment."

"If that's what you want to call it."

"I call it disillusionment. There is no divinity here. No grace. Conquest, killing—these are things which come from nature, not God."

"It's not natural to kill another person. God or no."

"Is it not?" the sheriff raised his brows.

"I don't believe we're born that way, nossir."

"It is true, we are born with nothing save the will to live. The goal to survive. Our every action bent toward it. A child crying for food, for sleep, for comfort. Yes, this is a natural thing. A thing the child does without choosing. But when the child grows, does its nature not change?"

"I can't say."

"But you can say there is a difference in a man and a baby, yes?"

Randall was growing impatient. He nodded.

"Well," the sheriff said.

"But that doesn't mean the nature is different. A man, even a bad man, is taught what he knows. And he can only know what he's taught."

"Is this true?"

"Yes, of course it is."

"A murderer must be taught to kill?"

Randall hesitated.

"Must his father also be a murderer?" the sheriff continued.

"I guess not."

"So why then?" the sheriff asked. "Why do we kill? A wolf pup, its small almond eyes barely open, can be held and nurtured and trusted. But a grown wolf? Less so. Nature has changed it. Hardened it.

"A man is not a wolf," Randall said, exasperated.

"Is he not?"

"You can't let killers go free."

"And you, if you catch these brothers and their faces, you will arrest them? Give them a trial by the law?"

"If I can."

"And if not?"

Randall was silent.

"We are all killers, my friend. Even those who have not yet pulled the trigger," the sheriff spoke and looked beyond Randall at some commotion outside. Randall heard shouting. The sheriff rose and walked slowly across the floor and stood in the doorway smoking.

"There is war coming," the sheriff said without turning back to Randall. "But already you know this. Who will be the winner? This you do not know. Nor do I. And so we wait."

"I couldn't care less about your war," Randall told him. "I just care about my son."

"Your son is my son, and your father is my father," the man said. "And this war belongs to all of us."

"Not me."

"Well. We will see."

* * *

Randall's frustration hung about him like mites on a cur, and the breeze moved the streamers and he could see the blood on the wood where the man had refused his help. He wanted a drink, but the town made him uneasy. He was wary of the saloon and its hardened men who would stab a patron, and the sheriff who puffed his cigar and flirted with girls, and so instead he bought a clear bottle from a comerciante, who insisted he also take a string of red peppers.

"Have you seen two men?" Randall asked the merchant, pointing to the poster. "Two brothers on horseback?"

"Hermanos," the man nodded.

"Yes, hermanos, have you seen them?"

"Hermanos," the man nodded again and smiled and began tying more peppers to a string.

"No, have you—" but the man was not looking or listening and his hands were orange and brown and red with dirt and peppers and he smiled and nodded and waved as Randall walked away.

The man at the stable was asleep in his chair. A lantern hung from the rafters and the boy sat squat in the straw, playing at some imaginary story with carved wooden pieces in each hand. Randall breathed in the fresh, earthen aromas of cut hay and thought of his own stables, where the men had let mold spread into the bales and the animals had sickened, and he saw his son's lifeless body and looked again at the boy. The child had come to the culmination of his game and smashed together the wooden figures until one broke.

From what Randall could tell, the horse had been brushed nicely and there was nothing missing from his saddle. He gave the boy five dollars and tipped his hat, and he'd only led Mara a few feet from the stable when the man awoke and took the money away.

Away from the square there were other structures, dimly lit with candles and girls leaned in the doorway and smiled. One girl asked Randall if he was lonely, and he kept walking, and the answer was yes. He was lonely and scared but if he turned back he knew it would eat him slowly, like a sickness, until there was nothing left of the man he hoped to be.

The town gave him caution, but so too did the desert. He made a small camp amid the saltbush and sage, not half a mile from the lights and music and reminders of life. He tried to pen a letter to Joanna but the words would not come and he stopped and blamed the clouds for covering the moon and hiding the light but in his heart he knew this to be false. He drank from the bottle and scrunched his face and it burned to swallow but was warm in his belly. After three laborious pulls he put the bottle in his saddlebag and said that was enough. A few minutes later he reached for it again and began to laugh and think about his time at Mormont, and he felt warm despite the cool night.

He missed the structure and uniformity of his younger life. There were no decisions to be made, and when choices did present themselves the impact was usually limited to a morning hangover. There was a freedom in the fact that his life would come later. His dreams knew no limits so long as they were only dreams. It is the great folly of youth, he thought, that we should believe our lives more worth the living as they go on. He drank to such notions. Soon he was awash with drunkenness and he embraced its call and danced alone, poorly, to the distant music. He cried and spoke to himself and to others and to ghosts, though none were present. He drew his guns and aimed them into the night and pulled the trigger. The hammer slammed down with nothing to strike, but he continued to massacre the desert specters until even his imaginary bullets had run dry. And when all was lost, from his knees he shook his fists and vowed his vengeance.

"I will have such revenges on you both,
That all the world shall—I will do such things—
What they are, yet I know not, but they shall be
The terrors of the earth."

He collapsed into the dirt. The clouds having moved on and the stars burning out above him, Randall listed the constellations in his head until he began to feel the spinning of the world. He rolled onto his side and shut his eyes, but the spinning lingered. He tried to think of Joanna and her naked form on his bed, but he saw only the woman from the doorway. The more he tried to control his mind the further into darkness it went, and there in a drunken version of sleep he was holding Harry's corpse, and the sheriff was laughing at him and smoking a cigar, and Joanna's arms were around both Bentley brothers, and his father lay dead in the street, and the great bear came to him and opened its mouth. "Are you lonely?"

7

For nearly two weeks since leaving Longpine we'd trekked desert country and mountain passes where roads wouldn't go, covering our tracks and keeping away from eyes not our own. Now we brought the horses down onto a trafficked path for the first time since Tucson, and I felt myself tense at the sight of passersby.

There were farmers headed to market, men and women working fields off the roadside, and children with makeshift fishing poles.

"Where in the shit you think they're going?" Shelby asked, craning his neck to watch the young anglers pass on.

"Fishing, I'd guess."

"Fishing, hell. I ain't seen no water for twenty miles."

"Maybe they got 'em a secret spot," I said.

Shelby spit and shook his head.

"You remember when we built that secret hideout off Christopher Creek?" I asked him.

There was no answer.

"Called it Fort Bentley," I continued. "Spent three days and nights out there."

"Then we ran out of beans," Shelby said.

"I told you we should've took more, but you were convinced we'd kill a bear and have meat for months."

"We might've done just that, if you weren't so loud with your whining. You missed Momma too damn much."

"I still do," I said, and neither of us spoke again for a long while.

We stopped in a town called Boracho, and Shelby traded his belt for a bottle of mash whiskey. His mood was sour as it often got, and whatever was eating at him he would try to drown it or, at the very least, put it through the trials of drunkenness.

"We need food," I told him.

"Shoot something then," he replied, turning the bottle up.

"The horses need food."

"To hell with the horses. And to hell with you."

"That's how it's gonna be?"

"You didn't love her no more than me," he said, wiping his mouth. "She was my momma too."

"Where the hell would you get that idea?"

"I know what you think."

"Well, bud, I sure do wish you'd let me know what it is."

"She loved you better."

"Now that ain't—"

"She did," he cut me off. "She loved you better and Daddy did, too, and y'all just thought I was dumb ol' Shelby. Don't say it ain't true."

"It ain't true."

"Well, I'm not dumb. I been watching folks my whole life. I know how they think."

"Alright then."

"I'll show you."

"Okay."

"I'll show you right goddamn now."

And with that he put a heel into his horse, and I watched the two of them grow small as they headed south from the town.

I followed, putting the horse at an easy trot and searching the desert for any sign of where Shelby may have quit the road. I was worried he'd found a bush to pass out behind and I would pass him by, leaving him to get snakebit. When I finally caught up with him, just two miles outside of Boracho, I wished for the damn snakes.

An old Mexican with a wide-brimmed straw hat and what I took to be his two daughters were just off to the side of the road. They were on foot and leading a pack mule and Shelby sat forward in his saddle with his arms crossed one over the other, grinning.

"Say hey, little brother," he said, his words a bit slurred.

The old-timer looked to his mule and up at Shelby and said nothing. The women stood still.

"Sir," I tipped my hat. "Ma'am, ma'am."

"Lord have mercy, look at that thing," Shelby said. "They sure do got it loaded down, don't they? I don't know that I ever seen me a mule that loaded down."

"Looks like it's handling the weight fine," I said, turning the horse in a circle in the road and looking back at where we'd been, watching it somehow get closer.

"Naw, I don't reckon it is," Shelby said, spitting and shaking his head. "I think it's only right that we help this poor animal by taking a little bit of that there load."

The man spoke and he offered that Shelby could buy whatever he wanted and then began to display his merchandise.

"Blanket my daughters make," he said, holding up a corner of blue and white.

"Don't want no blankets," Shelby said, and I called for him to come on and let's get moving. "Don't be rude, Caleb. This here businessman and me are doing business. Ain't that right, señor?"

"Sí, business," the man said and nervously pointed out a sack of cookware, some grain that he had traded for but would gladly sell, and a bushel of beans that he assured us had not been purchased at the poor market.

"What about that satchel there?" Shelby asked and the man patted at a leather bag.

"Ah, is pine nuts," he said, smiling. "Is for my wife. She make the pies."

"Pies?"

"Sí, es bueno. Very good," the man nodded.

"Well, I'm gonna need that satchel," Shelby said.

"No, no, is not for sell," the man said, still smiling. "Is for my wife."

"I don't give a good goddamn who it's for, you're gonna hand up that satchel."

The man looked to his daughters and then back to Shelby and his smile was gone. Shelby fished his pistol out of his pocket and the women screamed and he pointed it at the man.

"Pies, my ass. Now give me that bag 'fore I put your insides on the outside."

I stilled the horse who could feel the tension and watched as the women held each other and the man nodded his head somber and reached for the straps. He loosened the bag and walked slowly to Shelby's horse and stared up.

"Is not right, this thing you are doing," he said and lifted the bag.

"Not right?" Shelby said, his voice a mock surprise. "You hear that, bud? He says I ain't right."

Shelby crossed his arms again and the pistol rested in his left hand pointing casually into the desert.

"Alright, señor," Shelby said, snatching the satchel. "I'll make you a little deal then. If this here bag is full up with pine nuts, I'll toss it right back down to you, and everybody can be on their way. But if it ain't, I'm gonna put two holes a piece into you and your *mijas*. Sound like a fair trade?"

We were all of us silent and unmoving and the only thing we heard was the coins shifting as Shelby moved his hand through the bag of money. He tilted his head back and laughed.

"What'd I tell you, brother? I know about people. I'm a natural goddamn Peckerton."

"It's Pinkerton. And you're a natural horse's ass. Leave these people alone and let's go."

The old man dropped to his knees and brought his hands together in front of his face.

"Please, señor," he asked quietly, and Shelby laughed again from his belly and put away his gun.

"I ain't gonna shoot you, old-timer. My brother and me are just gonna ride off with your money, and you ain't gonna say nothing to nobody about it. Comprende?"

The man nodded and his daughters wept and finally Shelby moved his horse up the road behind me. I started out at a near gallop and had put some thirty yards in between us when Shelby turned back.

"You know, I always heard businessmen were lyin' sumbitches," Shelby said, approaching the man who stood watching him. "Just lie right to your face. You know who used to say that? Ol' Ben Hawkins. Folks called him Hawk back when he was cleaning out the Indians. Fought them redskins for damn near ten years, but you know who he hated even more than Apaches? Businessmen."

"Come on, brother," I called, but he ignored me.

"And any time old Hawk would catch a businessman lyin', well, he'd make sure it was the last lie that fella ever told. Now, what do you reckon Hawk would say to me right now, if'n I was to just let you walk on down this road here?"

"I don't know," the man mumbled, his head was down.

"Speak up, señor," Shelby said, hovering over him from atop his horse.

The man looked up and squared his shoulders to my brother.

"I do not know," he said, a resigned defiance in his voice. "I do not know of this Hawk. I do not know of you. But I will tell you now that you are not a good man. You are a wicked man, and God will judge you for your wickedness."

Shelby hung his head and sat his horse, and again the world was motionless and mute. When he looked up again his lips were stretched into a thin smile. I cried out, but my words could not stop the bullets, and the man's body jerked and spun and crumpled.

The shots spooked the animals. The mule turned and took off the way he'd come, while Shelby's horse reared and tossed him to the ground. I gave the horse under me some slack and let him run a piece, then slung my catch-rope over the mule before reining and turning back toward the chaos.

One daughter was crying over her father's body, and the other was screaming at Shelby, who dusted himself off, laughing. She ran toward him, her arms flailing, and he caught her and slung her to the ground.

"We got to go, Shelby," I pleaded. "Somebody would've heard them shots. Get back on your horse and let's head out."

"What about them?" he asked and the cries and screams stopped as the women awaited their fate.

"They bury their father," I said. "Now let's get off the damn road."

"They'll tell the law which way we went."

"Then we'll start out one direction and pick another once we're out of sight. But I promise you we won't have to worry about it if we stick around here one more minute."

He kicked one girl in the stomach.

"Shelby!" I called, pleading.

He mounted up and we headed off the road toward a grove of privet trees, and I thought the worst was over until Shelby pulled up short and spun his horse.

"I dropped the watch," he called as he raced away. "I dropped Daddy's pocket watch when I fell. I can't leave it."

"You can't go back."

"Got to, son," he said.

* * *

I pushed on and made the trees and dismounted and we stood, the horse and me, looking back up toward the road. I put my hands on my hips and spit and knew the old man was right about my brother being wicked. If there was a God, He'd judge Shelby, and I imagined He'd go ahead and judge me too while He was at it.

When I was a boy my father told me all men are the same. They're all scared, he said, and the meanest are more scared than the rest. I thought about this and concluded that I was destined to be mean and decided I would work a ranch somewhere and stay away from people so as to not spill my preordained meanness out onto them. Momma laughed when I told her.

They took Daddy's badge when I was fourteen, though it rightfully should've been much sooner. He would go on long drinking spells up in the hill country or down in Mexico, leaving the kid-deputy to manage things in his absence. The folks in town were sympathetic for a while, then concerned, and ultimately just angry and no one could blame them. No one except Shelby, who swore it was all Randall Dawson's doing. Dawson had paid money, of which he had plenty, to bring in some fancy lawman from back east. He also organized the vote to remove my father from his duties. After that, the drinking got worse—to the small degree it had left to go—and when Daddy up and left, Shelby swore his revenge on Dawson and said it was for the family. Shelby always went on about that—the family—especially when I didn't want to do something. He'd call me "little brother" and he'd say his piece and in the end I'd do the thing I didn't want, and I'd think about my mother and how we were both her sons.

* * *

And so I thought it now—family is family—as I paced the distance between trees, trying to think of any reason to not ride away and never look back. Family is family. My heart caught in my chest and I wasn't sure if it had stopped beating. My throat tightened up and I shook my head and said aloud, "Keep moving," and so I walked back to the horse and opened the saddlebag. My hands were trembling as I fished for the dandy brush at bottom of the sack. I tried to steady my breathing but each was quicker than the last and I braced myself against the horse and closed my eyes and saw the Dawson boy standing there in front of the stable, gun raised. His body spasmed and shuddered like the old man in the road and they were both dead and I felt like I was dying too.

I began to cry and couldn't stop and I stood brushing the horse and sobbing, and it must have been a terribly strange scene had anyone been there to watch. But there was no one. Only me. And when at last I wiped my eyes and put the brush back into the bag, my fingers hit something cold and hard. I closed my fist around the pocket watch and pulled it out into the world and stared at it without moving. My eyes widened and I turned again toward the road and waited for the gunshots to come. I didn't wait long.

The echo of murder was still in the air and I mounted my horse and rode hard into the hills, racing across traprock and shale, urging the horse forward through the unkind terrain. My mind was at once overloaded and blank, and when I suddenly pulled up on the reins and brought the horse to a skidding stop, I knew he probably took me for insane.

I sat the horse for what felt like hours. The two of us alone in the world. I wasn't sure if I couldn't move or if I didn't want to or both. I screamed out, and the horse perked his ears and twitched them and took a step. I sat, breathless.

* * *

At the top of a plateau about eight miles from the road, I looked down and could see his horse climbing. He sat an awkward saddle, and when he reached the top and saw me, he laughed.

"I knew you weren't about to up and quit on me," he said.

"I should."

He laughed again.

"I told you I wasn't dumb," he said, shaking the bag of coins at me. "I told you."

"And what about laying low? What about new lives? We ain't been in Texas two days and we're murderers all over again."

Shelby rolled his head back and groaned.

"You worry too damn much," he said. "Who exactly do you think is gonna tell anybody what happened? Nobody. I saw to that. Besides, the law's got more to handle than a few dead Mexicans."

He slid clumsy from the horse and took a few steps toward the fire and fell and lay there drunk for most of the night. I dug through the rest of what he'd stolen and found cold tortillas and dipped them in a can of beans and ate.

That night the moon was gone and the stars shone in earnest. Shelby snored, and I thought of the man back in Longpine who counted stars and named them. I thought of how he sold spyglasses out of his wagon and how I wished I had bought one. I thought of my mother and tried to remember her face. I thought of the family on the road and the boy in the stable and there I came into an unnatural sleep, and soon I was dreaming. In my dreams I heard the distant rumble of thunder as a storm gathered and the faces all returned, only now there was a girl. I couldn't see her, but I felt her there, and she felt like home. I tried to get to her, feeling my way through the darkness, but she stayed hidden. I called out to her but there was no answer, only the menacing faces melting into the sky and the growing darkness of the coming storm.

"Caleb," the girl whispered.

"Caleb."

I opened my eyes.

"Caleb," Shelby said. "Do you think He will?"

He'd awoken at some uncertain hour before the dawn. I watched him cry, and through his wailings he asked God to spare his soul. He rolled in the dirt and called out to God over and over but if anyone was listening They gave no indication.

"Do you think He will, Caleb?" he asked again, turning to me. He was covered in dust and snot and tears and his words were begging.

"No."

8

Randall awoke to the drumming of an infantry unit as it marched across his skull and lay siege to his brain with muskets and small artillery. He poured water over his head and saddled his horse. When he saw the empty bottle, its former contents churned in his stomach and were then expelled from his mouth in unceremonious fashion.

Heading east from Mesilla, the Organ Mountains rose up in the distance and masked the sun's ascent for the better part of the morning. The night's chill lingered a bit longer and Randall pushed Mara and the horse did not resist. Together they moved quickly up through the mesquite brush and cactus and followed a wash down into a canyon and at last came to the mountains, where they began a slow climb with the sun overhead.

In the afternoon both horse and rider took shelter from the heat in the shadow of a ridge topped with red rock formations and sparse flowers. In the evening they would make for higher elevation, where conifers and mosquito grass grew in the cooler climate. Randall found no creek nearby, so he watered Mara from one of his canteens and spilled much of it onto the horse's face and neck and the hardened sand below.

Finding his jerky dull he bit into a red pepper and was soon afire from mouth to midsection and he began to howl and spit and kick, and the water seemed to only make it worse. He cursed the comerciante and unbuttoned his shirt. Mara watched intently as he near emptied another canteen and then threw his hat into the dirt only to pick it up and brush it off. He slumped down against a rock and took short shallow breaths. He closed his eyes and they were wet with tears, and when he wiped them they stung and reddened and again he hollered and began to feel about the dirt for the canteen but was frozen by the report of a rifle.

"Don't shoot!" he cried, and from his knees he threw his hands into the air and tried to open his burning eyes.

"Don't worry, Mr. Dawson, she ain't shooting at you," the boy said, and for a moment Randall believed it was his son and he must still be dreaming.

"She shot the head of that snake yonder," the boy said and pointed, and Randall saw the blur of the snake's twitching body, and Mara stamped at the earth. "Saved your life."

"Wasn't saving him," the woman said. "Saving that horse. All tied up like that, couldn't have got away if it wanted to."

Randall was still breathing heavy and the sweat followed worn salt tracks down his face and he recognized the boy.

"Tadpole," he said, and the boy seemed pleased, and the woman began to comfort Mara and tell her it was alright. Randall saw that her skin was chocolate and her hair black and braided behind an olive hat. She wore brown breeches and a white blouse and her gun belt was rough, faded leather and when she turned to look at Randall her eyes were dark and unforgiving.

"Yessir," Tadpole said, "and this here's Miss Charlotte, and her paint horse named Storm. 'Course you already know ol' Pumpkin."

Randall and the woman looked at one another and he still was unsure what was happening but thought it important to climb to his feet. He turned back to the boy and his horse and the horse called Storm. Storm was gray and white and spotted with an almost silver mane and was well appointed with a dark leather saddle atop a green and white serape.

"How'd you all find me?" he asked.

The woman ignored him and turned back to the horse and resumed her comforting tones.

"Well, I heard all the fellas talkin', sayin' you'd probably get lost or die, or maybe get shot, or accidentally shoot yourself, or—"

"Tadpole," Randall said, and the boy took his meaning.

"Anyhow, I got started a couple days after you, but you weren't too hard to follow, and then I met Miss Charlie here on the road and she was nice enough to give me some food, and after I told her about Harry and about you, she said she ought to come with me to make sure I find you."

Randall looked again at the woman, and she was watering Mara from her hat and nary a drop had been spilled.

"We actually come up on you last night," the boy continued. "But it looked like you was having a go of it with that bottle, so we figured we'd let you sort things on your own 'til morning."

"How kind," Randall said, embarrassed.

"We didn't want to get mistook for whatever you kept shooting at with them empty guns," the woman said, and Randall could find no playfulness in her voice.

"Oh, well, I was just messing about," he managed.

"It ain't nothing to worry yourself about, Mr. Dawson. I seen drunk fellas before," Tad said. "Shoot, I even been drunk a time or two myself. That all don't matter though, we're here now and ready to help you track down them devil Bentleys."

"Now hold on, I didn't say you could stay. I'm on a personal—and dangerous—quest here. I gotta move fast and stay quiet."

"Move fast? Shit, Mr. Dawson, excuse my language, but you might as well be mounted up on a turtle, as slow as you been moving. Putting that horse to waste is what you're doing."

"Well, I didn't want to wear her out. I rode her hard the first few days."

"That's what you call hard? Jesus Christ." The boy looked incredulous. "I mean, Jesus Christ, Mr. Dawson. Them boys'll be having tea with the president in Warshington, DC, by time you catch up to 'em."

The woman laughed and Randall turned to her.

"You responsible for this?" he asked and her face turned back to hard iron. "You think it's a good idea to bring a boy on this sort of trip?"

She didn't flinch.

"I don't think it's a good idea for *you* to be on this sort of trip, least from what I've seen and what the boy's told me. And since you asked, no, I don't like the idea of him going off with you, and I told him as much before we rode up. But seeing as how he ain't gonna listen to neither one of us, I figured I better stick with him to make sure don't no harm come his way."

"Uh-huh, so you intend to ride with me as well?"

"Not riding with you, riding with the boy."

"Alright, well, I'll tell you what I told the boy. Nobody is coming with me. I forbid it."

"Forbid it?"

"Yes, ma'am, you heard me."

"Then you hear me, Mr. Dawson. This here is a free country. My father fought and died to help make it so. I ain't wearing no chains, and I ain't gonna act like I am, neither. This boy tells me these men killed your son. That ain't right. And as much as two wrongs don't make a right, there's a sense of justice to seeing them men pay for what they did. You may not think you need my help, but I promise you, sir, when them guns are loaded it's a different world. That's the world I live in."

Randall considered her words and softened his tone.

"I can appreciate your position, and I am grateful for your offer. However, I must decline. I cannot be responsible for putting a woman and a child in harm's way. I just cannot."

"Good," the woman replied. "That settles it. We'll just go on and put ourselves in harm's way, then you ain't got nothin' to worry about."

Randall shook his head.

"What's your name, ma'am?"

"Charlotte Washington."

"Where's your people?"

"In the grave. All except my sister. She went up to Chicago to be a lady."

"And that didn't appeal to you, I gather."

"Nossir, it most certainly did not. I headed west from a town in Texas called Jefferson, looking to make it all the way to California."

"Well, you know I'm headed the opposite direction, don't you?"

"There's always time, Mr. Dawson. That boy talks too much, but he's a good boy. I can't rightly let him go off with somebody like you. No offense."

"Hard not to take offense, Miss Washington. But please, call me Randall."

"I guess you'll have to sort that out with yourself. Either way, the boy's coming with you and so am I."

The woman walked past Randall and he watched her go.

"C'mon, Tad," she called back to the boy. "Let's get our horses."

Randall felt the boy clap him on the back as he passed by.

"I always figured I was meant to track down bad guys."

* * *

They rode east and the dirt road they followed turned from a deep-red clay to a brown sand and the foliage shrank before their eyes, mesquite and juniper making way for shadscale and rabbitbrush. There was a stillness to the country that stirred in Randall waves of anxiety and fear, as if he were trespassing through a time not his own, perhaps even a different world.

Randall thought the country a land of waste and unmet need. The dirt set thick upon his brow and breeches, and when the wind blew the dust rose up from the ground in spirals, as if the devil was reaching out from the underworld with long, thin fingers. The sky was neither bright nor dull, and no matter the passing of time and dirt Randall saw no change in the distant mountains, as if he and the others were bound to ride forever in some desert purgatory between worlds, never reaching a destination and never turning back.

The hills rose and faltered like the waves of a stagnant alien sea, and the three horses moved along dutifully as the sun gave chase to the moon and ascended to its position atop all the world and the world in turn embraced the change as it must, having no say in such matters.

The country before them was familiar in its sprawl, and no one spoke yet still the wind carried with it voices. When Randall looked about he saw no one and wished the ghosts would speak up so that he might hear their words. He wondered then about such a notion and about the language of the dead, and he concluded it was still his language or at least it was a language he would understand.

The vegetation, what little there was, began to thin and soon the land offered up only catclaw and creosote and the dried ash-gray stalks of dead yucca.

"The Lake of Souls." Charlotte pointed and Randall saw the expanse of crusted earth to his left. "It's a sacred place to the Strassi."

"How long has it been dry?"

Charlotte shrugged. "Since your people came."

Randall opened his mouth to speak but could think of no words worth saying so he nodded because there was nothing left to do. He turned to the dried lake and from it came a hot wind. The air washed over him and he heard one thousand voices and they spoke in Spanish and English and Comanche and he heard their screams and laughs and pleas.

Randall stopped and sat his horse and the others kept on and he listened harder. Soon the air was thick around him, and he reached to feel his heart where it pounded in his chest. Black birds flew overhead. He strained his ears but did not hear his son. The birds descended in a flurry of squawks and flapping wings and the voices rose with the dry wind and Randall could not move or breathe and soon he felt the feathers engulf him and the claws and beaks tore at his clothes and flesh.

"Mr. Dawson," Charlotte said, and he opened his eyes and there were no birds or wind, and Charlotte looked at him with concern. "Let's keep moving."

He nodded and put Mara forward and gave her her head and turned again to look at the dried lake. His horse soon fell into step with Storm.

They rode well into the night, but the moon was strong and the path clear and any ground they'd given by stopping was reclaimed and then some and there was game aplenty and Charlotte shot two rabbits and by Randall's estimation she could have shot many more had the need arisen. He watched her aim and fire and her body was so fluid, as if it were as comfortable with killing as it would be floating along in a soft stream. Who was this woman, somehow both graceful and terrifying?

In a narrow canyon draw where the water ran down after rains and the cliffs above guarded against the harsh desert sun, bands of chokecherry, wafer ash, and wild plum had grown into one another and it was there Charlotte said they should make camp. There was water nearby for the horses and a grove of wolfberries, which Tad began to pick and eat at a frantic pace.

Charlotte led the horses, following the headward erosion of the stream channel, and soon found trickling water that led to a greater source and there she filled their canteens while the animals drank.

Randall stacked wood and moved stones and lit a flame to warm the night.

Charlotte returned and roasted both the rabbits and they ate until they were overly full and tossed their bedrolls and blankets near the fire and there they lay with stomachs too large to sleep.

"My daddy says the Indians are still holed up out this way," Tad told them. "Says there's caves all through these hills and the Indians are just running through 'em, waiting to pop up and get 'em some scalps."

Randall drew on his pipe thoughtfully.

"I seen me an Indian back in Arizona," Tad continued. "He was all dressed up too, like how they do on war parties."

"And he let you live?" Randall asked, raising an eyebrow.

Tadpole looked down, "Well, I mean, it was a picture of an Indian, anyhow. But he looked real mean."

"Indians ain't mean. No meaner than any other folks," Charlotte told him, and Randall listened. "They's good and bad people, no matter if you Indian or African or any other thing."

"Well, my daddy always said black folks are lazy and dumb, but I sure enough know you ain't neither of those. So I reckon if he's wrong about that, he's probably wrong about Indians too."

That seemed to please Charlotte and she smiled and stood and went off to find a tree and Randall watched her go and tried to act natural when she turned and caught him staring.

He too stood and used the fire's light to gather more wood and he gathered more than was necessary. When Charlotte returned she eyed the large stack and scoffed, and Randall mumbled something about being prepared.

"Why you doing this, Mr. Dawson?" she asked him.

"Doing what?"

"Going off like this, chasing trouble."

"I'm out to bring the Bentley brothers to justice."

"Why not just let the law handle it?"

Randall hesitated.

"In truth," he said, "my wife, Joanna, insisted I go."

Charlotte said nothing.

"She insisted that a man—a real man, that is—would avenge his son."

"A real man?"

"Yes. Something I believe she thinks me not to be. Something she may very well be right about."

Charlotte was quiet again.

"In my heart, I suspect she may have sent me away in hopes of my being killed," he said. "Though I have not spoken that thought aloud until now."

The two of them lay on either side of the fire with Tadpole at their feet, his small frame no match for the Mexican blanket Charlotte had given him. Uncovered, she lay on her back with her arms behind her head and looked at the dark sky and her shirt raised just enough for Randall to see the smooth skin on her stomach and he quickly turned away.

"Do you believe this a fruitless endeavor?" he asked her.

"Can't say."

"Well, what do you think?"

"Ain't my place to judge."

"So you too. You don't think I'm a real man."

Charlotte propped herself on her elbows and leaned forward to look at him.

"I've known my share of fellas who I'd have a lot more faith in when it came to tracking and killing and all other matters of violence," she told him. "But that didn't make them worthy men. And so I don't think your wife, with all due respect, knows what a real man is."

"What makes a man worthy?" he asked.

"Kindness. Sure, it don't hurt if he's handsome and has a job. But most of all, he ought to be kind."

"I've always been told I was too kind. My father, my grandfather before him—they wanted me to be much more rugged than I turned out."

"No such thing as too kind, Mr. Dawson."

"Well, I wish my father could hear you say that," he told her.

9

In the morning we ate tinned fruit in silence and walked the horses down into a creek. The horses drank, and we splashed our faces with the cold water and ran our hands through our wet hair. We rode south through the Davis Mountains pass and came to a town called Valentine, where there was a mercantile and a smithy and a café all in a row. The short, flat buildings sat on dirt no different than the dirt before they started or the dirt that went on after they stopped, like somebody was walking and got tired and built a town.

We used the stolen money and bought a sack of oats for the horses and two cans of beans and one pack of dried beef, and Shelby bought whiskey even though he'd swore it off that same morning. He spit into the dirt outside the mercantile where the horses were tied.

"Not much money left from that old Mexican," he said, and I asked how much.

"We can ride another day or two," he said, "but we oughta find some work after that."

I nodded and heard the thunder and wondered if it was in my head again, but when Shelby looked up I knew it wasn't.

"Well," he said. "Can't outrun the rain, and I don't feel like riding wet. Let's go in and get us a cup."

The mercantile had a wooden-roofed porch but the café did not. Dirt followed us in and a Mexican woman pushed us out of the way with her broom so she could sweep the threshold. A man with a white mustache and a sizable midsection nodded from behind the counter. Shelby asked for two cups of coffee and the man could not hide his disappointment that we were not eating also.

Shelby splashed whiskey into his cup and winked and we sat by the window and watched the sky blacken. Three cowboys came in as the rain began to fall and ordered beef hash and eggs and biscuits and the mustached man happily obliged.

The cowboys ate and talked and laughed aloud. Their hats were tall with curled brims and they spoke of a woman with whom a man had been in love. And they laughed again and said she'd run away with an Indian and the man had said she was captured but everyone knew the truth of it and behind his back they called him Injun Joe.

"Say," Shelby said, turning his body in his chair to face them, "you boys know of any ranch work out this way? Me and my little brother are looking to catch on somewheres."

One of the men spoke and said not much work was to be had and he lamented that the cowboy way was ending and said we'd be better off heading east and cutting timber in the pines.

"Sad state of affairs this country finds itself in," he said, spitting on the wooden floor plank below him then staring up at the old woman with the broom. "Mexican vaqueros coming up and taking what little ranch jobs there are to be had. Cattle land being bought up by the oil men. Good cattle land too. Not any of that dusty shit like in New Mexico."

The man's companions shook their heads in agreement. Encouraged, he continued.

"Yessir, we're the last of a dying breed. Thought about heading down south of the border and trying to find some work cowboying on one of them big haciendas the vaqueros are always going on about. You know, sort of do to them what they done to us up here. 'Course now the Mexicans have decided they're gonna have them a civil war. Can't do anything on their own, always gotta steal our ideas."

The cowboys laughed and held up their cups for more coffee. The man rushed from behind the counter with a fresh pot.

The cowboy who'd spoken told us he and his bunch were headed west and offered that we might do the same if logging did not appeal to us.

"We'll take our chances," Shelby said, then asked how far to the timber country, and the cowboys conferred and said two weeks' ride.

They advised we head north first to avoid the Lobos, but when I asked if there were wolves they said no and the old woman made a cross on her chest.

"What's the Lobos then?" Shelby asked.

The cowboys looked to one another.

"Hard to say," the talkative one said. "They're outlaws, sure enough. Murdering thieves. But they're something else too. They ain't your regular grifters and lowlifes. A bunch of 'em are ex-military and the like. The Mexicans around here say they're led by a demon or something of the sort."

"You believe that?" I asked.

The man shrugged.

"Not particularly. But they are a spooky bunch, I can tell you that much. Had a run in with 'em out near Marathon. Come up on us right at dusk, maybe ten or so, howling like wolves, circling us with their horses. They asked if we was ready for a new world."

"What'd you say?"

"We said sure we are, that's why we're heading to California. Then one old boy came forward from the rest." The cowboy looked around the room, gathering in the eyes of his audience and perhaps also searching for that which he feared. "He had him a peppered beard and slicked-back hair. Told us California weren't no different than nowhere else. Said to come with him if we wanted to see what life would be like after the next revolution. Didn't much of it make sense to me."

The man took a sip of his coffee and pursed his lips.

"Anyhow, we politely declined whatever the hell it was he was offering, but he decided that wasn't gonna be enough. Started asking for our horses, our food, even our damn boots."

"You give 'em to him?"

"Hell yes, we did. They had us over a barrel, and I ain't getting killed over no goddamn horse, much less a pair of boots. 'Course, old Frank wasn't having none of it."

"Who's Frank?"

"Well, Frank *was* the fourth member of this here outfit. That is, until he decided he wasn't giving his horse to no man who wouldn't pay him for it."

"They shot him?"

"Nossir, they did not. Instead the old man just nodded, and they all rode off. Next morning, Frank was gone."

"Where'd he go?"

"Shit, if you're looking at me for answers you're on the wrong trail, bud. We got no idea what happened, but like I say, it's spooky business."

"That's a story if I ever heard one," Shelby told the man, who nodded.

"It is at that," he replied. "It got to where I couldn't shake what happened, so I started asking around. Turns out folks been disappearing all throughout the Trans-Pecos. Women mostly, but men too. Rumor has it the entire town of Diskin pretty much shut down overnight."

"The Rangers huntin' these fellas?"

"I expect they are," the man said, "but it's likely with heavy hearts."

"How come?"

"Word is, the old boy leading the Lobos is a man called Grimes. And Grimes, if it's to be believed, used to be a Ranger hisself. Some kind of hero back during the war too."

"Damn."

"Damn is right. But the strangest part is, he fought to clean out the Indians and now he rides with a few of 'em—blacks and Mexicans too."

"God dog," Shelby said. "Sounds like a bona fide wild man."

"Like we say, best stay north for a piece."

Shelby nodded and turned, and the cowboys went back to their banter.

"What do you think of all that, little brother?" Shelby asked me.

"Sounds like we ain't out of the woods yet. Let's head back north and then cut east. I don't want to run into any trouble."

Shelby added more whiskey to his coffee and swirled the cup with one hand and said nothing.

"Right?" I asked, prodding him.

"Sure, sure."

The rain passed and the earth drank up the moisture and the mustached man said something in Español and the old woman shook her head. The cowboys rode out, and I fed the horses from the sack of oats while Shelby spent the last of our money on a thermos of coffee.

"You see them gun belts them ol' boys was wearing?" he asked me. "First pay we come across, I'm getting me one of them suckers."

He reached into his pocket and pulled out the old colt and spun it halfway round in his hand, then lost control and cussed and seeing it gave me a chill and I heard thunder again but the storm was long gone.

On the outskirts of town there was a saloon and nothing would do but Shelby had to go inside. I followed him.

The tequila was from Jalisco. It was called Cabrito and had a sketching of a goat on the bottle.

"You drink," the barkeep said and poured two glasses.

"We do indeed, amigo."

"Vaqueros?"

"Sí, señor."

The barkeep nodded, solemn, as if he understood there was a certain nature to such an occupation, some regrettable calling to a faded and dying culture—the last, perhaps, of an entire breed.

"Where to now, brother?" I asked Shelby.

"East."

"How far?"

"Couldn't say. How big is Texas?"

"They say it's pretty big."

"Well. Let's see if they're right." Shelby tossed back the tequila and slammed the glass down on the bar, motioning for another round.

"Shelby?"

"Yessir?"

"There can't be no more of this."

"No more what?"

"Outlawing. Killing."

"You asking me or telling me?"

"I'm telling you."

"Telling me," he repeated and nodded his thanks to the barkeep who'd refilled his glass.

"Yessir."

"You know what Granddaddy used to say? About killing?"

"I know."

"Some folks can't help but be cannon fodder."

"I said I know."

"And do you believe that?"

"I don't."

"That means you're one of the casualties."

10

They passed along a red clay road, with wagon ruts and mule tracks carved out and preserved in the dried mud like tributes to a long-ago rain.

Charlotte rode at the lead, and Randall watched her. She sat tall in the saddle, her shoulders down and back in an effortless posture. Her dark curls fell halfway down her back until the heat of the day forced her to collect them under her hat.

Randall stared at the sweat on the back of her neck.

"What're you thinking about, Mr. Dawson?" Tad asked, and Randall nearly lost his seat.

"Nothing," he replied, embarrassed. "Just riding."

"Oh. Okay. I thought maybe you was thinking about Harry."

Randall turned to the boy and saw the downcast look he wore.

"Were you thinking about him?" Randall asked.

Tad shrugged. "Yeah, I guess. Been thinking about him a lot. It's just, he was my best friend. My only friend, really. He was always asking me questions about the horses and whatnot. I think he wanted to be a trainer."

"So you're the one who taught him?"

"'Course I am. You didn't think he was gonna learn something like that from you, did you? No offense intended."

Randall laughed. "I suppose that's fair."

"He was a natural, though," Tad said. "I'll tell you that much. A real hand."

"I'm glad he had you to teach him. I'm sure you made a fine instructor."

"Dang right. None of them lazy curs you got working for you know half as much as me."

Randall laughed again.

"Alright then," he said. "Teach me something."

"Now?" the boy asked.

"Sure. Why not?"

"Well," Tad looked around, then looked at Randall's horse. "I know Mara ain't hardly been rode outside of a pen before this."

"How's that?"

"Look there at her shoes. See how they're worn down around the outside? That's from turning in circles in a pen. She may have seen a pasture or two but not long enough to even everything out. You got to give a horse wide-open spaces, else them hooves will crack and peel and wear down."

"Is she in pain?"

"Naw. It ain't too bad just yet. And you been riding a while with her now, she's starting to find her own balance."

"That's pretty impressive."

"Harry would've spotted it too. He was as good as me, maybe better, before he . . ." Tad took a deep breath in through his nose, trying not to cry.

"I know, son," Randall told him. "It's alright."

* * *

There came what might have been a distant structure, and it shimmered and wavered on the plain before them as if it were meaning to dance in the sun but found itself instead tethered to the cruel immobility of the desert. They put the horses forward and with each rise and fall of the road the dancing building disappeared and appeared again closer and with added dimension until at last they saw it was a town and that the first building was flanked by others, though not as many as there may have once been.

They started down the main stretch and looked to one another for some acknowledgment of life beyond their own breathing and the breathing of the horses but there was none to be had on the street and they were ready to leave things to the ghosts when a young boy came into their path and there stood staring up at them, his faced shadowed by an oversized hat.

"Hello there," Randall said and his voice seemed to set the boy in motion, as if the child had been waiting for words—any words—so that he might know the travelers as true and not some apparition blown in from the desert on the rising winds. He gathered the horses without speaking and led them all, riders and mounts, past broken and boarded windows of faded and falling buildings.

"What happened here?" Randall asked, but the boy did not look back, instead pointing upward with his index finger as he walked, and they looked, the three of them, skyward and there they saw a lone buzzard circling and beyond it there were thin clouds fleeting in their makeup and, willing or not, soon to dissolve into the nothingness of the world below and above. They saw the sun as it held court over the land it had birthed and the land it would one day destroy and they saw, each of them, something from their past and all were silent.

The boy walked and though they had not gone far he dropped the reins as if he were too tired to go on bearing the weight of the horses and their passengers, and he turned and stood and again stared up at the strangers and it was any man's guess as to which party was the more curious.

"Are there no others?" Randall continued with his questioning as though each time the boy did not answer that was in and of itself some passing of knowledge and thus called for further inquiry.

"Momma," the boy said and pointed once more, this time toward the caved-in roof of what looked to have once been a café or mercantile of some sort.

"Your momma in there?" Charlotte asked, leaning forward on her horse as though proximity would wrest a more complete telling from the child.

"Momma," the boy repeated and this time pointed to a different building and all three riders leaned back in their saddles uniformly in an unspoken agreement of the boy's insanity and into the street came a pale man marked with boils and sores of a present nature and the scars of those past.

"My friends," he called, "come, join us for supper."

"Ain't even three o'clock," Tad said, looking at the sun and its position and finding the gaze of both Randall and Charlotte and shrugging his shoulders.

The robed man, who they each took to be a priest, looked also to the sun and there he stared for a long while and after that while he turned back to the riders.

"Even so," he said. "We do not get many visitors here and it would be a good thing, I believe, for the child to have the interactions necessary for a supper."

"He your boy?" Randall asked.

"The boy is of no blood relation to me, though he is a child of God and thus is my brother and my son and also my father."

"Well, hell," Tad said, "that don't make no goddamn sense a'tall."

"I see you have not taught your own son the ways of our Lord," the priest said, though not unkindly.

"He's not my son, but yes, he is not versed in many Christian customs, the least of which is taking the Lord's name in vain."

"Ah," the priest smiled, "so it is that we both find ourselves in the charge of young men not of our seed and yet bestowed upon us in one way or the other by God."

"I ain't been bestowed, mister, I rode my horse," Tad protested, and Randall shot him a look and that was the end of it.

"Please, sup with us and rest here tonight," the priest requested again.

"We'll break bread," Randall replied, "but seeing as it's early yet, we'll have to ride on after."

"I understand," the priest said, and if he was disappointed or desperate, neither showed. "The boy will show you the way to our stables, such as they are."

The stables, as suggested by the priest, were not stables but a makeshift overhang of rusted tin resting on reclaimed pine and oak which had at some time been cobbled together with no great care at a length wide enough for their three horses only, and all them near scraping the low points of the tin with their heads. The boy tied the horses and ran around the corner of one of the buildings as though being chased and returned sloshing a washtub of water thick and brown with film and flies. Randall waved him off and the boy had seen this gesture before and reacted in kind by dropping the tub and covering half his own breeches with water. The three of them watched, the horses too, as the boy stood in a motionless silence for a time and after that time he reached into a rusted bucket and from it produced a brush and made for the horses and Tad stepped up to stop him, but Randall held him back and they watched still as the boy ran the brush along the backs and haunches of the horses.

"Fine job," Randall lied when the boy was finished and he put two dollars in the boy's hand and Tad's dismay was audible.

"Fine job," Randall repeated and the boy closed his fist around the money and once more sprinted beyond the face of the buildings. This time he did not return.

The three of them walked back into the street and there the priest sat in the dirt, his robes folded about his knees and thighs and he arose at their coming.

"It was the railroad," he said and he lowered his head as if in some grand apology. "It was supposed to come and when it didn't the town moved on and the Indians and outlaws picked over what was left and fought among themselves and those who died I buried and those who lived I prayed for."

The priest paused and looked out over the ghost town and the country beyond it.

"Still, there were those who remained," he said. "Then came the sickness. A plague upon my flock. In the end I became a gravedigger, not a priest."

"And the boy?"

"The boy has been here since I can remember though I do not recall his coming, nor his mother or father. I cannot say that he is of the town or the plains or that he is not the second coming of Christ himself, and he can also not say these things, as he does not speak, though he hears very well. I have seen him perk up in the night at the sound of things far away, things even I can neither hear nor place. He is not a normal child, and yet I fear I do not know how to make him so. It is good you are staying."

They walked with the priest to the church he would not abandon and it was set into the world through the molding of mud and clay, the latter making it red in the sun, and above it stood fastened an iron cross and when Randall asked why it wasn't wood the priest stared up with one hand shielding his eyes as if he'd never before noticed or as if looking at the cross would bring forth the answer. In the end the priest shrugged his shoulders.

Though the sun was not yet down, the church was dark inside and they ate by candlelight. On the table was a single cut onion, a bowl of browned carrots, and a tough meat of which Randall did not ask the origin. Instead, he complimented the priest on a fine meal and commenced his arduous chewing and the rest of his party did the same.

There was also two-day-old fry bread warmed in a clay bowl and set in the middle of the table. Tad wrapped his meat in the bread and ate it as a sandwich.

"Momma," the child said to Tad and he copied the older boy's movements.

"I ain't your damn momma," Tad told him.

Randall looked at Tad and motioned to the priest.

"Sorry, Padre," Tad managed, his mouth full of food.

The priest waved him off.

"A word is only a word," he said. "Our Lord created the heavens and the earth and the things upon it. He governed life long before words and I do not believe He hears the thoughts on our tongue but rather those in our hearts."

The priest stared down at his own plate. The food was untouched.

"Yes," he continued. "There is no hiding what is in a man's heart."

"How come you didn't move on?" Charlotte asked him.

"I am an afflicted soul, ma'am."

"In what way?"

"I am cursed with a need for drink. A heavy need. And no doubt this is why He has punished me. To be spared when all around you are suffering will harden even the most compassionate of souls."

Randall watched as the priest pushed his plate toward the child who looked at it and grinned excitedly.

"Momma."

The priest smiled, weary.

"I am too ashamed to leave this place. I fear no other congregation would take me, and if they would, what kind of terrible things might come to pass? So I stay. I offer empty blessings in exchange for wine or ale. I am no example of God or even a man."

He shook his head and excused himself from the table.

"Father," Charlotte called after him, and he turned and lifted his brow in response. "We will stay here tonight, if that's alright by you."

The priest brought his hands together and gave a half bow.

"Thank you, my child."

They slept stretched out along old pews to stay off the cold floor. The wind howled through the cracks in the adobe walls where they met the slumping roof. Randall imagined his feather bed and the warmth of the stove and the smell of bacon and coffee in the mornings. The strange meat sat heavy in his belly and he heard Tad's snoring and the child's whimpering and at some point in the night Charlotte rose and went outside with her rifle. He was asleep before she came back in.

In the morning Randall felt a hand on his shoulder and he startled awake and Charlotte was before him with her finger to her lips. He sat up and she motioned for him to follow her. They walked out into the dawn and stood in the street and Randall wiped the sleep from his eyes. Once he'd done so, Charlotte pointed to the roof of the church and Randall turned to see.

The rope was made of horsehair and ran nearly twenty feet in length. It had been doubled back on itself and tied to a bosal like the ones Randall had seen his grandfather use to train young horses. It was looped and knotted around the base of the iron cross at the church's highest point and from it the priest swung and turned in a slow rotation a few feet above the doorway.

The two of them stood in the street and did not speak for a long while. The sun came on and its light shone brightly against the building and the span of the rope became engulfed in it and all but disappeared so that the body of the priest seemed to be suspended in air by some dark magic.

* * *

They stood—Tad, Charlotte, and Randall—outside the church. Charlotte had cut the body down and Randall dug a grave. He'd said a few words and quoted from the book of Matthew and that was the end of it and now there was nothing left but to push forward and so they would but different than they'd arrived.

"I don't like this one damn bit," Tad said, incredulous, looking at the boy as he stood in his typical silence near their horses. "That is one unnerving child."

"Well, we can't just leave him here," Randall said.

"Okay, then put him up on a horse and slap its ass," Tad argued.

"There aren't any more horses."

"If there ain't no horses, how the hell is he supposed to ride with us?"

Randall and Charlotte glanced at the child who was standing with his ear against the red-orange stallion.

"Oh, no. Oh, hell no," Tad said.

"He could be your friend," Randall said.

"He's too strange to have friends," Tad answered back.

"Them horses seem to like him alright," Charlotte said. "I ain't never known a horse to be wrong about nobody. Even Pumpkin took a liking to him."

"No, he ain't neither," Tad snapped. "Pumpkin does what I say."

"Pumpkin," the boy called from across the street and pointed to Tad's animal.

Tad rolled his eyes and scoffed.

"Well, hell."

11

We rode east and the desert rose up into mountains, though not as tall as the last, and we saw rams and mule deer on the rocks and I used my father's rifle to kill a rabbit for supper but there was little meat on it to be had. The sun was not as hot and in the mountain pass the winds came at night and we kept a fire going until morning and rode on without breakfast.

The grade was steep out of the mountains and the path narrow. We walked the horses along the cliffs and down into the valley and the air was cool here, but the water was still scarce. We led the horses along a dry creek and Shelby shot at a diamondback and missed and the horses breathed heavy even without riders.

The creek bed found a larger stream with something left to give and we drank from the shallow water, horses and men.

Shelby practiced drawing the pistol from his pocket and the valley echoed his curses as the gun tumbled from his hand. I sat near the water and watched birds dart in and out of the scrub brush and thought about my mother and if there was a Heaven. I remembered my baptism and could feel the preacher's hands on my shoulders as I shivered and Shelby telling me it would be the only way to see our mother once she passed, and the water was warm compared to the air.

I thought again of the boy and wondered how long my sins stayed clean and took stock of the stream and knew it wasn't deep enough to save me. Shelby said he was going off to dig a hole and I nodded and looked again at the water. The current was small and weak like a newborn, and I was a child once and my father a lawman and my mother not sick.

The bushes rustled behind me and it wasn't birds or Shelby, and the girl who emerged was scared and beautiful and staring at the horses. Her eyes found mine and they were dark and wild. She looked again at the horses, and I shook my head slow. She started after them and so did I and I was faster. I wrapped my arms around her and we kicked up dust and she yanked free and got in a good blow to my ear before I grabbed her again. The horses shied away from us, and I threw her to the ground and she kept at it from on her back. I pinned her arms and she kicked at me and screamed so I mounted her at the waist and we sat there. She had olive skin and black hair and I figured her for a Mexican or an Indian and her lips were dry and cracked. The sleeves of her white blouse had been ripped off and I could see the lean muscle in her arms as she struggled against my weight. She wore men's pants and they were held up with what looked like a tie string from a gunnysack.

"I ain't gonna hurt you," I told her and I asked if she spoke English, and she just laid there staring up at me and her face was sharp, both bone and brow.

"I ain't gonna hurt you," I said again, "but them are our horses. You can't take our horses. You understand? Comprende?"

She jerked her face to the side and out of the brush came Shelby. Without a belt, his pants sagged around his thighs and he rested his hands on his hips.

"Well, hot damn, Caleb."

He walked over to us and the girl's eyes stayed on him and he looked down and laughed.

"Hot damn," he repeated, shaking his head.

"She come out of the south," I pointed to the bend in the stream. "Caught her trying to steal a horse."

I followed her gaze to the knapsack tied to Shelby's saddle, and his horse stomped and shook its head.

"You could've just asked for food," I said, and Shelby shook his head and buckled his belt and walked to where our tussle, mine and the girl's, had ended.

"Food, horses—don't make no matter. A thief's a thief, little brother."

I stood up, slow, and the girl raised herself on one elbow and looked up at the two of us, her eyes squinted in the sun and I could see her shoulder had come clean out of the socket and her arm was hanging there like a dead branch.

"You want me to fix that shoulder?" I asked, and she looked down, as if just realizing she had a second arm, and then back up at me, curious.

"I ain't no doctor, but I seen my daddy do it to himself a time or two. He did it to me once," I said, and the girl looked confused.

"See, we used to have this little ol' corral and we'd break horses when I was a boy and they'd throw us about a dozen times a day and we'd end up beat and bruised and every now and then—"

"Shut the hell up, Caleb," Shelby said and then turned toward the girl. "Where you from? Ain't no towns we've seen."

The girl ignored him and Shelby spit and it landed near her boots and I saw they were also too large for her, like the pants.

"Have it your way," he said. "Don't really matter where you're from noways. Only thing matters is who you run off from and how much they gonna pay to get you back."

The girl tried to scramble to her feet but Shelby's boot found her ribs and she crumpled down again.

"You ain't gotta kick her," I said. "And how you know she run off from somewhere?"

"Well, why in the hell else would she be out here in the middle of nowhere good trying to relieve us of our food and horses? I imagine there's some old Mexican husband out there looking for her. Pretty little thing like that, I can also reckon he'll be willing to shell out a little re-ward money to the fellers who hand her over."

"But we don't know where she's from."

"That's true enough. Guess she'll just have to ride with us until someone comes a-huntin' her. If nobody shows, we may be able to sell her to a whorehouse in San Antonio. Either way, she ought to be worth a little spending money."

The dry, brittle catclaws rustled and cracked and the wind that came down to touch my face was hot. The girl stared at me and her eyes bore into my stomach and I felt the black sky crawling across the desert and it made me sick.

"Somebody looking for you?" I asked her, and she swiveled her head to each side as if she were surrounded by ghosts who warned her not to tell.

"She ain't gonna talk. Probably don't speak no English anyhow," Shelby said. "Now get her hands tied and help her up on my horse."

I didn't move. We stared at each other, the girl and me, and I recognized her face as my own and we were, both of us, scared of the coming storm and I could see it in my dreams and sense it on the open plains but what I had only imagined she had actually touched. Touched it and felt its teeth and they were sharp enough to bleed the world.

The girl's eyes went wide and thunder tore through my chest and I stepped back.

"Caleb, get her goddamned hands tied."

She shook her head as I moved toward her and her lips were moving and I stopped, inches from her face.

"He's coming," she whispered. "He's coming."

"Caleb!"

I blinked hard and took a breath and reached for the girl and she tried again to run. I wrapped her up and held her, my arms around her chest, and I thought maybe she was crying but she wasn't and instead she just kept saying it over and over: "He's coming."

"Hold still, and let me fix that arm," I said into her ear as I took hold of her shoulder. I could feel the socket and the bone out of place. We both closed our eyes.

12

The child rode with his arms around Tad and his cheek pressed against the older boy's back. The junipers followed the dry creek bed through the draw and the sounds and colors of life suggested the water nearby, but the mesquite that filled the sandy wash grew too thick and the riders turned the horses back out toward the desert to find a way around. They climbed to the halfway point of the south-facing ridge and saw the arroyo below and pointed to the trail leading down.

The rock shelf from the lonely ridge came down to meet the trees, which made for the riders a welcomed windbreak. They all—man, woman, and child—set about their routine and with the efficiency of those who'd been at such work over the course of many undertakings, as must be the case for any thing or things in life which are to ever be deemed routine in the first place.

At the finishing of the camp, Charlotte and the child walked with her horse toward the water, Tad sat and stared into the fire, and Randall found himself admiring his mount in a way he had not anticipated.

Randall knew naught of horses save that little which he read, which was mostly exaggerated accounts of deeds turned legend, and he placed such stories below him as the fantastical accounts of cowboys and book-sellers. But as he numbered backward the days and the riding and there was Mara, still profound in her regality, he thought again of these tales and at least entertained the idea of their truthfulness. He spoke to Mara and her ears flicked and his voice he thought must be a novelty as little of it had been given to her, and he apologized for this and other things and ran his hand along her neck and felt the strength of her breathing. His hand moved down to her shoes and the stout Arabian lifted her foot back in the learned way and Randall was remiss it had not been he who taught her. The shoe was still intact, but even a man who knew nothing would name it overworn and he found the same of the other three and suddenly there was a great indebtedness on his heart and again he asked the horse's forgiveness as if she were God Herself.

"You reckon that priest went to Heaven?" Tad asked, interrupting his admiration.

"It's not my place to say," Randall answered.

"You believe in God, Mr. Dawson?"

"I do. Don't you, son?"

"I don't rightly know. I guess so."

Randall studied the boy as he poked at the fire and seemed to pay no mind to the heaviness of the subject or the future of his soul.

"Tad, have you been baptized?"

"I ain't real sure. Daddy took me to a woman's house and dunked me in her bathtub and said I was baptized, but he was drunk so I don't know if that counts. I imagine he don't know the right words to say, anyhow."

The boy held his hand over the flame as long as he could, then jerked it back and shook it and appeared disappointed, as if in a competition with himself or the ghosts around him.

"Would you like me to baptize you?" Randall asked him.

"Did you baptize Harry?"

Randall smiled. "I sure did."

"Let me think on it a spell."

Randall nodded and they set for a time.

"What about Old Man Simpson?" Tad asked.

Randall shook his head, "Who is Old Man Simpson?"

"Old Man Simpson was this fella lived in a little cabin outside of Longpine. Daddy used to take me there and have me set with the old man's granddaughter while he and her momma went off and did what there was to do. Daddy would call it playing cards, but I knew it wasn't that. One time the little girl, I think her name was Mary, or Martha, she opened the door and we could see her momma down on her knees and—"

"Tad," Randall cut him off.

"Right. Anyhow, Old Man Simpson was deaf and dumb, so he couldn't hear nothing. Blind too, since birth, and he just set there in a rocker moving his lips while me and that little girl scooted a few playthings 'cross the floor."

Randall waited for more, but Tad was back at his hand-burning game.

"I don't follow."

"Well," the boy snatched his hand back and shook it. "If he can't see the Bible, and he can't hear no preacher, how's Old Man Simpson gonna know about God and Heaven and the like?"

"Surely in such a case, the Lord would make an exception."

"What's an exception?"

"It means not following the rules, but only in certain situations."

"So God gets to break His own rules?"

"Well, to an extent I guess that's right," Randall said, wondering if that was indeed correct.

"That don't seem fair."

"It isn't about fair. It's about faith—trusting in God and trusting He'll do the right thing."

"But sometimes He doesn't."

"He works in mysterious ways, but that doesn't mean He's wrong."

Tad poked at the fire and again looked disappointed, and Randall could not be sure if it was his answer or the dying embers that had upset the boy, and long after their talk both of them, man and child, would think about what was said.

Charlotte returned with the young boy who went and sat next to Tad. The older boy rolled his eyes.

Randall stared at the woman and took in her beauty—the leanness of her arms and the sharp edges contouring her face.

"Something wrong?" she asked and Randall shook his head, embarrassed, and looked away.

"So, uh, I was thinking," Randall said, hoping to deflect the awkwardness, "Charlotte, you know Texas. These men are headed there. Where will they go?"

"Texas is a big place, Mr. Dawson," she replied. "But if they don't want no part of the Mexican fight that's coming, I imagine they'll cross all the way through New Mexico, come into Texas around Gaines or Andrews County. That's the track I'd take, 'less we hear different."

"And you know the land in these places?"

"I know it a little bit. My brother was killed in Shafter Lake. A bunch of white men stripped him naked and strung him up."

"Good God."

"If you say so."

"Were you there?"

"I was," she nodded. "Hiding like a coward. The next morning I ran off to Carlsbad. Never looked back."

"I'm sorry to hear about your brother. But there was nothing you could have done."

"Don't speak, Mr. Dawson, on matters you don't know a thing about."

"My apologies."

She waved him off.

"Aw, I just get touchy," she said. "It's a good thing you did, taking that boy. Child like that shouldn't be alone in this world."

"We couldn't leave him," Randall said, confused by the praise.

"Some would have. A lot even."

"That's awful. I can't believe that to be the truth."

"Well," she said, "that's what makes you a good man."

Randall blushed.

"Y'all quit your dadgum courting," Tad said, crossing his arms. "Ain't neither one of you any good at it and I'm trying to get some shut-eye."

"Pumpkin," the child said, crossing his arms as well.

13

We rode east from the stream, nudging the horses out of the valley at a slow pace and the girl sat atop Shelby's horse, him behind her, arms wrapped around her waist to handle the reins. I didn't like it, seeing them like that, and I wasn't sure why and I didn't like *that* either.

The day was hotter than most and by noon we were, the three of us, covered in sweat and the girl's dark hair stuck to her neck and she saw me watching. The desert sand turned to dry prairie grass and the hills and mountains were dotted with short pines and scrub oaks and we nooned and took our lunch under their shade. We'd seen no game since the rabbit, so we rationed a half a can of beans between the two of us, Shelby and me, and our stomachs grumbled even after but there was nothing to be done. I gave the girl a few bites of beans and a piece of dried meat and asked how her shoulder felt and Shelby cussed me as wasteful and soft.

I ignored him and fed the girl from my spoon.

"You have brothers or sisters?" I asked her.

She swallowed and spit into the dirt.

"What are you doing out here in this country alone?"

She did not answer.

"What happened to you?"

I asked her where she lived, if she was on the run, if she'd done something wrong.

"How about a name?"

She spit again.

"Alright then, good talk."

* * *

The heat only worsened and Shelby complained and said Texas weather was no good and he missed the territory and he put the girl off his horse and told me to deal with her.

"C'mon," I said and offered my hand and she refused.

I dismounted while Shelby sat his horse and watched, and I untied her hands and pulled an eight-foot basswood rope from my saddlebag. I wrapped two feet around the girls hands and asked if it was too tight and she glared at me and with every movement I felt like an oppressor, like I was a murderer and a kidnapper and a horse thief and the weight pressed down on me.

"None of this is right," I said, holding the rope in my hand and the girl on the other end. I stood by the horse. My chest grew heavy and my throat began to close up. "I can't breathe."

The girl looked at me and for the first time her face softened and she leaned forward as if she wanted to comfort me, but thought better of it. Then she ran. I felt the rope snaking through my hands and I tightened my grip just before it was gone. The girl had momentum, but I dug my boot heels into the ground and as soon as the slack disappeared the girl's feet flew forward from under her and she twisted in the air and landed hard on her side. She rolled onto her back and looked up at the sky. I walked over to her and her breathing was heavy and the sky blue and with only one cloud. I thought it looked like a bear, but the bear was being stretched thin and soon it was nothing and there was just sky again.

"If you two are through playing cowboy and Mexican, how 'bout we get on with it," Shelby said.

I felt weak and dizzy, but I helped the girl to her feet and saw her shoulder had pulled out again and she held her lips tight and made no sound.

"I can pop it back again, if you want," I told her and she thought and gave a single nod, and this time the going was a little smoother and she stayed on her feet and screamed, which I thought was a good sign.

"You really ought to ride. It's hell-hot out here and plus them boots is too big for you."

We both looked down at the worn, black cow leather.

"You take them from somebody? Your father? Your husband?"

I took off my hat and wiped the back of my arm across my forehead.

"Listen, I'm not here to hurt you," I spoke slowly, as if she was a child. "If you're running from somebody, you gotta let me know. I can protect you. You understand? Keep you safe. I'd like to do that for you. Would you like that?"

Her face scrunched and she began walking up the trail and me behind her with the rope and Shelby laughing on his stolen horse.

"Looks like you're the prisoner now, little brother."

And maybe I was.

* * *

That night I tended the fire for hours even when it didn't need tending. As hot as the day had been, the darkness brought with it a chill and it added to my sleeplessness. I watched the flames eat away at the wood and the logs consumed from their middle and then split in half by the fire. One piece became two and I was a whole log once.

I didn't know I was crying until I felt the girl's eyes on me and awareness came like a wave and I wiped my face and stared back at her. I'd tied the basswood in a knot around my old calf lariat made of horsehair, then tied one end of the lariat to my ankle and the other to one of the junipers in the stand where we'd made camp. The girl couldn't run without me feeling it. I wiped my eyes and took her water and watched her drink and when she had her fill she handed back the canteen and studied my face with concern.

She motioned for me to come closer and when I leaned down she kissed me. It wasn't wet or passionate or exaggerated like I'd seen in the Tanglefoot. It was soft and sweet and over too soon.

She sat back against a fallen red rock and looked at me and I felt a strange comfort until I thought of the things I'd done and wondered how I could have deserved a kiss as perfect as that one, and the tears came again and I did not stop them. I wept in silence as Shelby slept and the fire burned and the wolves closed in and the girl saw it all.

* * *

Shelby was into the whiskey early the next day. At first it had him talking about ranches and outlaws and the guns he would buy. But soon the talking bored him, and I could see in his face the sinister things that were taking hold and the way he stared at the girl did little to curtail my worries.

I thought back to the two women on the road with their father and wondered what might have happened before the shots rang out and again I felt sick and I tried to think of my mother but all I could see was Shelby's face as it grinned and I wondered if there was any good left in him.

By noon he was far gone and angry at the world and dumped out the half can of beans and said he was tired of eating at the poor table and he cussed the lack of game and cussed the girl for slowing us down.

When we set off again he jerked the girl up onto his horse and said it was so we could make better time and we all knew, the three of us, it was a lie. Within minutes he had nuzzled his face into her neck. She squirmed and ducked and he clouted her ear and went on kissing her shoulder and grabbing at her small breasts and laughing.

"Hey, don't do her like that," I said.

Shelby threw daggers at me with his stare and continued his fondling, challenging me to do anything about it.

I could feel my face heating up, some mix of embarrassment and anger and I tried to look away, patting my horse and running my hand along his mane, whispering to him and congratulating him on being a good horse.

I rode ahead, escaping the things to come, which I knew I could not stomach. I dismounted and led the horse up a stone-cut path that I figured the Indians had put there all them years back. When we reached the top the vistas showed the places we'd come from and the way we were headed and I could see Fort Stockton, less than a day's ride, and the lonely country that stretched east from there.

The world whole seemed to sit below, and I fought against the feeling that the dried salt flats and the scrub desert and the canyons and plains beyond were all there was, all there ever had been. No beginning, no end, just a sprawling, staggered overlay of what the earth once was, and perhaps would be again.

I pissed in a dying cluster of fiddleneck that had grown up around the rocks and drank water from my canteen to replace what I'd lost. I knew I ought to eat but I wasn't hungry and I kept imagining Shelby and the girl and his hands on her and I told my horse I was sorry and that I was a damn fool and then I led him back down the path to confront my brother and my fears.

* * *

The country sloped east and I imagined it covered with snow and knew there were cold days ahead and wondered about the weather in East Texas and if I might make a good timberman. I walked the horse back down the Indian steps and I didn't like them being there, something made by man in otherwise untouched country. I knew no land was left virgin, but my boot prints were alone in the dust and that gave me a great comfort unlike I had felt before. I looked out again and thought of how far we could go, the Missouri and me, and it was something beautiful. But there was still Shelby and the girl to see about and I had made up my mind, so I kept down the ridge toward the valley and there a man appeared in my path and it was as though he had manifested onto the trail with no horse and without making a sound.

My horse pawed at the dirt and shook its head, and I held it with one hand and tipped my hat with the other. The man wore no hat and no gun belt and had dark-gray hair which hung back across his scalp and his skin had been turned leather by the sun and his days under it. He was draped in a blue-and-black poncho and the man nodded and stared at the nervous horse and moved toward it. I said nothing as he reached for it and stroked its nose and we all stood still, horse and men.

"Fine animal," the man spoke and his voice was deep but kind and his eyes shone bright blue.

I agreed and asked if he was lost and he laughed and said we all are and I figured him a drunkard.

"Fine country, too," he said, and I couldn't discern from his tone if his words were meant for me or himself or perhaps the horse, and there was something that unnerved me about the man.

"You alone?" I asked and the man ignored my question, walking past me and the horse and the patches of alkali grass to where the ridge looked out over the empty land below.

"You ever hear of the Caddo?" the man asked without turning around.

"They were Indians, I think," I answered, strangely drawn to this man and his casual display.

"Yes, Indians, very good," he said.

"Did they build these steps?"

The man shook his head.

"No, the Caddo people lived in East Texas. Along the rivers and among the pines, where the deer were too many to count and the smell of the forest was bitter in their nostrils but sweet in their souls. I lived in these places once."

"How come you're out here?"

Again the man ignored me.

"There is a story—a legend if you will—in Caddo lore," he said. "It's the story of Lightning."

"Lightning?"

"In the first days of the people, Lightning lived among them, free upon the earth. But he was too strong and too powerful and the people feared him. So they banished him to the spirit realm so that he could not hurt them."

The man turned from the cliffside and faced me. He stared at me, into my eyes, and continued.

"But then a great monster came from under the ground and laid waste to the people. They fought it, bravely, but could not kill it. Then other monsters came. Finally Lightning appeared again to the people and told them, 'I will kill these monsters, if you will but allow me back into your world.' And the people were afraid, but they let Lightning return because only he was powerful enough to rid the earth of those things that wished to destroy it."

The man spoke no more but continued to watch me and the horse to my back.

"Well," I said, "alright then."

"We're all lost and we're all alone. But we don't have to be," he said and looked at me like he knew me and everything and more. "You just keep that in mind when the time comes."

I didn't know the appropriate response and so I gave none. But the man smiled anyway, his demeanor instantly changing, loosening.

"Now," he said, with a grin and a wave, "get on down there to that girl, 'fore the fella you're riding with does something he can't take back."

The man turned back toward the vista and spit and shook his head and said again that it was damn fine country. I mounted the horse and rode it hard into the valley.

* * *

I heard screams and followed them and the Indian grass swayed and parted as the horse charged through. I didn't see the cactus grove but the horse did and moved to the side of it without so much as shifting the saddle and I told him again he was a good horse and I meant it. The screams grew louder, and I burst into the clearing with my rifle raised and there was Shelby's horse tied to a tree and the girl tied also and there was blood but not her own.

Shelby screamed and it sounded like dying cattle and I saw him on his knees frantic and digging his hands through the dust as blood poured from the side of his head.

"I can't find it!" he shouted and then screamed again and his horse whinnied and I asked the girl what happened and still she didn't speak.

"Stupid bitch bit my goddamn ear off!" Shelby yelled and then sunk his head in his hand and cried. "My goddamn ear."

I could see the front of the girl's shirt freshly torn and the tie string on her pants undone but if there was fear in her it did not show and I looked at her for a while and the blood on her lips. She was beautiful and ferocious.

"I can't find it," Shelby moaned and rocked back and forth and we looked up, the girl and me, onto the ridge and there was the shape of a man against the sun.

"Brother," I called to Shelby. "Stand up. Now."

Whatever strength the girl had shown in the face of my brother quickly dissipated and she began to tremble where she stood.

"He's coming," she said.

"My goddamn ear."

"Now, Shelby!"

Howls began to echo through the valley and the dry brush and tall grass swayed with no wind and the girl struggled against her ties while Shelby sat in the dirt.

"Damn it, Shelby, we got trouble," I pleaded with him. "Use the ear you still got and listen to me: get your ass up."

I heard movement behind me and a man sprang from the underbrush and knocked the rifle from my hands. He caught me with one fist, but I blocked the next and kicked his knee out from under him. He pulled a knife and came up slashing and I grabbed his wrist and we stood pushing against each other in some sort of backward tug-o'-war. I kicked his knee again and it buckled and I brought the blade down from his own hand and it went into him somewhere near his ear and drug across toward his neck. He went limp and fell and the girl screamed and pointed up.

I looked at her and then back at the top of the ridge and there was no one and Shelby stood and wiped his face and drew his gun and the howls grew louder. The horse turned a nervous circle and I put my hand on his neck to calm us both and the girl shouted something but her words were drowned in the yips and yells all around us.

I picked up the rifle and there was everywhere to aim but nothing to see and Shelby, the only one moving, stepped toward the girl with his pistol in hand.

"My goddamn ear," he said and the girl's eyes grew wide.

I took two steps and leapt at him and our bodies collided, us brothers, and we were there in the dust, where we'd always been, and Shelby's eyes were sad and confused with betrayal.

The girl shouted again and I turned in time to see the butt end of the rifle as it closed my eyes and I was back in the territory and the rain fell like a sheet over the mountains and my mother said not to worry.

14

The eastern light summoned from the darkness a world of shapes turned to stone and the wind blew at nothing, but it blew unsparing, and the four riders found no shelter or mercy as the cold came into the land like the flowing of a river into the sea.

A herd of antelope crossed the flat plain and the dawn saw the life-breath from their nostrils and the dust of the earth come up from their feet and they paid the riders no mind save a glance before moving on into the mist of morning.

Randall felt the iron at either side shifting as Mara moved under him and his gaze was to Charlotte and he felt something else. Their horses moved in unison, as if being called home into the rising sun, and soon his look of adoration was returned—and even a smile—and so they were as a pair, horses and riders.

"People coming," Tad said, and they sat their horses, watching the specters grow taller in the distance.

"Pumpkin," the child said.

"Shut up," Tad told him.

The images appeared on the horizon as if born from the morning and moved slowly on foot and a mule behind them carried what little there was. The man among them saw the horses and their riders and sent the rest of his party scurrying mouselike into the cover of the underbrush and that cover would not have been enough and the man knew it.

He raised a shotgun and called out and took a few steps toward the unknown, then thought better of it and stood sentry midtrail. Randall put the horse forward and called "friend" to the man, who kept the shotgun trained on the rider even so.

The distance between eroded, and Randall put both his hands out near his shoulders and again called "friend" and the man lowered the gun, nervous, and each motioned to their companions and there they all met in the road, in the desert, in the world.

With the man were a woman and two girls no older than ten years.

"Y'all bandits?" the man asked of Randall in a scratched and low tone, and though the sun was at his back his eyes were squinted almost to closure.

"Nossir," Randall told him.

"Alright then, Geanie, go on," the man said, nodding, and shoved forward the woman, who kept her head down as she spoke.

"You like to go yonder behind them bushes with me?" the woman asked softly, and only when she was finished asking did she tilt her eyes up enough to see an answer.

Randall looked to Charlotte, who shook her head in a sad way, and to Tad, whose eyes had grown double their size, and then back to the woman.

"No ma'am," he managed, at a loss for what else is to be said at such a strange encounter as this, and the man in front of him grabbed the woman and pulled her back behind him, where she began to cry.

"Shut up, whore," the man said and turned back to the silent onlookers. "Well, I would offer up the little'uns, but I imagine I'll get more for 'em if they ain't ruint."

Charlotte moved as if she were made of lightning. Before Randall could turn his head, she had a pistol drawn and lowered at the man's head.

The man looked at first confused, then angered.

"You better tell this nigger to holster that thirty-eight," he said to Randall. "These is my women and I'll treat 'em however way I please, as the Good Book says is my right."

"Put it away, Charlotte," Randall told her.

"He don't deserve to live," she replied, thumbing back the hammer.

The world around them moved, but they did not. Then forward came the woman called Geanie and she stood in front of the man and looked up at Charlotte.

"Please," she asked. "Don't shoot him. He's my husband. He takes care of us."

The man smiled a crooked smile as Charlotte lowered her gun. He spit and it landed in the dirt near Mara's hoof.

Randall eyed the man and felt his own violent urge growing.

"We're gonna head on down this road the way we were going," Randall nodded to the man. "I suggest you do the same."

The man grunted and hurried his wife, or his whore, or both, down the road and the two girls in rags trudged behind and Randall's bunch all just sat their horses and didn't say anything and when somebody did it was Tad.

"Sorry sumbitch we just crossed paths with," he said, and no one argued. "Sure hate if he was my daddy."

He spit and shook his head.

"Pumpkin," the younger boy said in a matching tone and he too spit and shook.

"Let's get on down the trail," Charlotte said. "I don't much care to be no closer to that man than I got to."

* * *

They rode in silence and nooned off to the side of the road and there was no shade and, the cold of the morning long gone, they began to sweat. A fire seemed too much trouble and time, so they ate cold beans and dried meat and there were berries fallen from bushes along a retired fence line and they ate those too.

"You would've killed that man," Randall said to Charlotte as if she herself were wondering.

She nodded.

"I imagine I would have," she said.

"That's murder."

"It is," she nodded again.

"And the woman and the children? What would have happened to them, alone in the desert?"

"They would have been free," she snapped.

"Free to die, maybe."

"Death is better than some things, Mr. Dawson," Charlotte said, her voice cold and cutting. "Maybe you didn't learn that growing up with money spilling out your ears. Some painful things in this life."

Randall was silent for a moment, then he nodded.

"There are indeed," he said. "Some of the men on my ranch, they had to drag me away from Harry's body. I wouldn't let anyone near him that night. I could smell the burning trees and hear the shouts of the men, but I just sat there, holding him. We were going to go hunting, once the weather cooled. This was going to be the year he took his first buck."

Randall swallowed his tears.

"It was my pistol," he said, soft and choked. "It was my pistol he tried to stop them with."

Charlotte came to him and put her arm around his back and his head slumped and he wept.

"I'm so sorry," she said.

Randall raised his head and took a deep breath and opened his mouth wide. He stood.

"I'm fine," he said. "I'll be just fine."

Charlotte watched him walk away and felt inside herself both pity and desire. Desire to comfort him, to watch over him, somehow. Or perhaps, she thought, it was her failure to save her brother that was driving this need to protect the helpless. And Randall Dawson was nothing if not helpless.

Randall left the camp for nearly half an hour and when he returned he acted as if nothing had happened. He fastened the strap under Mara and called to the others to mount up.

"We oughta get off the main road," Charlotte said. "There'll be more water and better places to make camp if we head north a piece and then cut east."

"Too many banditos on the main road, anyhow," Tad added.

Randall drained the last of a cup of coffee and flung the crud from the bottom of the cup and squatted down on his haunches, bounced, and then stood back up and shook his head.

"We can't afford to lose time. Not to mention we have to ask the whereabouts of the Bentleys and the best place to do that is in towns along the road."

"Them boys weren't going through no towns, Randall," Charlotte said.

He smiled. "*Randall?*" he repeated, then nodded. "We're still sticking to the main road. If you all disagree, you're welcome to head back."

He took his empty cup and swung himself atop Mara and put her into the road.

"He must be feeling better," Charlotte said and clicked her tongue.

"Pumpkin," the small boy said and clicked his tongue in turn.

15

The world was black and in the blackness I saw the flames.

The fire would clear out the ranch and send the men up into the hills with buckets and no one would be left tending the herd. Shelby said we'd pick what we wanted, horses and cattle, and ride out laughing. I told him there's not much worse in the world than a horse thief, and he said ol' Dawson had more than any one man ought to have. He told how Dawson had shamed our father and turned the town against him and asked if I loved my family and I thought of our mother and said yes.

I asked about the law, and he said Dawson was a dandy and he'd be too scared to say anything. He told me most folks hated Dawson anyway, so we'd be heroes and the whores would bed us no charge and the men would buy us whiskey, and I said I didn't too much care for all that, but I would like a horse of my own.

The saddle had always been a harbinger of joy, the horse a bellwether of freedom. Growing up in the territory I'd ridden ponies and mules, then mustangs and quarter horses. We kept a corral in back of the house and it sold with the land and the horses too after my mother turned ill. Sickness is expensive. Sickness and sadness and drink and all the horses gone.

Our spread was part of Dawson's now. Our house rented to tenant farmers when my father refused the offer to stay on. Our horses were Dawson's horses, and I watched our lives dissolve into his and I knew I would never bring back my father from the bottle nor my mother from the dirt, but a horse to call my own sounded as fine a consolation as could be offered and so I went along with Shelby's bad plan and in the end I killed a boy.

The fire was set and, like my brother said, the men raced toward it with buckets aplenty. But the flames were too close to the stock pens and the horses were first unnerved and soon horrified and they cried and kicked and climbed atop one another in a wave of chaos and flesh. They crashed into the gate, which could not hold, and they went sprinting in all directions. The cattle had already made for the far prairies when the fire was little more than smoke, and so we stood, Shelby and me, motionless in the empty yard.

"What now?" I asked, my eyes darting, my breathing fast.

"Shit," he said and kicked the dirt.

"Let's just go. Let's get out of here before somebody sees us."

"Shit," he said again.

"Come on, brother, let's get."

"Naw, there's bound to be horses in that fancy stable barn yonder," he said, pointing. "That's where I'm headed."

Light was showing through one of the windows in the big house. I watched it, wary and anxious, but nothing moved. Reluctantly, I followed Shelby to the barn.

Inside, the animals stamped and snorted and were all-around skittish on account of the smoke and commotion nearby. The barn was lit by a single oil-burning lantern and the shadows of beasts rose up against the walls. To Shelby's dismay, only two of the stables held horses. The rest were filled with goats and pigs. He grabbed a saddle from the wall and ran the strap under the belly of the bigger horse and fastened to him a jaw rope. I stopped staring and went to work on the other horse and within two minutes we were mounted and free of the stalls and in the center of the barn.

The light from a second lantern uncovered us and our misdoings, bringing us forth from out of the shadows. The boy stood in the wide doorway, a lantern in one hand and a pistol in the other.

"The hell are you all doing in here?" he called, and I knew he could not be more than twelve.

"Taking these here horses," Shelby answered. "Now go on and get, before somebody gets hurt."

"My ass," the boy hollered, then he turned his head out toward the twilight. "Hey! They're in the barn! They're stealing the horses! Hey!"

I looked at Shelby.

"Now or never, little brother," he said and put his heels to the horse and together they plowed down the middle of the barn toward the door.

The boy was taken aback and stumbled out of the way and onto his bottom. I had frozen, but now I put my mount forward toward the outside world. Before I reached the door the boy rose and leveled his pistol at Shelby's back. I raised my rifle and flipped it as I rode. I swung the gun toward the boy just before he fired. My intention was to knock the pistol from his hand. Intentions, of course, are only hopes. And I should have given up on such things long ago.

The boy tried to turn toward me and I could feel the butt end of the rifle meet his wrist or hand or arm. I couldn't tell because the flash of gunpowder from the pistol caused me a half second of blindness and when I looked back the boy was slumped against the door frame, his face unrecognizable. Unhuman.

Men had come into the yard and were unsure of what to do as we charged past on our stolen mounts. No one fired a shot or even yelled for us to stop, and then there was Randall Dawson, bucket still in hand, and we looked at one another. I saw his eyes and he saw mine and for the briefest moment we were connected by this awful thing, and I knew then that we always would be.

That night I killed a boy made of flesh and a boy made of soul and together we died and one moved on to whatever comes next and the other was left to wander in the desert as a shell of skin and bone with only blackness beyond. And each day I became more convinced of my soul's departure, believing it to be already in Hell or, perhaps, on the run somewhere, like me but in another world. And if all worlds are the same then I imagined my soul might find me again, in some familiar way, and maybe we'd be happy to see each other, or maybe it would kill me on the spot and hope that redemption is attainable through deeds, lest we both burn forever.

* * *

"Alright then, boy. Come around nice and slow. I ain't figure Tom meant to kill you, but he sho'nuff got close."

The sunlight dimmed my eyes as I looked up and tried to make out the shape of the man speaking and the earth was spinning and my throat was raw. I moved to touch my head where it throbbed, but my hands were tied behind my back and I settled for the canteen as the man pressed it to my lips and tilted it back. I choked and the man laughed, though not unkind, and he said, "Easy, easy," and laughed again and called out to the world behind me, saying I was awake, and his shout cut into my head and I tried to stand up but instead slid into the dirt and closed my eyes again.

When they opened, the bearded man from the vista was in front of me, sitting on the ground with legs crossed and a blue-and-cream blanket laid out between us. My cheek rested against the red dirt and the man turned his head almost upside down so that we saw each other on similar planes.

"Guess you weren't alone," I managed, and the man found great humor in this and asked that I join him for a drink.

"Marcus," he called and a man came to cut my ties and it was the same man from before. He smiled, the man called Marcus, and helped me into a sitting position and told me he was glad I was feeling better and I was confused but nodded.

"Do you know who I am?" the bearded man asked and produced two clay cups and a bottle and set them on the blanket and Marcus took that as a signal to leave, and so he did.

"Where's my brother?" I asked and I tried to turn and look around but I moved too fast and had to steady myself against the earth. "Where's the girl?"

"The girl is alive," the man replied. "Thanks to you."

"And Shelby, my brother?"

"Him too. For now."

I caught sight of the horse and my rifle, at least twenty yards away—too far to make a dash. The bearded man poured from the bottle and the cups filled quickly and he emptied one himself and motioned to the other with his hand.

"Do you know who I am?" he repeated and I shook my head and he studied my eyes.

"I know you," he said, and I didn't break my blank expression. I held his gaze and kept my voice steady.

"I'm Edward Crawford," I told him, and he laughed. It was a warm laugh, both boisterous and friendly and his eyes were in a perpetual smile and I felt at ease even in a situation where I should have been fearing for my life and the life of my brother.

"Edward Crawford," he said the name and tasted it on his tongue and it swam in his mouth until he could not contain it and it burst from his lips again as another laugh.

"Well, I'll be damned," he said and shook his head and pulled from his pocket a paper. A paper I did not need to see to know what was on it. "Apparently there's a fella named Caleb Bentley that looks an awful lot like you."

I was silent.

"What's more, this Bentley, the one from the wanted poster here"—he tapped the likeness of my face with his forefinger—"he's got a brother that looks an awful lot like the fella we got tied up over yonder by the creek."

"You a bounty hunter?" I asked.

"I am," he replied. "But not the kind that's looking for you."

"What kind are you?"

"My bounties aren't collected in dollars, son. They're collected in the souls of wicked men. Are you a wicked man, Caleb?"

The light of the sun can do many things to a man's sight, and a concussed state does not always provide images that deal in reality, but the fact remains: I watched the bearded man's blue eyes fade to black as he stared at me, into me, and I could not move or speak and my breathing came heavy as the world around me spun.

"No," he said, as the darkness slipped away from us and a smile returned to his face. "I don't believe you are."

He motioned again to the cup and this time I did not hesitate. The liquor was dark and warm and it slithered down inside of me like it was looking for a place to hide. The man clapped his hands together once and nodded and then spread out his arms.

"Now, since you're not a wicked man, and since you've shared this drink with me, I am obliged to answer whatever questions you may have."

"Where's my brother?"

"That's a good first question. It shows loyalty to family, concern for others—very good, son. He's just down the slope here from us, where the rest of the fellas are camped. He's a little beat up, though to be honest he didn't put up much of a fight, and as you may remember he is short by one ear, which of course was not our doing."

"Who are you and how come you run up on us hot like that?"

"Yes, I apologize for that, and I know Tom just feels awful about that whack he gave you. It was purely precautionary, especially after you all but cut off poor Jacob's face. But don't feel badly about that. He disobeyed an order."

The man paused and shook his head as if reliving some grave disappointment.

"He never listened," the man said, then shrugged his shoulders. "Anyway, we weren't sure of your intentions nor what would be your reaction when we took back what was ours."

"The girl."

"That's right, the girl who you saved. An action, by the way, for which I am indebted to you," he said, holding his arms out. "Now, as to who we are. I myself am General Lawrence Grimes. You've met Indian Tom, a name I've tried to get him to part with, but alas, he is a most stubborn breed of Apache. And Marcus Freeman, the dark-shaded gentleman who has looked after you so as to not have you do something stupid, like die. There are nineteen other men in our current camp, and a few dozen more down south, waiting patiently for our return. I could give you all of their names but it seems an exhaustion in both time and practicality."

"The Lobos," I said, and the man nodded, pleased.

"You've heard of us," he said, almost giddy with delight.

"Y'all gonna kill us, then?" I asked plainly, and the man measured either the question or his response.

"Things like that are difficult to say. While I don't intend to kill you, I can't know that my hand won't be forced. I can't rightly give you my word, on account of there's a chance I'd have no choice but to break it. But I can cut a deal with you that says as long as I have no cause to kill you, I most assuredly will not."

"Ain't that the deal all men make with one another just by being in the world?" I asked.

"Oh no, son, killing goes on without cause more often than not. But I promise that won't be how you end," and the man moved his face forward toward mine and there were tobacco lines down the white of his beard and overhead the buzzards waited for something ill-fated and when he spoke again it was with the voice of prophecy. "When you die, Caleb, there'll be a cause."

I swallowed hard and waited until the man had settled back and then I pointed toward the makeshift camp down the ridge.

"Alright. Let me go. My brother too," I said. "And the girl. We'll ride out today, and you won't follow, and we won't speak to a soul about any of this and that'll be the end of it."

Grimes rose and brushed off his breeches and stared up at the circling birds and they called out and the man nodded and for the briefest moment I gave life to the thought they were conversing, the man and the buzzards. I lifted myself off the ground and squinted my eyes under the pain in my skull.

"Well, now, that's not quite what I had in mind," he said.

I stood in silence and waited. We stared at one another but somehow it felt as though I was the only one present, watching from some other dimension as Grimes stared at the real me.

"I could always use good boys. Are you a good boy, Caleb?"

"I'm a boy who wants to collect his companions and get on down the trail, with all due respect."

Grimes wore no gun belt but I took note of the leather sheath that hooked around his neck and shoulder and fell at his side and inside held a bowie knife of considerable size. I tensed, and Grimes stayed with his studious approach, always watching and considering and contemplating and then he threw his hands up in mock defeat.

"Fair enough. You go get your brother and y'all ride on out."

"And the girl."

Grimes smiled.

"You know what your brother was doing to her, don't you, son?"

I nodded, "I'll handle him."

"Will you? What do you reckon would have happened between you two if we hadn't ridden up when we did? Were you gonna kill him?"

"He's my brother."

"Is that a no?"

I didn't answer.

"A woman's place is with her family," Grimes said. "Do you agree?"

"I suppose it is."

"Then I think it best if my daughter stays with me."

I hesitated, then said, "She don't seem to feel that way."

His face flattened out and the way he looked at me set a lump in my throat and I felt the familiar panic sliding up my spine. The thunder in my mind was as loud as it had ever been and I could feel the darkness around us despite the bright sun and even the horse seemed spooked, but Grimes never moved.

"Get your brother," he said. "Sophia stays with me."

Sophia.

* * *

They had Shelby tied back-first against a tree and his head was slumped and bloody but he smiled when I said his name.

"Looks like you was right, little brother," he said, almost proud. "The murderous Bentley brothers was famous enough to get caught by a band of bounty hunters."

I studied his lazy grin and the mash of pus and dark red crust on the side of this head where it seemed no ear could ever have been.

"How come they turnt you loose?" he asked, suddenly confused, and I looked around to see how many eyes were on us before I answered.

"They ain't bounty hunters," I half hissed at him. "It's the Lobos. The ones them cowboys were talking about."

Shelby scrunched his face and considered the information.

"They gonna kill us?" he asked.

"I don't know. Grimes said they ain't."

"You talked to Grimes?"

I nodded, "Says the girl's his daughter."

"He's gonna kill me for sure," Shelby said, panicked.

"I don't think he is, but I ain't for certain one way or the other. Now lean up and let me get them ropes off. I don't wanna hang around and find out I'm wrong."

I helped Shelby to his feet and we found Bullet with the other horses in a grove of stunted oaks near the creek. His bedroll and saddlebag were attached, and he went through the two satchels slung over the old Mexican saddle and cussed and said the sumbitches had stolen his pistol.

"Forget it," I told him. "We still got the rifle."

"To hell with that. They can't get away with that."

"They sure as shit can, unless you're looking to die for that gun. And even then I reckon they'd oblige you and get away with it just fine."

Shelby looked around at the hardened warriors milling among the tents and small, scattered fires.

"That pistol didn't shoot straight anyways," he said and he spit and we walked Bullet back up the ridge where my horse sat near Grimes's tent.

Grimes had lathered his face with a shave soap and was half bent over a wooden bucket of water gliding a straight razor down his cheek when we walked up.

"Boys," he said like an old friend who'd been awaiting our arrival for some time. "Y'all sure I can't get you to stay for a while?"

Shelby looked at me, confused, but I said we were just here to collect the horse and rifle.

"And my pistol," Shelby blurted out, and my heart sank as Grimes lowered the blade and looked at him blankly.

"What pistol's that?"

"The one your men down there took off me when y'all jumped us by the creek."

"That sounds like something you'll need to take up with them," Grimes said and turned back to his bucket.

"Well, ain't you the boss?" Shelby asked.

Grimes stilled the razor once more.

"The boss?" he said. "Are you under the illusion this is a business enterprise of some sort? There is no boss here, son. No workers. That's not how we do things."

"Like Arthur and his knights," I said.

I don't know why I said it. I can't even be sure where I'd heard it, but Grimes beamed through his lathered soap and pointed the blade in my direction.

"That's right, Caleb. Just like Arthur."

"Who the hell's Arthur?" Shelby asked, but we both ignored him and again found ourselves in an unannounced staring contest. Grimes broke first.

"I knew you were a smart boy," he said.

"We're gonna be on our way, Mr. Grimes. We appreciate the hospitality, and the fact you're letting us leave outta here in one piece."

Grimes held his razor and his stare and no one moved and I felt Shelby shifting anxious beside me. From our right, Marcus approached with three men, one of them an Indian in full native dress who I assumed to be Tom. They were each of them armed. They stopped a dozen or so feet away, and we all stood in silence, every eye on Grimes, waiting.

"Almost," he said at last, and his face was straight and still no one moved.

"Sir?" I asked.

"Almost in one piece," and he pointed to the Indian with his razor and grinned and his men laughed and I saw then that Tom had also adorned himself with a necklace from which hung a severed ear.

I looked back to my brother. Shelby laughed, nervous, and touched his hand to his wound and grimaced and then laughed again.

"Alright then," I said and mounted up and bid Shelby do the same and as we rode over the ridge to the east I could feel Grimes watching us and I thought about the girl and her fear and I knew we'd all see each other again.

16

They rode, the four of them, up through a mountain pass and down the other side and across sand so white it looked like milk had spilled in the desert. Randall rode ahead, pushing the pace while distant plateaus became reality, and the rabbits and lizards and desert foxes fled from the pounding hooves.

In the desert valley west of the Guadalupe peaks, he reached a town with no name in which a wedding was taking place and a crowd of well-wishers blocked the road. There was only one street and on it four buildings, one being the church, and Randall looked at the people and wondered where they'd come from but did not ask. He sat his horse, the others yet to reach the town, and watched as the people threw rice into the air and it fell onto the groom's black jacket like a light snow and blended with the bride's white dress and veil and Randall remembered his own wedding and how Joanna was upset to be leaving so soon for the territories and he'd told her their whole lives were waiting for them in the West.

The groom was short, but well built, with soft tan hair that seemed to match his skin. He beamed to each ear and whispered to his new wife and she laughed and shook her head. He pulled away from her and she reluctantly let his hand slip away, leaning toward his absence as he went. The man bounded up the church stairs and waved his hand to the crowd. He motioned for the bride to follow and she blushed and the crowd clapped until she joined him atop the steps, atop the world. The man began to speak and Randall was not close enough to hear or if he was it didn't matter.

Randall thought of the last time he and Joanna had been truly happy and it was long ago and it pained him to admit, but even then he considered it was not her happiness but her desire for a different life that bound her to him. He had said all the things she hoped to hear and they, the both of them, had painted a future in the setting sun. Years of disappointment had stained their dreams, but Harry was the saving grace. He brought them back together, gave them purpose and the colors to draw a happier ending than the one for which they were destined.

"If only you could go back," a man said and Randall jumped in his saddle and considered for a moment the possibility of God but found only an old man with a well-kept gray mustache astride an Indian paint horse and the old man motioned with his head toward the newlyweds, who were making a second pass through the line of rice throwers.

"They got no goddamn clue what life's all about," the old man said. "Too bad they can't keep it that way. Ain't that right, partner?"

"I suppose so," Randall answered and moved to turn his horse.

"That's my granddaughter up there. Happy. In love. No goddamn sense in her brain. I'm the richest man in a hundred miles," the old man said and then laughed at himself. "But in case you hadn't noticed, there ain't nothing much around for a hundred miles. Anyhow, I told her, I said, 'Darling, I'll give you the money, you just go on and take a coach to El Paso, then catch you a train somewhere.' North, east—hell, I didn't care— just away from here, from all this dust and nothingness. Instead, she goes and does the dumbest goddamn thing a person can do. She falls in love. And to a sodbuster of all people. Dumb sumbitch has land not far from here. I know 'cause he bought it from me. Just like I know not a thing's ever gonna grow on that land—or anywhere else out here. Only thing can grow in this desert is the weight on a man's soul."

"You made money, though," Randall said, and the man laughed again.

"Aw, hell, I just got lucky. I come out when this place was full of luck, and we used it all up long ago. I made my money off the ones who come too late. And the ones still coming."

The man looked at Randall and Mara and cocked his head.

"I don't know you, stranger," the man said, and it was a statement not a question.

"I'm Randall Dawson, out of Longpine in the Arizona territory." Randall stuck out his hand, and the man met it with his own and held onto it as he thought.

"Dawson. That ain't kin to Travis Dawson?"

"Yessir, it is. The lieutenant was my grandfather."

"Sumbuck," the man said and slapped his thigh, causing his horse to stir. "I'll be goddamned straight to hell, you're Travis Dawson's grandson? Well, where the hell were you when my Priscilla up there was set on finding her a husband? You know, your grandpappy was a real mean sumbitch, but boy, he was good stock. We cleaned out the Comanche, the Apache, even some of the damn Yankees before they sent the army out this way."

The man laughed and coughed and hacked from his throat.

"I'm drunk and ornery and sending my only grandbaby out into the world with some sorry kid who don't hardly have a row to hoe, and here sits the kin of Travis Dawson. Why don't you come on and enjoy some of the festivities I paid for?"

Both men turned at the sound of horses, and Tadpole and Charlotte pulled their mounts up alongside Randall, the child still clinging to Tad's back. Charlotte's hair fell loose and curled from beneath her hat, and Randall studied the shape of her face as she took stock of the scene ahead.

"Can I help y'all?" the old man asked and Randall noted a change in his tone.

"These are my companions, Miss Charlotte Washington and young Tad . . . Tad . . ."

"Roberson," Tadpole said and he sat tall in his saddle with his chest out.

"The child is in our charge as well, but we don't know his name or his story," Randall said, worrying how that might sound.

But the old man barely heard him. He sat stunned, staring at Charlotte, his mouth agape to the point Randall worried he may have been taken by a stroke.

"A nigger," the man mumbled, and Charlotte stiffened.

"Sir?" Randall asked, and the man blinked and spoke again.

"You telling me the blood of Travis Dawson is out here riding the country with a goddamn nigger?"

"We best be moving on," Charlotte said, but Randall waved her off.

"Oh, I don't see the hurry," Randall said, not taking his eyes off the old man. "This gentleman here just invited us to his granddaughter's wedding celebration."

The old man's face grew two shades of red.

"I sure as hell didn't invite no nigger," he said, and Randall mocked a look of disappointment.

"Well, that's a shame," he said, then leaned closer to the man. "Because if you think my grandfather was mean, you oughta see what I'll do to you if you say one more word about that woman."

Randall folded his arms across his waist and let his right hand rest on the butt of his Colt.

The man considered this, and in the seconds he took to think, Randall felt as if his hard-beating heart would betray his false display of confidence. His hand began to shake and he slowly lowered it to his side. He tried to control his breathing, but the world began to shrink around him.

"Well, fine—this is already a goddamn disaster of a day," the old man muttered as he nudged his horse toward the crowd.

Randall's pulse showed in his neck, and though he wasn't quite strong enough to form words, he looked at Charlotte and nodded.

"What are we waiting on?" Tad said eagerly. "Let's get us some of this wedding grub. I ain't had no cake since I asked Daddy where my momma was."

"Pumpkin," the child agreed.

They tied their horses and filled their plates with grilled corn and paper baskets of fruit from a buffet line stretching through a courtyard in back of the church. Long wooden tables had been moved outside and they sat and ate in silence and ignored the puzzled or angry glances that came their way. Tadpole left his seat on a quest for cake and Randall looked at Charlotte and smiled and she said nothing.

"Not even a 'thank you?'" he asked.

"Thank you?" she repeated, her jaw tight. "I don't know these people. I don't need this food. All I see is we're wasting time with a bunch of folks who don't want us here. And what was you planning on doing if that old man decided he was gonna get some boys to ride us outta town? You gonna draw them pretty pistols and start spilling blood?"

"No, I just . . . I thought maybe you would think I . . . That was hard for me, to stand up that way. I'm not used to it. I think I was trying, maybe, to impress you."

"Why on God's green would you be trying to impress me? I done told you, Mr. Dawson, I'm here for that boy and nothing else. You're a married man. And if you weren't, going around picking fights ain't the way to court me."

"What is the way?"

"What?"

"To court you," he said, and she noted his eyes, desperate and searching, like a lost child.

"Don't be foolish," she said, dismissing him.

"Well, I wasn't gonna let him call you that," Randall said, then stood.

"Where you goin'?" Charlotte asked.

"To see if anyone has a bottle."

"Well, don't get drunk and go to shooting ghosts again," she snapped. "We ain't got time to bury 'em all."

She watched him go. He was slight, but sharp. Handsome even, she thought as she tried not to smile. She had not been with a man in more than a year. She had no desire to, as most men were foul and obnoxious. Still, something ached inside her and she could not convince herself Randall Dawson had nothing to do with it.

Randall returned empty-handed, while Tad showed up with cake crumbs still on his lip. The child stuffed his pockets full of corn and they rode, the four of them, away from the town, leaving the wedding and the people and the sun behind them.

* * *

The road, like the country it ran through, pitched and tilted and flattened out only to pitch again and Randall studied the map and Charlotte studied the sun and both knew they were making good time.

They stopped only once the rest of the day, near a wooden marker with an arrow painted on it in a color once red. The child flung himself from Tad's saddle and stood up, apparently unharmed, and stared at the post. When they circled back around for him he wouldn't get back on the horse. He shook his head like a dog throwing off water and then commenced with slapping his own skull with open palms.

Charlotte slid off of Storm and tried to calm the boy but it was slow going. Randall tried talking to him and that too brought no results.

"Looks like he wants to stay," Tad said. "Might as well let him."

They stared at him until the guilt came, and he sighed and got off his horse.

"Goddamnit all," he said, and reached out and took the boy by the hand and the boy quieted on the spot and Tad helped him up onto the horse.

Charlotte and Randall stared at each other and at Tad and he looked at them with contempt and lost patience.

"Don't say a word," Tad told them. "I'm just ready to get on with it."

He put the horse back into the road and Charlotte and Randall followed suit and the boy whispered, "Pumpkin," and Tad shook his head.

17

The desert prairie in front of us was pocked with scrub brush and we raced through it, toward the darkness in the east, pushing the horses away from the thought of the Lobos giving chase. By nightfall we decided if they'd followed, they'd done so as ghosts.

We made no fire, and I studied the distant mountains, shoveled up against the setting sun, deciding the horizon. The charred, orange glow of the dying light outlined their peaks and in that moment they were aflame and perhaps it was beautiful to others, if there were others to see. To me it was hellfire and it burned eternal and there among the desperadoes and demons was a trapped soul and here I sat, a shell of a boy. I thought of repentance but found no comfort in a savior or a rebirth, and decided I had been wet in a river and nothing more. And so it was only a fate as twisted as the bare mesquite posts dotting the plains where a fence once stood, perhaps would stand again.

I waited until night overtook the world, killing the fire with cold and black, and I untied the horse and told him he deserved better than me and it was true. I mounted up and slipped away and the night was still and there was a finality in my mind that brought me great peace. I would die, there was little doubt as to that, but maybe the girl would live, and I saw it not as an eternal bargaining of the soul but as a human notion of right and wrong. If there is a darkness, I thought, I am bound to it after death no matter what course I take from here out, but if I could save the girl from the coming storm, I could face my death and my fate, the two of them, having lived a human life—where consciousness and stardust meet and we try to do right and we fail and we try again and again until the trying becomes the memories we look back on at the end.

The hills loomed larger as I drew near and I hoped for stronger winds to cover my approach. I moved south to the first sandy draw and began to follow it up and there I heard a rider coming on hard from my rear. I led the horse around a jutted rock formation and dismounted. The rider didn't slow and as he came into view I lay the rifle across the saddle and trained the bead on his chest. I recognized the horse before the man and lowered the rifle as Bullet climbed into the draw and led my brother to me.

"What the hell are you doing?" I asked him.

"I knew you was gonna go after that girl," he said. "You're too goddamned soft, Caleb."

"I'm set on it. Don't bother trying to stop me."

"I ain't here to stop you. I'm here to help."

And there it was, the light I'd been searching for since Longpine. Family is family, and my big brother was standing by his words. Of course, I couldn't let him do that.

"We ain't gonna be no help to nobody if we both get ourselves killed. Let me go in alone, and I'll send the girl your way. Give her the horse, then you and Bullet go a different direction. Be harder for them to follow her if there's two sets of tracks."

Shelby didn't say anything but nodded intently.

"Shelby," I said his name and looked into his eyes and spoke in a way that gave feeling to every word. "Do this for me. Help her. Don't talk to her. Don't touch her. I'll forgive you for everything you've ever done. Just help her, please."

"Alright then, little brother. I swear it."

* * *

I scrambled up the south side of the ridge and took off my hat and put my stomach in the dirt. There were a few fires smoldering below, but the camp was quiet and motionless and I realized then I had no plan to speak of. I didn't even know which tent the girl was in. It was only by chance, as I lay there on the hill, that she appeared. With Indian Tom at her side she emerged, dressed in a gray cloth shirt and a long ruffled skirt. She emptied her bladder and I watched the light from Tom's swinging lantern as they walked back to the center of the camp and disappeared inside a tent. A few minutes later Tom came back out and I cringed as he unfurled a bedroll in front of the door flap and blew out the lantern.

An hour later, I left my hat and the rifle on the ridge and moved slowly down the hillside. I took a route that put me at the bottom of the camp, where there was more darkness but less chance of a misstep that would send rocks tumbling into the tents to announce my arrival.

I made my way along the back of the outermost tent row and heard nothing to suggest I'd been spotted. I picked an opening between tents and crept through, my eyes half watching each step while also taking note of the big Indian asleep up ahead. I reached the back of the tent and the wind finally picked up but now it was a hindrance as I tried to speak softly to the girl.

"I have a knife," I said. "I'm going to cut a flap and help you run."

I was crouched in the grass with the small pocket knife in my hand when Indian Tom rounded the corner of the tent and looked down at me. I froze and he smiled and unsheathed a foot-long blade with a curved end. I prepared for the fight, knowing it would end quickly, and I tried to tell myself this wasn't a mistake but somewhere inside the fear outweighed it all and I thought about begging for my life.

"Don't shoot!" Shelby's voice called out and we, me and Tom, decided to put our tussle on hold.

"Don't nobody shoot!" Shelby yelled again. "We're unarmed. We ain't looking for trouble."

Men began to emerge from their tents, guns in hand, wondering whether to follow Shelby's instructions.

I backed away from Tom who saw fit to let me do so and met my brother in the middle of a tent row. His hands were straight up in the air and a dozen or so men were watching. I saw the girl's head stick out from her tent and I couldn't be sure but I thought maybe she was happy to see me.

"What is this?" I asked him, but he looked past me to where Grimes stood above the camp.

"We decided to join up with you," Shelby called to him. "Turns out you just asked the wrong brother." And with that he looked at me and grinned and I knew it had been his plan all along and I would never forgive myself for being so ignorant.

Grimes stood for a while and some of the men went back in their tents and finally he called down for Jimmy to find us a spot and a blue-eyed man with thinning hair walked toward us with the look of sleep about him.

"You boys sure made an entrance," he grumbled. "Come on to the pack mules and we'll cut you some cloth. Y'all don't mind sharing a tent?"

"Not at all," Shelby answered. "We're blood. We share everything."

* * *

We didn't speak, me and Shelby, and my anger made the work go faster. The tent wasn't much: two pine posts—one crooked and knotted in the middle, the other too short—and there hung the torn fabric thrown at us by Jimmy.

"This should be big enough," he said. "If not, don't wake me up. We'll sort it in the morning."

"Say, y'all got any grub left from—" Shelby began, but Jimmy stopped him short.

"Morning," he repeated and was gone.

The cloth, which looked to be actual tablecloth like you would find at one of those hotel restaurants in San Francisco, was too short and the wind played at it and me and Shelby sat on either end and I had never hated anyone as much as I hated myself but I thought maybe in that moment I hated Shelby more.

"You lied to me," I said, breaking the silence and trying to resist the urge to break his nose.

"Lied to you?" he acted shocked and hurt and it only made it worse. "I saved your goddamn life. That big ol' Indian was 'bout to add your scalp to his belt 'fore I came up."

"Don't deny it, you selfish bastard, you just wanted us both in camp so you could volunteer to be the outlaw you always dreamt of. You knew I wouldn't be able to object or they'd probably shoot us both on the damn spot."

"You gotta trust me, little brother. You're the one always going on about us not having no plan. Well, by God, here's one that just happened upon us. Ever' one of these sumbitches is wanted for something. Hell, the number one priority of the whole outfit is to stay away from the law. They got food, whiskey, and by the looks of it, plenty of money to go around. We could do a whole lot worse."

"It wasn't supposed to happen like this. Momma, the boy, none of it."

"I know, Caleb. I know you're hurting. But this is a good opportunity, and we ain't even gotta do nothing but say yes."

"You almost had me convinced, you know it? Those nights out in the desert. I thought, we make it to East Texas, catch on with a logging outfit, I could build me a little cabin somewhere. Maybe by a river."

"You can still build a cabin," Shelby started, but I wasn't listening.

"Put in a week of work for a week of pay. Go fishing on Sundays, or maybe just ride out on a lake trail and feel the sunshine warm my face. I told myself, maybe, just maybe, I could find some sort of peace."

Shelby looked down and shook his head.

"But that never was the plan, was it?" I asked. "Not for Shelby god-damned Bentley."

"Naw, peace wasn't the plan, little brother. Not in this life. But this is gonna be real good for us, little brother. Real good."

"It wasn't your choice to make."

"Aw, yeah, like when Grimes asked if we wanted to join up and you told him no without talking to me?"

"He didn't want us. He wanted me."

"Horseshit."

"Believe what you want. But go on and ask yourself why a man like that would want a dumb son of a bitch like you riding with him."

"You watch yourself, Caleb."

"You ain't gonna be no famous outlaw or no rancher or nothing else.

You'll live and die as the same sorry shit you've always been. I know it, you know it, Daddy knew it—that's why he left us."

"Shut your goddamn mouth!"

"And Momma knew it too. She told me before she died. Said I'd have to be the one to look after you."

Shelby came out of his crouch and met me where I sat and the two of us went rolling into the loose cloth and took most of it with us as we tumbled across the ground. I grappled my way around him and took his back and held him and told him to calm and he put an elbow in my ribs. We traded some half-blocked, short-range punches and there were words hurled as well and I couldn't tell you what they were, but rage was controlling the puppet strings and there was no reason or hesitation. The violence came and it came natural and I caught my brother with a sharp left hand and he was stunned long enough for me to mount him. Once I had the position, I could've stopped it. My whole life I'd been putting a stop to Shelby's bullshit, or worse, I'd been getting caught up in it.

"What would you have done?" Grimes's words echoed in my head. "Would you have killed him? Killed your brother?"

Men talk about fighting—saloon stories to impress the whores or, more likely, to impress the other men. They drink and laugh and the fighting talk comes easy, but it shouldn't. It's not a normal thing and you need look no further than the sound. Until you hear the dull thud of your fist on a man's bone, you don't know fighting. Sit and laugh at the stories but don't think you know the fight and what it means and what it does. I knew fighting and I'd always tried to stay away. But sometimes things just find you and it found me that night and I had the chance to stop it and instead I took a quick breath in and I went to work.

I was sure my right hand was broken, and maybe my left, and the sound had changed from bone to mush and I realized later I would have killed him, killed my brother, had a giant hand not enclosed my shoulder and tossed me backward.

Only then did I realize I'd been crying and I stopped and looked up at Tom. His face was concerned and he looked at Shelby, squirming and moaning and coughing blood, and then back to me.

"Grimes," he said and motioned for me to follow.

I staggered to my feet and felt a little dizzy and wiped the blood from my lip and inspected my raw, red hands.

"You got brothers, Tom?" I asked, almost sheepishly, as we hiked up the hill to Grimes's camp.

"I have many brothers," he replied.

"Where are they now?"

"There," he said and pointed out at the rows of tents that shrank behind us.

A few paces from Grimes's tent, Tom told me to stay put.

"You were going to kill me, right?" I asked. "Earlier."

Tom smiled and his mouth was big even on his sizable face. I nodded and put my hands on my knees and bent forward, exhausted and hurting.

"You are looking to die," Tom said, still smiling. "Your brother says you want to be here, but your eyes say different. We will find out."

"And then you'll kill me?"

"We will find out."

Tom pulled the flap back and entered the tent and I saw a lantern burning and soon he reappeared and motioned for me to come inside.

"Welcome back, Caleb," Grimes said, not looking up from his rolling tobacco. He sat shirtless and cross-legged on the ground, his hair slicked back and his face red in the absence of the beard and he looked both older and more alive. His muscles were sagging but sinewy and a bullet-sized scar on the left side of his chest caught the light from the lantern.

"Yessir," I managed.

"Change of heart, huh?"

"Yessir."

"Well, I doubt that, but we'll leave it for now," he said and then licked the paper holding his smoke. He motioned for me to sit, and in case there was any confusion, Tom's big paw gripped my shoulder and shoved me down.

"Tom says you have an interest in my daughter. I say the same. What say you?"

"She seemed scared to be here's all. I wanted to make sure she was alright."

"See, Tom, that's what I like about the boy. He's a straight shooter," he paused and considered his own words. "Well, for the most part. Tom also tells me you about killed your poor brother down there just now. You reckon he needs a doctor?"

"I can't rightly say. But like you already know, we're wanted men. Don't know that I'd trust a doctor or no one else with them posters out. Lucky we didn't run into trouble in Valentine."

"That's not a problem, Caleb. We have our own doctor here, in this very camp. Another two down south. Well, really another doctor and one dentist, but old Jeffries gets ornery, don't he, Tom?"

The two men laughed and Grimes lit up the cigarette and breathed it in and the fire ran down the paper, smoke chasing after it.

"You have an outlaw doctor?" I asked.

"Sure, and lawyers and cooks, a few smittys—hell, we even got a sheriff. Or a former sheriff, I guess." And again the two men laughed and Tom said something in Comanche and Grimes laughed even harder.

"And you were a Ranger."

"I knew you'd heard of me last time we chatted. I knew he'd heard of me," he looked to Tom and then back to me. "That's right, and I was a Ranger."

"What happened?"

"You want me to send for the good doctor, or just let your brother lay there bleeding?"

I lowered my head and there were my boots, folded up with my legs beneath me and covered in blood. I knew what it felt like to kill and it wasn't like that with my brother. I knew he'd live, but I nodded anyway.

"Yessir, I reckon somebody ought to take a look at him."

"Alright then," Grimes said and nodded at Tom and Tom disappeared outside the tent and I wondered if that was all but didn't move.

Grimes stared at me and by now I was getting used to it, and the smoke crawled from his nostrils and hung in the air and I thought about the way a soul is said to leave the body and how some folks believe you can look down at yourself.

He tapped the burning paper and the ashes fell to the ground and one was still lit and both of us, Grimes and me, saw it and he smiled and brought his boot down on it.

"The people of this great nation saw fit to call me a war hero." He spoke and I listened and he looked at something far off, as if he could see through the tent cloth. "I wasn't much more than your age. A child in many eyes, but I killed men and eventually led men and in the end they gave me medals and honors and glorified my deeds in ways unnatural. Death is natural. Killing is not. Do you understand the difference?"

I nodded.

"The ghosts of those fellas, the ones I killed, followed me back home to Nacogdoches and in the daylight hours the good people of East Texas would call me a traitor and a nigger-lover and a murderer, all on account of me fighting for the Union. Then at night the ghosts would come and make sure I didn't sleep a wink. That was bad enough in its own right, but I could manage it, until the bastards started following me around during the day too. So I've got a racist redneck hollering at me, a ghost mocking me, and I don't know which one to fight and which one to ignore. Anyhow, a doctor gave me some magic cure—a bottle of syrup he said was cooked up back east. It worked for a while."

"What happened?" I asked, and Grimes was back to looking at something I figured only he could see.

"You ever carry something so long it becomes a part of you?" he asked and ashed what little was left of his cigarette. "See, that medicine did what it was supposed to do, but something didn't set right with me. I found myself missing the things that haunted me. A man carries his deeds with him, in this life and the next, and the way I saw it, I didn't want no exemption. I figured the best thing for me was to go back to work, and seeing as how I was a hero and all, I caught on with the Rangers with no questions asked. At first I was just rustling up cheats and cutthroats in San Antonio, but pretty soon they sent me out west to clean out the Indians so as the respectable, God-fearing folk wouldn't have no native problems when they rode their wagons into the great unknown."

He licked his finger and thumb and brought them together over the cigarette end and he looked down and studied it or studied something in his mind and his face was pained.

"You ever have any run-ins with Indians up in the Arizona territory?

They're a fierce bunch. Brave. 'Course, courage don't mean all that much against rifles and cannons and a well-supplied army. We rode with the army for a spell. Our job was to hunt down the natives then call in the cavalry. Turned out I was good at that too. Wasn't long before the ghosts started getting mighty crowded. Then a miracle happened. You believe in miracles, Caleb?"

"I can't say, sir. I been doing some thinking on 'em lately, if that's what you mean."

"I didn't believe either. Not in God, not in miracles. I'd seen too much of the opposite, to tell you the truth. But one day, a few of us Rangers came across a camp of Apache. Small camp, mostly older folks, a few children. We were just north of Mexico, where the river dips down and bends for days before starting up again. The army was camped about a half day's ride, and I knew that if we went on and did our jobs, by morning that little group of Indians would be dead or rounded up and sent some-wheres else to die. There was five of us that day. Men I knew, men I cared about—respected even. I told them right then and there I was done with it. Said I didn't have the stomach to fight for freedom in one war and fight for slavery in the next. I said a few other things, but in the end my companions disagreed with me and started talking pretty loose about a court marshal and a hanging and whatnot. One decided it would be a good idea to draw his gun. I killed that man, and one other before he could clear leather. A third fella had the drop on me, but he hadn't counted on Marcus. My little speech had made sense to Marcus, no doubt on account of his being a Negro. Marcus blew the majority of that gentle-man's brain matter out through the side of his skull. So the two of us stood there not saying a word, and I don't know how long the standing would've went on, but out of that sad little camp come one of the biggest Indians I'd ever seen. He'd heard the shooting and found us there with a pile of dead Rangers, and I guess he figured out the score without our help. He grabbed one of the bodies and started to drag it off. We followed suit and before we knew it, we were burning the dead in the camp we had scouted. The Indian spoke a little English; said his name was Tom. No idea where he learned that name, but he insisted on it, so we obliged. I knew the Rangers would come looking, so me and Marcus took Tom and his people high up into the mountains. We killed every man they sent until they stopped sending them. And with every soul I collected, my ghosts started to leave. That was my miracle. I'd found my purpose in this life."

"As an outlaw."

Grimes looked annoyed but continued anyway. "As a savior of the downtrodden. We rode out, raiding supply wagons, spreading our message, and recruiting like-minded guns. We picked some bad apples, but they ripened up after a while. These may be hard men, Caleb, but they're men of principle. Like you. Let me help you the way I helped them. I can give you something you've never had."

"What's that?"

"Power. The power to shape things the way you want them to be shaped. The power to create a new world, where all men are free and equal. You believe in that, don't you?"

"Yessir, I reckon I do. But I ain't sure robbing and killing folks is the best way to go about it."

"We rob the army and the government, not the people. We kill who we have to."

"Like that cowboy in Marathon?"

Grimes laughed.

"You mean Frank? Hell, he's back at our border camp right now. We recruited him, we didn't kill him."

"Everybody thinks you did," I told him.

"Of course they do. That's because the US government is doing what they do best. Propaganda. They're painting the Lobos as the scariest thing since the Plague, making sure it's hard as hell for folks to trust us. Control the people, Caleb, and you control the world. You break a horse because you want it to be yours, bend to your needs, listen to your directions. You break a horse because you believe it needs to be broke. What purpose can that horse serve if unbroken? What use is it to you unless you can control it?

"It's the same with men. These leaders of ours—from preachers to politicians, ranchers, and Rangers—they want to break you. They want to break you like a horse because they need you. They need you to never question. They need you to fight their wars, kill their enemies, and be part of the world they're building—not the one that already exists, the one that existed long before them.

"They break as many men as they can and then the greedy bastards start breaking the land. You understand what I'm saying, son? This is the last of it. The last of the American frontier. They'll make states out of the whole lot and they'll break the people and the country and they'll use it all for the next great cause, the next big war to kill boys and line pockets. I swear to you I've seen the very nature of these men and it's soulless and dark. You think I'm a murderer. Maybe that's true enough. But it's them who made me this way. I pranced and trotted and ran at their every command. I was broke, sure enough. They made the mistake of letting me see the other side and the freedom that thrived here.

"When I got here, to the West, everything was different than what I'd seen back home. This place was untamed. The horses, the cactus, hell, the goddamn weather. It was all wild and unbroken and uninterested in the rest of the world. It was the freest country I'd ever seen."

"And you think now it ain't?"

"Yessir, Caleb, I think now it ain't. It's already overrun with government and churches and drunkards mining gold or cutting timber and soon enough, thanks to the railroads, folks will start poking holes in the ground looking for oil and nothing will be left wild."

"Wild don't always mean good, Mr. Grimes. Some things are better left alone, I'll give you that. But I imagine there's some things better off being broke."

Grimes smiled and leaned back, patting his hands on his knees.

"And you, Caleb? Are you better off wild or would you fall in line with all the others as they bleed this world dry?"

I tried to choose my words carefully, the way my mother had taught, but I couldn't quite turn 'em the way I wanted, and before I knew it, my thoughts were out loud and unprotected.

"I can't say that it's that simple," I told him. "It ain't free or slave, not no more. And it ain't wild or broke, neither. I imagine it's somewheres in between that a man can find his place. That's what I'd aim for, if it come down to it. A place to call mine, sure enough, but also a place where folks are pulling together. I guess what I mean is a place where there's some sort of balance."

"Between what?" Grimes asked.

"Between everything."

He stood and I with him and he moved close and put his hand on my face in the way a man might caress his lover, but there was no smile or tenderness and his words grew more urgent the more he spoke.

"I like you, Caleb. There's something about you, and it draws me in and I want to know more. But hear this now: the people in this world, all of them, they aren't like you. They can't abide by balance, by nuance, by circumstance. They must be all or nothing, one or the other, and they will slit their brother's throat without hesitating if it feeds their narrative of destiny or desire. They don't want harmony, you understand? They actively work against it."

"And so you work against them."

"Like I said, you're a smart boy. Now, as for this situation with your own brother, is this going to be a problem?"

"Sir?"

"I know you didn't come sneaking in here tonight to join up with us. The way I figure it, your brother sold you down the river and you let him feel it. I know you don't want any part of this."

"Then why—?"

"Because I want you to ride with me, Caleb. Not just with my men, but with me. I don't want your brother. I don't want him, because of all the things you already know to be true. I was willing to take him if it got me you. I was willing to help him. But now I find for the second time in as many days you may mean to kill him yourself. Is this so? If it is, say the word and we'll take care of it. Or if you'd rather, you can finish things yourself and I doubt anyone here would blame you. Hell, I doubt anyone who has ever met Shelby would take too great an offense. The choice is yours but whatever you decide, it sticks. If you both ride out with us, you both become part of a family that's even greater than blood. And I won't have my family quarreling. So make your choice, then live with it."

"Yessir."

"And one more thing: I can appreciate your wanting to protect a young lady in danger. But as I hope you can see now, my daughter is not in any danger here. Take my meaning?"

"Yessir."

* * *

Tom walked a few steps ahead of me through the camp. He was as imposing a man as I'd ever seen—and not just physically. He had the air of man who would not die quietly.

"How come Grimes's daughter hates him so much?" I asked him.

"Enough talk," he said, continuing forward with long, effortless strides.

"I reckon that's not the first time she run off."

He stopped and turned to me. He hesitated, searching for the words.

"Sophia misses her mother. Very much."

"Where's her mother?"

"Enough talk," he said again.

18

They made camp a half day's ride from the trailhead at Guadalupe Pass, tucking themselves in a mesquite grove near the base of the first mountain and overlooking the floodplains and salt flats to the west. The young boy took the horses without being asked and began to brush them and press his ear to their sides and no one told him different. Randall gathered wood and Tad took to some of the brush with a hatchet and soon they had a fire and were heating tortillas and beans and rabbit meat and when they had finished, Charlotte gave the boys fruit tins and motioned for Randall to follow her and he did. She grabbed his hand and he fought against the shiver snaking through his spine as they touched and by the dying light she led him through the ocotillo and tall-stalked agave and above to where the roots gave way to fallen boulders and lava rock, and though he would have followed her anywhere she stopped and pointed to an overhang and when he looked he saw nothing but the face of the cliffs overhead.

"See the drawings?" she asked and he shook his head to say no but stopped short of speaking as the images began to appear.

"Indians," she said, "but not Apache or Comanche or even Mescalero. They call themselves the Strassi. In their language it means 'those who emerge.' Like other tribes, they believe their people originated from inside the earth. 'Course, unlike the others, they haven't exactly come out yet."

"They live in the mountains?"

"They live underneath."

Randall studied the pictures. There were suns and spirals and great horned beasts. There were humanlike figures who floated above jagged lines and horses who stood in rows.

"I've never heard of these people," Randall said, touching the drawings and feeling the cool stone on his fingertips.

"Not many have," Charlotte replied. "It's how they survive. How they hid from the Comanche all those years. How they hide from the whites now."

"How is it you came to know this?"

"I lived with them," she said. "For more than a year, after my brother was killed."

"You lived with Indians? Doing what?"

"Just living. Training as a warrior, farming in their underground fields."

Randall laughed, "What is an underground field?"

"In the caverns, there are great rooms with light from sinkholes and tunnels. The sun warms the room, and with enough soil from above, many things can grow."

"Underground fields," Randall repeated. "Well, is that where you learned how to handle those guns?"

"The Strassi don't use guns. The guns were my brother's. He wanted me to be safe. But I wasn't. Instead, I was foolish. I thought guns made you powerful just because you had one. I ran into some trouble with some men who were too young for the Civil War and figured roughing up a nigger woman would be the next best thing. They left me for dead, but a Strassi boy found me, nursed me back to health. We were going to be married, and I was to become a Strassi woman."

"What happened?" Randall asked.

"I didn't want to live in a cave."

"Makes sense; seems a bit claustrophobic."

It was Charlotte's turn to laugh.

"Not like that," she said. "I didn't want to live a life hiding. I wanted to see the world, and to help people."

"Like you're helping me?"

"Something like that, yeah." She smiled.

"Why are you here?" he pressed. "And don't say the boy."

She sighed.

"I found that kid in a bar, where some degenerate had decided to let him drink. He was talking loud about how his friend had been killed by a couple of cutthroats. He kept saying there was a man chasing them too, but that man wasn't no Wild Bill Hickok."

"I'll have to thank him for that."

"When I asked him about the man, he said it was his friend's father. An educated man from back east. A man out of place in a cruel world. A heart too good for such violent delights as those that are commonplace in an untamed land. A handsome man, with a kind disposition, who does right because he should, not because he has to."

"He said all that, did he?"

"He said enough."

She looked away into the night sky and grinned and turned back toward him with a mischievous look.

"I still have the scars," she said.

"From the relationship?"

Charlotte rolled her eyes.

"From the men who almost killed me."

She lifted her shirt almost to her breasts and Randall could see the tissued marks across her skin.

"My God."

She loosened her belt and began to slide her pants downward. He looked away.

"It's okay," she said, stepping toward him. More scars ran the length of her thigh. She took his hand and pressed it against them. He shuddered.

"I see the way you look at me," she said, her voice soft and yearning. She moved his hand.

Randall's words caught in his throat.

"I . . . we shouldn't leave the boys alone at night," he said, and her face became twisted and confused and then hurt.

"I'm sorry," he said, "I . . ."

"Don't be sorry," she told him, fastening her belt. "Let's just get back."

"No, it's not what you think—"

"Please stop talking," she said, and hurried away.

That night she slept alone, away from the fire.

19

I barely recognized my brother. His face was swollen and colored with purple and yellow and his skin was mangled near his missing ear and there was a pathetic look to it all that gave me guilt and might have made me hate him even more.

The man looking after him was young. He wore spectacles and a bowler and was in the midst of growing an orangish beard to cover his freckles. He reached out a pale hand and I took it and his grip was stronger than I expected.

He walked me through Shelby's condition and injuries. The man's knowledge of the body and how it healed further cemented the out-of-place nature of his presence and when he was done I nodded and thanked him and understood little of what he'd said.

"Can I have a minute with him?" I asked, and the young doctor looked uncomfortable so I promised I wasn't gonna kill Shelby and he didn't laugh but left the tent anyway.

I sat near my brother's bedroll and his body stank. I reached out and touched his hand.

"I guess if you could help it, you would," I told him.

Shelby's body rolled toward me and he groaned and the eye that could open did so at half mast. He gripped my hand and held it and there we stayed, Shelby and me, until the sun brought with it the dawn of a new day.

I woke sitting, my back jammed against the tent post. The fog of sleep and dreams and uncertainty hung about my eyes and I could not be sure where I was or how I'd gotten there. My hands throbbed.

"Caleb," my brother said, and his voice was soft and weak and a hundred miles away.

I looked at him. He stared at me through swollen eyes.

"You reckon I'm evil?" he asked. "The real kind, what comes from Satan."

I blinked my eyes and looked around the tent.

"I don't reckon much in the way of Satan," I told him.

"That's ignorant," he said and winced at what pain there was and there was plenty.

"How come?"

"All that's wrong with things—Momma dying, Daddy, the way we had to grow up—them ain't good things."

"Lotta folks worse off."

"That's what I mean. So much is wrong with so many," he said. "And wrong with me."

He motioned for the steel flask propped against his satchel and I shook my head and fetched it for him.

"I can't help it, you know," he told me, taking a pull and choking it down. "I get these thoughts, and they make sense to me even though I know they ain't supposed to. You ever think things like that?"

"I think about killing that boy."

"What about it?"

I took the flask from his hands and drank deeply.

"It weren't no goddamned devil killed him," I said. "It was me. You understand? And whatever unnatural thoughts you got, there ain't nobody put 'em there but you."

Shelby groaned. "So that's it then, you think I'm evil."

"I didn't say that."

"You might as well have."

"Well, I didn't. Fact is, I don't think nobody's evil. I don't think there's such a thing that even exists. The way I figure it, there's people, some of 'em better than others, some of 'em worse, and every one of 'em has to make a whole bunch of choices, and then in the end it's someone else gets to say whether them choices were good or bad."

"So you reckon I made a bunch of bad choices?" he asked.

"I sure as shit wouldn't call 'em good."

"You talk to the old man last night?"

I nodded.

"And?" my brother asked.

"And thanks to you, we're Lobos now."

"It's good to have family, Caleb. Have people to look out for us."

I shook my head and took another pull and tossed the flask back onto his bedroll.

"How could I forget: family is family, right?"

* * *

Shelby spent two days riding in a wagon with the redheaded doctor. We headed southeast toward the Mexican border and I marveled at the efficiency of the Lobos. Scouts rode ahead to make camp and keep lookout for the law or the army, a cook manned his own wagon full of supplies, and old ranch hands rounded up any stray horses or cattle we encountered along the way.

Grimes rode a chestnut-colored palomino mare that looked to be some line of Tennessee walking horse. He pulled alongside me and the Missouri early on the second day and asked how I was settling in and I told him fine, I guessed. He asked if my horse had a name and I said no and nothing more.

"Bad luck to ride a horse without a name," he said.

"What's *her* name?" I asked, and he stroked the neck of his horse.

"Doesn't have one," he said, laughing. "I don't believe in luck."

I smiled despite myself, and he reined up and waited for one of the wagons and I rode on near the heart of the column and wondered what I was doing and who these people were. I was already an outlaw, whether I wanted the title or not, but this seemed like more of a militia than a group of bandits and I couldn't help think maybe Grimes wasn't the sort of evil I'd imagined him to be. Still, Sophia was scared of something, and I reminded myself that's why I'd come back in the first place.

She rode a brown Morgan with a yellow mane and sat as natural a saddle as I'd ever seen. With Grimes falling back to check on the wagons and Tom nowhere in sight, I pulled even with her and tipped my hat.

"Howdy," I said and smiled, and she burned a hole through me with her eyes before opening her mouth.

"You are the dumbest cowboy I ever met," she said, and it was the first time I'd truly heard her speak and her accent was Spanish and though her words were not kind, they played in the air like music and I drank them in.

"You might be right about that," I told her and smiled again despite her icy stare. "It was you I come back for, you know."

"You should stay away from me. And tonight, after we make camp, you should ride far from here and never come back and hope he doesn't chase you."

"Who, Grimes?" I asked. "He's a little on the radical side, and there's definitely something spooky about the man. But so far he's treated me pretty good, all things considered."

"He wants to collect you, to make you part of his army of the wounded. He takes these broken things and tells them they are wonderful and they love him for it and he hypnotizes them with his words and soon they do everything he says. He holds their souls in his hands and watches them turn dark."

"You think I'm here for him? Like I said, I came back for you."

"The dumbest cowboy," she said.

"Alright then," I nodded my head and looked out toward the east, where the horizon still swooned from the sun's kiss. "Let's you and me go. We'll leave tonight and we'll ride until we can't ride no more. How's that?"

"He will always find me. I belong to him now, and he doesn't like when things are taken away."

"I imagine I wouldn't want my daughter running off, neither."

The girl's face grew even fiercer and she hissed at me, "I am not his daughter.

"My mother was his woman, yes—another one of his broken toys who worshipped him like a god—but I was already ten years old when he found us. He wanted my mother for his own, but my father—my true father—would not let him have her. My father, Hector Francisco Montez, shot Grimes through his heart, but he did not die. The devil has his soul and he breathed life back into him and Grimes returned with his men, but even then my father outwitted them and escaped into the river near our village."

"And Grimes took you and your momma?"

"Yes, he took us to his camp and made my mother his."

"But didn't she hate him, for running off her husband like that?"

"It is like I said: he can control a person in ways you do not understand. Not yet."

"Well, it don't seem like he can control you."

"Because I have no soul for him to wrap his fingers around," she said and turned away from me and stared across the desert plain and further, to where the mountains sprung from the river and blockaded the Mexican border.

"That makes two of us," I told her.

"You have a soul, dumb cowboy. And it is going to get you killed."

Sophia's eyes darted left, and I turned to see Tom riding along beside me.

"Howdy, big fella," I said.

"Howdy," he replied stone-faced, then rode on past us.

"I don't care what you think of me," I said, turning the Missouri away from the girl. "You want to run, let's go. You want to stay, then here I am. I ain't gonna let anything happen to you one way or the other. That's a promise."

A promise I wasn't sure I could keep. A promise I wasn't sure why I felt the need to make. But there was something about Sophia that called to me and I wanted desperately to answer.

* * *

That night, Tom pulled back the flap of my tent and I figured he may have been there to kill me but I didn't move, instead I just stared up at him and gave a sort of half wave.

"Grimes," he said, and I figured by now I knew the routine.

"You and me are gonna tussle one of these days—you know that, right?" I asked him as we walked.

Tom didn't smile, and I was beginning to think no one here did until Grimes greeted me outside his tent and reminded me that wasn't true.

"Caleb," he said and he sounded thrilled to see me and somehow it always felt like he meant it and I kept Sophia's words in mind as he took my hand. "Come on, let's take a little ride."

"We both coming back?" I asked, and he laughed heartily and slapped my back and I felt pulled between opposing forces.

We untied our horses and mounted up. I followed Grimes down a game trail that led out of the desert valley and into the foothills of the Sierra Santiago. He stopped his horse and me behind him and the two of us dismounted into the dark night.

"I know what happened back in Longpine," he said.

"Yessir, I reckon it's there on the poster."

"No, I mean I know what really happened. Shelby told me everything. Even said it was all his fault and you didn't hardly have a thing to do with it."

"You been talking to my brother?"

"Well, yes, isn't that what you wanted? To help him. To make him a better man."

I was quiet.

"I know it's weighing on you, what happened to that boy. And that's good, Caleb. It's a good thing. If you weren't twisted up over it then what kind of person would you be?"

We walked in silence for a while after that, leading the horses through bear grass and winterfat and there was a coldness to the night and the temperature with it.

"I don't want you talking to my brother no more, Mr. Grimes," I said, finally.

"As you wish," he replied. "And unlike you, I'll keep my word."

"Sophia," I said and he nodded and again I was quiet.

"Aw, don't get all flustered. Hell, who am I to say who you can and can't talk to? In fact, I been doing some thinking. You two are about the same age—probably the youngest in camp—it makes sense for y'all to spend time together. I guess I was just being overprotective."

"She's not your daughter," I said and closed my eyes at the stupidity of my own damn mouth.

"No, not by blood, that's true. But I loved her mother, and I'm all she's got to look after her now, whether she wants to believe it or not."

"She ain't got no other family to take her in?"

"Her no-good pap is probably up in Austin somewheres, drinking and gambling. But he's a lowlife, and even if she don't remember it that way, he did terrible things to that girl's momma. I saved them, and I would've killed that son of a bitch if he weren't so cowardly as to run when he saw me coming."

"Is it true he shot you?"

Grimes nodded, "Yeah, that old bandito drew down on me when I was unarmed. Shot me in the damn chest. I figured that was the end for me, but somehow the bullet came out clean and if there's a hole in my heart, it hasn't stopped it from beating yet. But we ain't out here to talk about me, son. I wanna know about you. I wanna make sure you're alright with all this."

"All this?" I asked.

"It's true, me and the boys believe in everything we're doing, but that don't make it legal. And riding with us makes you a part of it, and after talking to your brother, which I won't do again without your permission, it sounds like you might not be the type."

"And if I'm not?"

"Well, then I'll give you a blanket and some food and wish you well. Of course, I'd half expect to see you crawling into camp again, like last time you were supposed to ride off into the great beyond."

"I'll tell you straight, Mr. Grimes, I don't know what type I am. And with all due respect, I don't know what type you are, neither. Things are really mixed up in my head and they have been since my momma died. My brother damn near raised me on his own, but I know, in my heart I know, he ain't worth the air he breathes. But to say that, what the hell kind of brother does that make me?"

Grimes stopped and put his arms around me and his embrace was warm and familiar and before I could stop myself my head was on his shoulder and I was trying to hide the tears.

"Listen to me, Caleb. You take the time you need to sort things. You can ride with us as long as you want and you can leave when you want. You understand?"

I nodded and wiped at my eyes with the sleeve of my shirt.

"Now, with your blessing, I'd like to keep talking to Shelby. See if I can't help him get his priorities right. Would that be alright with you?"

"Yeah, I reckon it would."

"Come on," he said, swinging up into the saddle. "Let's run these horses wide open on the way back."

"That don't seem too smart," I replied. "Wrong step in the dark and they're liable to come up lame."

"Aw, hell, son, you just gotta trust 'em."

* * *

The next morning I took coffee to Sophia and she eyed both me and the cup suspiciously. I felt Tom's stare on us from across the camp and I slipped him my middle finger behind my back. Sophia's hair was up in a bun and a few strands fell down and outlined her face.

"You again," she offered without much warmth, but it didn't deter me from giving a hearty "good morning" to which she rolled her eyes.

"Listen, you may not be real happy 'bout your current lot in life, but that don't mean we can't have a pleasant morning together drinking this here coffee. Now I done beat up on my own brother, risked my neck, and become an outlaw—all just to see you."

"Nobody asked you to do these things."

"Naw, but you did kiss me. And that might not have meant much to you, but it damn sure meant something to me."

"Out there, you were different."

"You didn't know me. Hell, you don't know me now."

"I know you were scared. I saw it in your eyes. I saw the same storm that fills my dreams. I could feel your fear as you felt mine.

"You think I'm not scared now?"

"I think Grimes is sliding his poison into you. I think you like it here, even if you won't admit it to yourself. I know that feeling. I know what it is like to weigh the choices. In this life, we have only the choices we make and I have made mine. I will run again, and this time I will not let some stupid cowboy stop me."

"Fine then, you run whenever you feel set, but until then I'm gonna bring you coffee and pester the living shit out of you."

For the first time I'd seen, Sophia let a smile creep across her face.

"That will only make me run sooner."

* * *

And so it went, the closest to a routine I'd had in some time saw me spend the mornings sitting with Sophia, trying to make her laugh. I passed the noon hour playing cards with Marcus, Jimmy, and a fast-healing Shelby. My brother was embracing the outlaw life with gusto, bragging to the others about the gunslingers he'd served or the women he'd bedded. His stories were mostly exaggerations, if not outright lies, but to my surprise the men in camp listened intently and laughed when appropriate or gave him satisfying nods. I suspected Grimes had told them to take it easy on Shelby and in a way I appreciated it.

Most evenings I was summoned and it got to where Tom would just stick his head in my tent and I'd be ready for our walk. Grimes talked to me about his days in the army and asked me how I got to be so good with horses. I told him I didn't know I was, but he assured me I had a gift and I wanted to believe him.

One night I entered his tent and found him counting out stacks of paper bills by the dozens.

"That's more money than I've ever seen in my life," I said.

"Well, don't get a hard-on, you'll scare away the girls," he answered without looking up.

"My entire life," I repeated.

"It's not stolen, if that's what you're thinking. We have a particular investor. He sees that we're well provisioned."

"An investor?"

"The whole of this world answers to something or somebody. The Lobos are no different. Revolutions cost money. So does whiskey."

* * *

"You're enjoying these talks with Grimes," Sophia said one morning and it wasn't a question.

"I don't know that I'd say I'm enjoying anything," I replied, "except maybe your company."

"Stupid cowboy," she said. "You are becoming his."

"Well, at least somebody around here finds me interesting."

She rolled her eyes.

"You will only know when you see it, and by then it will be too late."

"Fair enough, but what if you're wrong? What if Grimes loved your momma, and what if he just wants the best for you? Hell, what if he wants the best for all of us?"

"Do not speak of my mother when you know nothing, Caleb. He did not love her. He killed her. And he will kill me too."

"I thought a fever took your momma?"

"A fever he gave to her."

"What you mean like a curse?" I said, and a laugh betrayed my attempt at a somber delivery.

"Laugh now, vaquero. You will see."

"I just don't see how come, if he's all the things you say, he'd even want me talking to you."

It was only when I saw the look on Sophia's face that I realized what she thought. There was some anger and sadness, quick flashes, then she hardened up and sealed off like the day we'd first come across one another.

"Aw, hell, I don't mean it like that. I want to be talking to you, you know that. I just mean he said he's alright with it. It don't seem to make sense. He's gotta know you're telling me all these things, right?"

She glared at me with a mix of pity and impatience.

"And he also knows you would defend him," she said. "And that if I loved you, keeping you here would mean keeping me too."

"Love me? Shit, Sophia, I wear myself out trying to get you to even talk to me most mornings."

"Stupid cowboy," she said and she turned to go and I let her.

Sophia didn't speak to me the rest of the day, and she took her coffee with the young doctor the following morning. Whether she meant to make me jealous or not, it damn sure worked. So, as it were, I was full of piss and vinegar when we rode into Perry Springs and all hell broke loose.

20

The gun was heavy in Randall's hand, as it should be in any hand, and heavy with the weight of decision and consequence and the destruction to come. It was, he thought, a machine constructed to kill and spill the blood of nations and become a commodity for the powerful, and another tool with which to control the weak and later the same tool that would make the weak believe they have power when in truth they have none. Only a gun, heavy in their hand.

Randall's gun was polished steel with gold plates clasped to the handle—added weight, added worth, he'd been told. He missed his first three shots and his ears rang with the embarrassment and his face grew as hot as the gun itself and Charlotte offered no words of encouragement or advice.

"Again," she said, and again he fired.

They'd eaten the last of the tinned fruit that morning with beans charred over the fire in a clay fry pan. They warmed tortillas in the pan and it was hot enough from its first encounter with the fire that it did not need another to toast the thin saucers of wheat flour while they soaked up the remaining juices from the beans before them. Charlotte gathered the empty fruit cans, taking the last one out of Tad's hands as he attempted in vain to scrape a final meaningful bite from the bare tin.

"Tad, look after the horses and don't get spooked when you hear shooting," she told the boy, him still sullen over the empty can. "C'mon, Mr. Dawson. Bring your guns."

She's going to kill me, he thought. He'd deflected her advancement the night before and now she was out to exact her revenge.

She led him out from the cottonwoods on foot and together they scrambled up the rocks of a stunted plateau and then more carefully navigated the steep descent of the far side. With a wall of rock at their back Charlotte told him to walk and so he did and thirty yards later she called, "Stop," and he did this as well and turned to see her and thought she was beautiful at any distance.

"Seems far," he said.

"If you can shoot far, you can shoot close," she replied, and he had nothing to say to this.

The sun was up in full but it had not yet heated the air and it sat low in the sky as a spectator to the earth and its happenings. What was left of an oak long since fallen had been bleached by the dust and the sun and upon it Charlotte placed the cans in a row, and there they rested as if on an altar and Randall charged with defying God.

Charlotte moved to the side though not so far as Randall would have liked, and Randall drew one of the Colts and fired and missed and took a better aim and missed again. He stared at the gun, inspecting it as though the fault could not have been his own and to further this suggestion he holstered the weapon and pulled the second pistol from his belt and took even longer still in the aiming before he fired.

"Again," she called, and again he sent a bullet whistling into the dirt and rock of the far ridge while the cans stood defiant in tribute to their oaken God.

"Move back," she called.

"Don't you mean forward?"

"Back," she repeated, and he complied with growing frustration.

He fired two more bullets and was now growing accustomed to the failure in the way a betting man is accustomed to the loss of his money.

"Back," she called again and believing it could get no worse he diligently walked further from the cans until she called stop.

A whiptail lizard darted across his path and disappeared into the sagebrush, reemerging on a small rock some ten feet away to assess this unfamiliar predator or perhaps just to sit on the rock and watch the strangeness of the world as it unfolded.

Randall raised his arm and searched for the cans and they were visible but barely and he shot and missed as was his routine.

The smell of smoke and powder filled the air in ten- and fifteen-yard intervals and Charlotte told him once more to step back and even the lizard had grown tired of the procedure and moved on.

This time Randall used both hands and squinted into the growing distance and found the cans smaller than the sight on his pistol. Aim. Squeeze. Miss.

"Come here," she called and Randall prepared for his lesson, hoping the woman had noted some error in his act which had caused the bullets to fly false. He kept his head down as he walked, lost in his own analysis of his regrettable performance and was only pulled from his thoughts when Charlotte yelled stop.

He did so and looked up at her and she motioned to the cans and called, "Again," and the tins were now so close that he may well have counted the ridges on their sides and he drew and aimed and fired and sent the middle can spinning backward violently. Without waiting he fired again and it was another hit and he holstered the gun and looked back to Charlotte.

"We should've started this close," he said.

She pointed to the ground around him and there he saw his own casings—not two, but several—and when he looked back up, Charlotte had gathered the fallen cans and started back up the ridge. Randall smiled and followed.

21

The town sat south of the Sierra del Muerto, where the winds wash down from the peaks to taunt the Apache plume and the earth slopes inward on all sides, as if trying to close its fist around a secret. Nestled deep in a hidden valley of dogwood trees, the brightly colored rooftops of Perry Springs reflected the soft light of the morning as we made our descent.

What began as a spiritual community founded by those who believed the hot springs possessed healing powers and more, grew into a village of artists and gypsies and outcasts and, because of its location in this remote twist of desert, became a vital trading post for western travelers.

We stopped and sat our horses on the last ridge above the town and I tried to catch Sophia's eyes but she wouldn't look my way and instead Shelby met my stare and nodded and licked his tongue across his chipped teeth.

"Alright, fellas." Grimes rode to the head of the column and there was an excitement in his eyes, a fervor-like longing that I couldn't place. "Tom, Grant, Beau, and Tall Boy, handle the coats and extra duds. Jimmy, you and the doc and Shelby help Cookie with the food. The rest of you, get what you need. No more than a shot and an ale. We got a lot of riding 'fore we get back home. I don't want you walleyed if we end up having to shoot our way out of here."

Some of the men laughed and Grimes grinned back at them. My blood went cold.

"Marcus and Caleb, y'all stay here with Sophia. We'll be back by noon."

"Tough break, little brother," Shelby said as he and Bullet passed, and I saw his face was still colored with bruises but no longer swollen and the doctor had sewn what looked to be a cotton flap to the inside of his hat so that it hung down over his missing ear.

"Now you will see," Sophia said and pointed her horse toward the shade of an old spruce.

I stayed mounted on the hillside, watching the riders move slowly down the winding trail that led to the east end of town and they moved like one, a great dirt worm slithering over the land with Grimes at the head.

"Come on now, young Caleb," Marcus called to me. "We best get these wagons ready."

Ready for what, I wasn't sure, but I followed Marcus nonetheless and it occurred to me now would be the time for Sophia and me to make our run.

The long snake of men had reached the town and the body began to split off in different directions. Marcus lifted a piece of cut oak from the wagon's back and handed me a stack of Indian blankets.

"Fo' blankets in each wagon, then come help me cut this rope. Gone need eight, maybe ten pieces."

Marcus moved methodically and with his eyes down and I recognized his manner and it reminded me of Shelby before he did something stupid.

"What are we doing here, Marcus?"

He looked up at me, confused. "We gettin' the wagons ready, and making sure Miss Sophia don't run off again, I reckon."

I stole a glance under the spruce where Sophia sat and talked to her horse. I hadn't given much thought to the chance of her fleeing without me, but all of sudden my stomach started to knot up and I realized I may need to make a choice pretty soon.

Marcus was a former Ranger, but his demeanor didn't suggest it. He seemed gentle and kind and I knew better than to believe any of it. He'd gun me down if I ran. I'd have to overpower him, maybe kill him. I didn't like the thought or my odds.

When I finished with the blankets, I walked to where Marcus sat in back of the first wagon and took stock of the rope being cut and the large blade being used. My rifle was in the saddle holster and Marcus looked too comfortable with that knife for me to try anything. And what if Sophia was wrong? I'd met a handful of cutthroats in Longpine and they didn't have the mind Grimes did. They didn't long for a better world where folks were treated equal and peace was a priority. There was something happening here, bigger than myself. Maybe he really could help my brother. Maybe once folks saw his vision, enough people would join him and the outlawin' would fall by the wayside. Maybe a lot of things, I thought. Maybe I'm a damn fool and falling for everything like Sophia had talked about. I was pulling myself in both directions and felt the panic waking up and stretching its arms through my body and my knees buckled up on me and I steadied myself against the wagon.

"You alright, there, Caleb?" Marcus asked and kept cutting the rope in identical pieces and there was thunder so loud in my head I had to grit my teeth to keep from screaming.

"What's the rope for, Marcus?" I choked out, gripping the large wooden wheel with white knuckles and trying to control my breathing. "How come they didn't take these wagons into town to load 'em with supplies?"

"Easy now," Marcus said. "You don't look too good."

"What's the goddamn rope for?" I yelled and I saw Sophia move around the opposite side of the wagon and I saw the small medic blade in her hand and remembered her morning with the young doctor and I knew this was it and it was all I could do not to vomit.

The first gunshot echoed up the ridge like a fast-moving blizzard to freeze us all. We waited, the three of us, looking to one another for confirmation or denial as if we weren't sure of the sound or its legitimacy or our own sanity. But soon enough the second report came, followed closely by a third, and the adrenaline of the moment shocked us into motion. Sophia turned and quickly tucked the scalpel somewhere in her long skirt just before Marcus leapt from the back of the wagon. I was already running toward the horse to grab my rifle when, my senses heightened, I heard Marcus cock the hammer on both his pistols.

"Hold on, boy," he said and I stopped a few feet from the scabbard and put my hands up.

"You heard them shots, something's going on down there," I told him.

"Yessir, I reckon it is. But I can't have you riding in causing a mess."

"A mess is what it sounds like they already got."

"They be just fine. Now come on back over here and set on this wagon with me 'til them boys get back."

I could feel Sophia eyeing me and Marcus too and I knew we could overpower him but at what cost and whatever I thought of Shelby I wasn't sure I was ready to have him dead, or maybe I was afraid it wouldn't be me that killed him, and all these thoughts shattered in another flurry of gunfire.

"You'll have to shoot me in the damn back, Marcus," I said. "I'm going down there to see what's what."

I swung my leg up and into the saddle and turned the horse down the trail to town and gave him the full heel and we flew forward and no shots rang out behind us.

The guns grew louder and the world hotter as I raced into the canyon and there was a rider coming on hard and fast and before I could unsheathe the rifle the distance had closed and I could see my brother's face and it was wild with fear.

"Shelby! What's happening?"

"We got to get, little brother," his head shook. "We got to get now. They're fighting the whole damn town."

More gunfire and it was slung against the canyon walls and echoed around us and no man could tell if there were two shots or twenty and they seemed to sound from all directions and Shelby's head turned, frantic, as he searched for danger and found it everywhere and none of it to his liking.

"We got to get," he repeated, and with both heels digging into Bullet they retreated, horse and rider, into the hills at a frightened and furious pace.

I pulled the rifle and rode with it in one hand and rode the way my brother had come and rode into the town, where there was death immeasurable.

The bodies lay crooked and inhuman, as if in a child's drawing, limbs splayed in unnatural positions and smatterings of deep scarlet covering holes from which their souls had surely fled. No living thing walked the streets save a few dogs who appeared to not share my panic. The shooting had stopped but I recognized the horses tied near a square and put mine that direction at a quick trot.

A man in a bowler cap with a dark mustache and a fine suit burst from a building and out onto the wooden thoroughfare. The chain from his watch swung as he ran and he looked over his shoulder and must have seen nothing, but ran faster still. He saw me and froze and neither of us spoke and he looked behind him again and then took to running once more.

I looked at the faces on the ground as I passed and none of them were familiar to me and yet in them I saw my mother and the boy and myself. I counted in their still eyes all the sunsets of a lifetime and when I was finished I counted the lifetimes themselves and saw that none of them ended or began but rather they were as I was. All of us breathing and bleeding and freshly dying like the flowers of the field as they push through the dirt and grow and bloom, and a man points at the field and remarks on the beauty and never does he single out a petal or a plant, and so it is we all live and die as one and none and together and alone.

I did not tie the horse and trusted he would not flee and if he did I wouldn't blame him and I entered the saloon on the square with rifle in hand. A man I had seen in camp sat behind the piano and had just begun to play and Jimmy behind the bar was counting bottles into his arms and the men dotted the tables laid out across the wood floor and the scene itself may have been almost common were it not for the women and children and a few men gathered to the corner and, in it, huddling against one other, with some crying and shaking and others bleeding and all of them staring out at the men smoking and drinking. Their eyes trembled and were blinded by what they'd seen and what they might see again.

"Caleb," Grimes said and there was little emotion in his voice. "I see you came a-runnin'."

"Thought there was trouble."

"Well, there was a little, but it didn't last. Get Jimmy to pour you a drink."

"I'm alright."

"Are you? Your brother didn't seem to have the stomach for this after all."

"What is all this?"

"We can't very well create a new world without women. It's pretty basic biology, son."

"You're kidnapping them."

"We're liberating them from a world they have been enslaved by. When they arrive in our camp they'll have more freedom and choices than they ever had here."

"But they can't choose to stay or go."

"That's correct. No liberty is open-ended, and as always, freedom comes with a price—usually paid up front."

"You killed so many."

"Apparently folks don't take kindly to people taking their women. But that's alright, this way we won't have to worry about anybody tracking us when we head into camp. Sort of a two-birds situation, wouldn't you say?"

"You're a goddamned madman."

"Caleb, don't be so sullen," Grimes said, and he appeared hurt by my words. "Remember the story I told you, about Lightning? If you truly want to rid the world of monsters, you need something stronger and scarier to lead the way. Well, here I am."

I could feel the multitude of eyes watching me. No one moved except Grimes who simply leaned back further into his chair and smiled. I thought of Sophia and Shelby and even my own life, which I came to realize in that moment I wasn't ready to let go of.

"Well," I said, looking around the room with a wide grin. "I hope they at least got some good whiskey."

The men laughed and stomped their feet and banged their glasses on the tables. Grimes never took his eyes off me as I moved toward the bar.

One of the men in the corner, he looked to be the bartender displaced by Jimmy, came out of his crouch and pulled from his apron a small pistol likely slipped to him by one of the women and he rose with it aimed toward Grimes.

No one seemed to notice and the world slowed and at once I was outside of myself, watching me swing the rifle toward the corner. My spirit reached out to stop my body but there was nothing to be done and so I turned away from myself and asked forgiveness not from God but from the man, as I was sure to see him on the other side, and if he was a vengeful man he would be waiting for me and even if he was a man of peace he may be waiting still.

My shot buried into the man's chest and exploded from between his shoulder blades and the bullet lodged deep into the wall behind him and his lifeblood was distributed on the others and there were many screams and shudders. The men all turned to watch the man die in the corner, but Grimes never took his eyes away from my face and I felt them there and returned his stare and he nodded and I nodded back.

"Boys," he called, and everyone was silent. "Meet your new brother."

And again the men hollered and cheered and soon the saloon was filled with howling and I played the only part I could and I tilted my head back and let flow all that was inside of me.

22

Randall had taken to watching the stars on most nights and his feelings for all that looked back at him were changing. The expanse of the universe had once filled him with anxiety and uncertainty and brought with it in its enormity a questioning of faith and purpose and other ego-driven notions which he in turn rebelled from, shutting away the immeasurable illimits of all that is, and focusing rather on what he could control.

Yet the more he forced himself to look the more he saw, and though he understood no greater truth than before he now found a calmness to the magnitude of the night sky and the sweltering symbols upon it. Each constellation the same and always creeping up from the horizon and taking its turn and then settling back into the abyss and leaving the supremacy of the night to some other cluster of brilliance and all the while ignoring the shooting stars as they emblazoned their legacy across the sky in an extremity of drama and dying, never to be seen again by this world or another.

The constellations are strong and sturdy, Randall thought, and he kept that in his mind and he told himself he would work in every moment to display the steadiness of twilight and when he woke in the morning he would face his first test.

"People coming," Tad said in a manner more frantic than the last and he shook Randall awake. "Coming hard."

Randall's sleepy eyes were slow in adjusting and when they did his mind was still a fog and it was all he could do to look in the same direction as the others and when he did he saw nothing. He and Charlotte and Tad watched the western horizon with intent but the sun had yet to touch the far side of the world, the things in it still forsaken to darkness. The small boy seemed unaware of any happening and stood brushing the horses in his underwear and boots.

They had crossed the plains and flats and forests beyond the Organ Mountains and had seen no trouble, and Randall in his life had laid eyes upon very little of the world's wickedness and these things together made him blind. A man who has found fortune the once will attempt to see it again in every prospect, just as a man who has felt sorrow will brace for it at every changing of the winds.

"I don't see anything," Randall said and it was true all around.

"They're out there," Tad replied, and Randall closed his eyes and felt his son tug at his sleeve.

"They're out there, Father," he heard Harry's words replay in his mind, "in the barn with the horses."

When he opened his eyes again he saw the first of the riders as they began one by one to emerge onto the far plain as if some portal had swallowed them up and dropped them here without a single horse breaking stride.

Randall extended his spyglass and confirmed the uneasiness of the boy.

"Banditos," he said aloud at the same moment he thought it and barely was the word spoken that Charlotte was beside him with the long rifle.

"How many," she asked, not looking up from her loading.

"Eight. Ten, maybe."

"You reckon they might not of seen us?" Tad asked, scared but hopeful.

The riders in the distance began to fire their pistols into the air and let loose high-pitched yells and crows.

"They seen us," Charlotte said, raising her rifle.

* * *

By full sunup the gun smoke was drifting east toward the light, and Randall lay on his back and tried to look at the stars but found only a swirling dawn of pale blues and pinks and he muttered to himself memories of long ago and moments before.

"Quiet now," Charlotte said and turned her head to one side and inspected him and he saw the orphan boy still brushing the horses.

"I don't know why," he said and he wasn't sure what he meant but he said it again. "I don't know why."

"It's alright. You're alright," Charlotte said, and he might have believed her if not for the fire in his stomach.

He looked down and regretted it and was dizzy.

"Tad," he said and she nodded.

"He's fine. He's over yonder spilling up the breakfast he ain't even had yet. He done good though."

"I'm sorry," Randall said and he closed his eyes.

* * *

The pines near the ranch followed the slope of the ridge and it seemed every other tree had its branches turned up or down and to look through the limbs it was like lattice work and from it came the short green needles of spring, each bunch pointed upward in offering to the sun or the sky or nothing at all. The deer migration was ever the spectacle and the gray beasts called timber ghosts in the winter were now brown and their antlers velvet and Randall's grandfather took his hand and pointed at one of the bucks moving through the high wood.

"It's a rebirth, boy," he said in a gruff whisper, leaning down to where his face was near Randall's. "Every year. They shed and grow and shed again. Changing, but never changing. Do you understand?"

Young Randall shook his head.

"The Indians out here, they got their ways. White folk, we got ours. Something has to give, you see. It'll be the ones who can change, who can evolve—that's who'll rule these lands. The rest will just be velvet on the ground."

* * *

Randall opened his eyes and must have still been dreaming, he decided. The young Indian man hovering above him blocked out the sun so that it seemed the outer edges of the man's body were radiating with some magic glow to hold in his spirit.

"You drink deep now," Charlotte told him and held a bottle to his lips and he swallowed and his throat immediately set fire and the pain in his gut was overwhelming and he longed to close his eyes again but knew if he did it may well be for good, or at least forever.

"Can you dig it out?" he heard Charlotte ask, and the man answered in a language unknown to Randall and Charlotte in turn spoke the same tongue and Randall felt his sanity slipping.

There was black and then sky and then Tad over him wearing a concerned face.

"You don't want that Indian coming close to you with a knife, you just let me know and I'll kill him like I did them banditos."

More black and then agony so great it forced open his eyes and he cried out and Charlotte and Tad held him down as the Indian dug for the bullet.

"Alive!" Randall screamed and the adrenaline for a moment felt soothing and so he continued screaming.

"Alive!"

The Indian held up the bullet and judged it under the sun as if to ensure he'd taken out the right one. He held the knife over a flame and the blade turned to steel fire and he pressed it against Randall's stomach and this time it was too much and Randall fell back onto the cold ground and screamed no more.

"Alive," the small boy said and pointed at Randall.

23

"Come on, sit down, son." Grimes motioned to an empty chair in the Perry Springs Saloon. "You play any cards?"

"Nossir, but I've set around with some boys."

"Good, you ought not start. Put you in a bad spot with worse people, playing cards."

"Yessir."

"Come on, sit down."

"Yessir."

Jimmy dealt the cards, five a man, and the room was silent as the players studied their fates and weighed their choices.

"Now see, you watch old Marcus there, son. He'll ask for four cards. Don't matter what he's got. Hell he'll put back a host of aces if he's got 'em. You watch him."

"Four cards," Marcus said and grinned, and Grimes slapped the table with his palm.

"I always think there's something better out there," Marcus said, "I reckon I'm just a dreamer."

"A dreamer who catches more damn cards than a magician," Jimmy said.

The betting made its way around the table and stopped on a man they called Rigs and Rigs stared at his cards and at the pile of money and back at his cards.

"Fold," he said and moved to stand from his chair, but Grimes slapped the table again and this time with a closed fist.

"You sit right there," he said, and even the lanterns seemed to darken with the mood.

"Sir?"

"You heard me. Sit down and play your damn hand."

"But, Mr. Grimes, I folded." Rigs laughed nervously and looked around at the other men for some sort of reinforcement.

"Yeah, I saw what you did. But that ain't honest is it?"

"Sir?"

"Goddamnit, boy, you sit down and play those cards."

"Mr. Grimes, I'm sorry, but—"

"But nothing. Sit or I'll tell the boys out back to dig a bigger hole, you understand me?"

"Yessir."

Rigs sat and picked up his cards and matched the bet on the table.

"You don't want to raise it up?" Grimes asked, fire in his eyes.

"Sir?"

"I know you can hear me. What I asked was, Don't you want to raise it up?"

"Nossir, I'm just calling."

"I see what you're doing."

"C'mon now, Lawrence, let the man play the way he wants," Marcus said.

"You stay the hell out of this. I know how he wants to play and I can't abide by it. He's trying to curry favor by losing at cards and that ain't the way a man behaves. Is it, Caleb?"

"Seems like there's worse things," I replied. "At least he ain't losing at chess."

At that, Grimes erupted in laughter and the table followed and even Rigs allowed himself a nervous grin.

"Well, alright," Grimes said, still smiling. "Let's see 'em."

The cards were laid and Jimmy with a pair of jacks lit a cigar and shook his head. Marcus's four new cards held two queens to go with the one he'd kept. He winked at me.

Grimes had yet to show and he stared at Rigs and nodded and Rigs took a breath and laid his cards and they read nine to king in order and the table was silent again.

"You scared to beat me at poker, boy?"

"Nossir, I just wasn't sure I had the best hand."

"You wasn't sure?"

"Nossir."

"That's mighty cautious of you."

"I guess so."

"You guess so."

"Yessir."

"Easy, fellas," Jimmy said. "It's getting late. Why don't we go on and call it a night?"

Grimes leaned back in his chair.

"Yeah, I imagine you're right, Jimmy. It is late."

Rigs closed his eyes and let out a long breath and it turned out to be his last. Grimes cleared leather, fired a single shot and tucked away the pistol in a motion so fluid it made the running of a river seem cumbersome and unnatural.

I flinched at the sound and watched Rigs slide from his chair, the bullet lodged somewhere in his brain. The other men at the table looked down and were silent.

For a while we sat and no one spoke or moved, and Tom at hearing the shot had come and stood in the doorway and looked down at the body and then walked away again, satisfied. The sound of shovels came through the open air of the swinging doors and we all listened and to each of us they played a different tune. Somewhere in the hills far beyond the town a coyote howled and when his cry was not returned he howled again. The blood flowed from Rigs and dripped from his face onto the floorboards and pooled and soaked and grew dark. His eyes were still closed in relief.

"I'm gonna go check on Tom and them boys, then hit the hay," Marcus said, rising.

"I'm turning in, too," Jimmy agreed.

"Fair enough, boys, fair enough," Grimes said and he leaned forward but before he could stand my hand shot forward and grabbed his forearm.

All three men paused and looked at me.

"What did you have?" I asked, letting his arm go.

Grimes flipped his cards and showed us five spades, his flush beating Rigs's straight.

Marcus shook his head and he and Jimmy made for the door.

I stayed seated and Grimes the same.

"I'm not stupid, Caleb," he said, and I gave him a quizzical look. "I know you're still weighing all this, and I know that was a little show you put on earlier. But seeing as how you saved my life, I'm not going to lose my patience with you. So let's talk."

"Them people didn't deserve to die," I told him.

"No, son, they didn't. But they had to. Do you understand?"

"Nossir, I can say it certain that I do not."

"The world is full of wolves and sheep and when the sheep are killed the wolves are blamed. But why? Why are the sheep not at fault? Man stood on two legs and walked from a cave with club in hand. We conquered fire and beasts and sickness. We are meant to be wolves, and if the sheep of this world cannot evolve, what worry is that of mine?"

"That's a mighty bent way of looking at it."

Grimes hiccuped a laugh.

"It is, you're right. I get drunk and angry and the weight of a sinful world presses heavy on my heart. But these people, Caleb, they're rotten. They make slaves of their brothers and sisters, steal land that isn't theirs, destroy the earth with pen and paper and malice and war and . . ."

His words trailed off and he stared into his glass of whiskey and gave it a swirl and watched the dark brown liquid circle itself along the sides.

"Seems to me you're doing the same," I told him. "Making slaves. Taking what isn't yours."

He stilled his glass and looked up at me thoughtfully.

"Then look closer, child, and see the world we are creating," he said. "The wagons you prepared with Marcus will take the women we left alive. You can't start anew without children. But understand the killing is not for sport. I drink on nights like this one because I cannot face myself and what I've done."

"Then why do it?" I asked.

"The early stages of any civilization are the most important. We need supplies. More than we can steal," he said. "I've made a business agreement with a powerful man who can give us those things. Money, food, even protection from the government to a certain degree. But he asks for blood in return, and blood I will give him."

"What man? Why does he want people dead?" I asked, understanding things less the more I sat and listened.

Grimes ignored my questions. He narrowed his face and the lines upon it grew pronounced and he leaned toward me and I could see he was proper drunk.

"Let me tell you something, son, and come close now so that you might hear it and know it to be true. God is what you make of Him. Do you understand? God is what you make of Him because this world is what you make of it and this world is God. I will make things the way they ought to be, and I know it's all of it right and just. I know it, because it comes from within me. It was put there by God."

"How do you know?"

"When you're but an infant, you scream and cry until your mother's breast is at your mouth. Why?" Grimes asked. "Is this something you've seen and learned and grown accustomed to? No. It is a hunger inside of you which is not learned but necessary. The evil things in this world were taught and over time we learned them all too well. But what can be trained can be retrained and so we will be the ones. We will be the first."

I nodded, uncertain. "And you reckon God has chosen you?"

"Not me, not you, not any one of these men or women," he slurred his words and waved his hand out at the empty saloon.

"Then who?"

"All of us, Caleb. All those here and not here, alive and dead. God has chosen man because we once chose Him. When the first men dreamed, they awoke and told the others what they had seen and all agreed it was surely God who had put these images in their mind. This was the purest form of the relationship between men and God because we did not presume to know His will. There were no books, no priests, no men to conjure images they knew nothing of. I strive to be like these first men, Caleb, I crave it. I have practiced the abandonment of all I know, which is both impossible and enlightening and I have felt God move inside of me as a child kicks in the womb. I have cast aside the teachings of men who grew greater than God, greater than the world. These men led us all, past and present and future, away from that first encounter with God."

I shook my head.

"Folks hear a man talk like that, they call him mad," I said.

Grimes hammered his fist down on the table and his eyes went black and I felt the earth still, as if it were waiting for something to pass before turning again.

"Not mad," he said. "Extreme, yes. But not mad. There is no subtlety here, Caleb. From the mountains that spring up from nothing to the rivers which are dry in the afternoon and flooded by nightfall."

He stood and stumbled toward the door. A sideways dance with himself and the world outside of him.

"Look around," he said, again waving his hands. "This is a country of extremes. The moderate man will never succeed. Nor will the moderate God. Nature to its very core will only respect radicalism and the extreme actions born of it. A moderate wind cannot bend a tree, nor can a moderate wolf run down an antelope. Moderation is for the weak. It is good only as a tool for evil men to control populations. Peace without fighting is a mirage, a fantasy that has never been. Always we will fight, but it is up to us to choose what for."

The doors swung open and he disappeared into the night and I was left sitting, alone and near shaking. From the street came his voice and with it a question.

"What will you fight for, Caleb?"

24

Randall had frozen when the banditos were on them. Charlotte had taken four with the long rifle and three more with her pistols. The boy hesitated but then began firing wildly and had shot one man from his horse, and shot the horse too, she believed. The band of robbers had not expected a fight. They rode up firing their guns in the air, and by the time she was picking them off with the rifle they were struggling to reload their weapons. Randall had all time in the world to shoot, but he never did. She yelled at him, but he did not hear her or likely anything else, she thought. He had never seen such a thing, of this she was quite certain. It's one thing to shoot cans and this was another thing and she pitied him. She'd finished off the last of the cutthroats and the boy was whooping and hollering and the small child was jumping up and down near the spooked horses and screaming, "Pumpkin!"

Randall had not moved and when she looked into his eyes they were gray and his face pale and only then did he fall, or perhaps more accurately he stumbled into a sitting position on the ground and put his hands to his stomach and felt the blood.

Once the smoke cleared Tad grew quiet and then she heard him throwing up in the brush and she looked at Randall's wound and applied pressure best she could. He would die without help and it was help she did not know how to give.

"We have to go," she told the two boys, and they helped her lift Randall onto the front of her saddle near the horn and she rode behind him and they set out to look for help. In the end, help found them.

A young Indian rode down from the hills and there in the middle of the desert west of Guadalupe Pass he made a fire and started to work.

The Indian, she saw, was little more than a teenage boy and she asked where the healer was and he said he was the healer and that Hiushenuah had been dead since the last snows. I am Tuhallinho, he told her.

"Where are your people?" she asked and the boy waved her off and held his hand on Randall's wound and closed his eyes and spoke into the sky in soft tones.

"Can you dig it out?" she asked.

"You gonna let that dadgum savage stick a knife in Mr. Dawson?" Tad shook his head.

"Pumpkin," the child said and shook his head likewise.

"He will die," the Indian said and rose and walked toward his horse.

"Wait," Charlotte begged. "You are Strassi? The Strassi people?"

The boy hesitated and turned and looked around as if the desert might be listening. He nodded.

"Please," she said in the boy's native tongue. "This man's heart is good. Heal him."

The Strassi boy looked at her.

"Chenina Wasqua," he said, nodding. "My sister."

* * *

The boy had finished his work and led them to the mouth of a network of caves and Charlotte recognized it all, as if she had dreamed it or perhaps lived it in a life past. The clomping of the horses echoed off the wet walls of the cavern and soon they were in the barn room and small Indian children, boys and girls, took their horses and led them to the naturally occurring troughs and tied them to pillars of dolomite.

They continued down on foot and in the great room both Tad and the child stared up in awe at the height of the cavern roof and the number of Strassi who moved about the underground village. The Indian healer stopped and spoke to a group of men, and they looked at the newcomers and nodded. Soon the chieftain came forward and smiled and put his hands on Charlotte's shoulders.

"Chenina Wasqua," he said. "Welcome home."

They were taken to a low passage and all but the child ducked to enter and the walls to either side were barely wide enough to fit the travois which held Randall's body. A dozen yards down the dark tunnel the cave opened up into a small room with rounded rock walls and a ceiling which never rose above six feet. There were many blankets covering the cold ground and animal skins hanging on the wall for insulation. A small fire burned in a clay pit near the corner of the room and the smoke rose and disappeared into a hole in the wall near the rock roof. An Indian girl sat naked in the center of the cave and the low light from the stunted flame cast her shadow upon them as they entered.

The healer spoke to her and when she answered her words were unpleasant. The two began to shout at one another and eventually she stood and stamped her bare foot and then pushed past the group and disappeared into the dark passage. Tad and the child watched her with wide eyes as she left, then continued to stare long after she was gone.

They laid Randall on a pile of blankets and covered him with deer hides. Charlotte pulled from her bag a layer of bandaging and showed it to the healer.

"More," she said, and he nodded and left the room.

* * *

She gently rolled Randall to his side and continued to wrap his wound in fresh cloth. He lay with his eyes open. It had been two days and he was beginning to heal. A fever had come on the first night, but the Indian boy had given him herbs and soup and his skin had cooled and his breathing steadied.

"Your boyfriend the one who fixed me up?" he asked her.

"No."

"You talk to him?"

"Why?"

"Just wondering."

"Mm-hmm."

"You imagine a world different than this one?" he asked her.

"You mean like Heaven?"

"No."

"Well, whatchyou mean?"

"I mean a world, this world, but different."

"You catching another fever?"

"No, I'm not." He paused. "I don't think."

"Well, you ain't making much sense."

"You believe in God?"

"I don't know what I believe, to tell it straight. My family, and all my people, they was in chains a long time and they didn't stop praying and singing and worshipping God."

"You think God gave them freedom?"

"I think Lincoln gave them freedom, and a bunch of dead soldiers, and maybe they had some help from God. I couldn't say."

Charlotte was quiet for a moment, then spoke again.

"I couldn't say if God let black people out of their chains, because if there is a God, He must have put them there in the first place."

"You think God has failed the world?" Randall asked.

"I might. You reckon the world has failed Him?"

"I might."

"Well."

"You are devastatingly beautiful, did you know that?" he said, looking up at her.

"Randall." She turned her face away from him.

"No, you are. You are the warrior queen of the West."

"Warrior queen?" She laughed.

"Yes, ma'am."

"And what are you?"

"I'm the court jester."

"What's that?" she asked.

"A fool."

"Well."

"I should never have stopped you," he told her. "By the river."

"Randall."

"I was scared of my own feelings. That's all."

"You were right. You got you a wife back home."

"I don't believe I have either of those things—a wife or a home."

"Don't talk like that."

"You've saved me, Charlotte, in so many ways. I'm sorry I let you down."

She leaned over him and put her hand on his cheek. Then she rose from the pile of blankets and left.

* * *

She was in love with him. She knew that. She'd been in love once before and recognized the symptoms and was even less happy about it now than she had been before. She had seen his mother in the big room of the cave but the woman ignored her and she wondered if he was dead or on a hunting party or perhaps just staying away from her. He was married, she thought. If he was not dead, he was surely married.

Tad found her near the west-facing mouth of the hidden caverns.

"I gotta tell you, Miss Charlie, these Indians ain't half bad. You tried any of that fry bread? Lord have mercy."

She smiled at him.

"Pumpkin's took a shine to 'em, and he seems to be a good judge of character. He's down there with the little'uns playing some kind of game I couldn't make no sense of. How's Mr. Dawson holding up?"

"He's gonna be fine."

"Well, I imagine his old pride took a bullet too. 'Course it can't be every man who just has them instincts like mine," the boy said, pulling his shoulders back with a long sigh. "It's not like I learned 'em or anything. Some fellas was just born from a different cloth."

"It's cut," she corrected him.

"What is? Never mind, it don't make no difference. What are you doing up here anyhow?"

"Just looking."

"At what?"

"Things."

"Alright then," Tad said and the two of them sat in the quiet of the dusk and looked out over the prairie.

The sky turned yellow and orange and streaks of red were cast across the grasses. They moved together to the symphony of the wind and flowed back and forth as does the sea, and they covered what parts of the earth they could and left the rest to the dirt and rock and clay.

"What was his boy like?" Charlotte asked, breaking the silence.

"Who, Harry? Aw, he was a good'un. Little more rough around the edges than Mr. Dawson, which ain't that hard. Harry spent a lot of time with the horses. Preferred 'em to people I'd imagine. Me and him used to make forts in the wood with bed cloth and when his momma would see the sheets all dirty and stained she'd wear out his backside and I'd always think that was the last time, but then he'd come find me in a few days with an armful of linens and we'd do it over again."

"He love his daddy?"

"He did, sure enough. Don't know about his momma, to tell you the truth, but he respected Mr. Dawson in a certain way."

"What way?"

"Hard to say. I was afraid of my daddy, so I had that sort of respect for him. Harry wasn't afraid of Mr. Dawson at all but he still looked up to him or something like that. I think that makes it better, when you're not afraid."

* * *

That night Charlotte was summoned to the great room and there the Strassi elders asked to hear of her travels and they sat patient and attentive as she talked. They asked of her companions and their purpose and she told them and they nodded and spoke among themselves.

"It is good you are here, dark daughter," the chieftain said. "My soul is happy to see you, and many have told me the same. But the whites cannot stay. Their place is not here."

Charlotte nodded.

"The wounded white loves you. So too does Shaytaomo. He will return soon from his hunting in the mountains. This is not good. The whites must leave."

"They will," she assured him. "And I will leave with them."

The old man nodded.

"This is what I knew. You love the wounded white. Many have seen this in you."

Charlotte turned her eyes to the floor.

"They have seen something else, dark daughter. Something in the white man."

She looked up.

"His path is crooked and bent. It turns in a way that is hard on the soul. He is a good man, many have said. But he will not always be."

"I will watch over him," she told the elders. "I will make sure he is a good man, always."

Again they spoke among themselves.

"The healer has seen the path this man will walk. He walks it alone."

"I will go with him," she insisted.

"This is what I knew."

One of the men spoke low to the chief and the others nodded.

"There is one last thing," he told her. "We have seen the men you are searching for."

25

Pitted up against the slope of the closest gorge the ranch appeared as some modern-day David and the Goliath mountain rose there above it. Grimes at the column's head held up his hand and moved his finger in a circle. He then put his horse out of the road and into a field of bluestem. The horses followed with their riders and me with all of it and as the grass spread thin the main house grew larger and the bunk barracks multiplied and I sensed this was no poor man's hacienda. We crossed more than a mile of salt flats and in them standing water which had no doubt come down from the mountain and I walked my horse so that he might not step unknowingly into a false pool and have it deepen on him.

"You gonna twist an ankle thataway, hero-boy," Shelby said as he slowly pulled Bullet in step.

"I was already slower than the horse," I replied and he spit and shook his head and when some of the men laughed he rode on angrily and I hadn't meant to make mock of him but some things are as they are and I wouldn't apologize.

Shelby had come slinking back to the column the day after the dustup and asked forgiveness for fleeing and while Grimes allowed him to stay, the men were now hard on him. They called him coward and they called him soft and my elevating standing only served to further his feeling of outcast.

I had not spoken to Sophia since Perry Springs. She avoided me for a time, then rode with the scouts ahead to the ranch. The rest of us approached it from the north on the following day.

The ranch unfolded near the base of the mountain, pushed in from the valley with a few sand dunes and sparsely vegetated hills between the last of the structures and the red slate rock of the Sierra de Angar. The front gate alone seemed an oddity of some far-off time brought current and refusing to change. Its posts were pillars of carved stone flared out at top and bottom and upon each sat a lion and a lantern and within one lantern burned a flame but not the other. The iron slats on the gate were thick and black, and the row of Italian cypress flanking the pathway beyond stood tall and straight like sentries beholden to their post now and forever always.

The line of horses headed straight for the casa grande and then followed the path left, curving around the adobe plaster walls of the court-yard, where a host of young Mexican women peered out and watched the procession with sharp eyes, as if it might be an invading force.

I reined up and let the rest of the column pass and from the men there was either no notice or no mind and so I put my horse through the arched entry to the yard. The women turned to watch the young gringo, and I touched my hat and rode along through Bermuda grass cut short and kept green as the color itself. The desert and the mountains and the dust had stolen the color from the world and turned my eyes only to brown, and it filled me with a strange joy to see such grass and the women in white dresses which had stayed white and had been stitched with flowers of blue and red. Their black hair fell long against their pale skin and they looked at me with a great curiosity and I at them and the prominence of their surroundings.

They were preparing for what appeared to be an event of some impor-tance. They hung streamers and lights and set out paper lanterns of all colors, some with designs cut into the bags. There was fruit by the pound cut into squares and placed in bowls and it mixed with the candles and piñon wood burning in the outdoor stove and the air smelled as sweet as I could remember. An older woman nervously oversaw the preparation from the clay-tiled porch coming off the front of the house. The woman leaned on a pillar furiously puffing at a cigarette and called to them words of direction in Spanish. When the woman saw us, the horse and me, she shooed us away from the tables and their fine silver and white cloths.

"Lo siento," I mumbled and rode beyond the courtyard and under a larger archway connecting the main house and a smaller structure, the latter of which was padlocked and heavily chained.

There was a metal tank on the far side of the house and it was surrounded by roses of several colors and other flowers whose names I did not know. In the tank were lily pads and koi fish and the horse sniffed at both and began to drink and I let him, checking over my back for the woman. I dismounted and led the horse away from the water, lest he inhale the fish, and together we walked the fence line of the house and I could see the dust where the riders had gone and the barracks where they'd stopped.

"We could go on right now," I told the horse, and he did not respond. "Go out to East Texas and saw on them logs. Forget all this outlawin' business.

"I know," I said. "I can't leave 'em either. I don't know which one I'm staying for, or if one's just an excuse to be with the other. I'm pretty mixed up about everything, to tell you the truth."

The horse tossed his head.

"Yeah, well, you ain't exactly hating the steady food and water, are you?" I asked him. "I'll tell you what, I'm gonna tie you to that post yonder and see if there's somebody in that big house that can spare a biscuit or two for us."

I stopped at a side door and knocked but no one answered. I pulled the handle and it wasn't latched and the door swung open and the house was laid out before me in a great chain of connected rooms and hallways that disappeared in all directions.

The man was older than a man should be and he sat alone with his elbows atop a long cedarwood table and I saw him there, slumped over, and his attention tethered to his gaze, which traveled to a mantle at the far side of the room. He looked up and saw me and waved me over casually but with great care so that his delicate positioning was not compromised by his motion.

I walked to the table and he patted an empty chair with a shaking hand. I sat.

"You follow the man Grimes?" he asked and his English was for most intents and purposes better even than my own.

"I don't follow no one in particular. But I'm riding with him for now."

"You follow God?"

"I tried a time or two. I got dipped in the water, if that's what you're asking."

The man nodded.

"The man Grimes believes he follows some higher calling. Higher even than God."

"You don't reckon he does?"

"A man follows himself and calls it what he will."

I nodded and leaned back in the chair and motioned to the house and beyond.

"You own all this here?" I asked.

The man shrugged.

"A man owns only his decisions," he said.

I stared at him for a while. If he was wondering who I was or bothered at all by my presence he didn't once show it.

"I ain't what you think," I said. "I ain't no outlaw like him."

The man nodded as if he accepted this as truth just by my saying it.

"And me?" he asked.

"Sir?"

"You think me an outlaw like Grimes?"

"Well, if you're the man pulling the strings—the one Grimes talks about—then I guess you're as much a part of it as any."

"I pay for horses, for food, for other things. What do you do?" he asked.

"I don't do much of anything," I replied.

"You have not killed for the man Grimes?"

"I didn't say that."

"And yet you say you are not an outlaw."

"Fair enough," I said.

"Nothing is fair, boy. Do you agree?"

"I'm not sure I can speak to that, señor."

"And yet you are speaking. You say you do not follow God, nor the man Grimes, but here you are and so you must be speaking to something, yes?"

The woman from the porch entered the room and was aghast at my presence and she stepped forward with a flurry of Spanish but the man simply raised his hand and she stopped.

"Huevos rancheros," he said, and the woman turned and huffed and disappeared.

We set there, the old man and me, him slumped over the table in a frail arch which looked as if it might collapse at the slightest weight upon his back, and who knew what weight it might already bear. Behind him on the buffet was a handful of books titled in Spanish and a picture of a young man in Mexican military dress.

"That's you, yonder," I pointed, and the old man didn't turn but raised his head and lowered it in some motion akin to a nod.

"They took this country from us," he spoke and he closed his eyes as if there was a memory there he was trying to find or perhaps trying to hide from.

"Who did?" I asked, but the man did not answer, he only lifted a hand and waved it once through the air.

"Do you know of revolution?" he asked, his eyes raising just enough to find mine.

"Schoolmarm read to me once about the fighting with the British. I seen a bit of the trouble brewing down south."

"Do you believe one is like the other?"

"Sir?"

"The fighting changes, yes—the land and the weapons and the color of the flags—but is it not all one revolution?"

"I imagine the cause separates things some."

"The cause."

"Yessir."

The old man paused and seemed to consider this for a while and then a while longer, and then the woman returned to the room and brought with her two plates of bone china with yellow and blue birds painted round the rim and a gold line encircling it all.

The woman's presence or perhaps the plate in front of him seemed to reanimate the old man.

"There is one cause," he said, and he spoke with the certainty and sadness of the old.

"What is it?"

The woman came again into the dining room and placed on the table a silver bowl filled with scrambled eggs and another bowl filled with black beans. From a clay warmer she produced a slightly burnt tortilla and set it on the old man's plate and used a silver spoon to scoop eggs and beans on top of it until the man raised his hand.

A young girl hurried into the room and the woman gave her a stern look and took from her a small bowl of salsa and ladled a single spoonful onto the man's plate. She placed the salsa bowl on the table among the rest of the grub and turned to me. She let the spoon fall from her hand and it clanged noisily onto my empty plate and the woman raised her head high and looked down at me with spiteful eyes.

The man groaned and spoke to her in Spanish and she spoke back rapidly and with much frustration and pointed at my hat. I imagine she would have gone on at some length had the man not brought his fist down upon the table with what I thought to be considerable strength for his specimen.

"Enough," he said, and the woman was gone again and there we set, young and old, and he motioned to the food and insisted I eat and I did so with a great fervor, the juices from the beans soaking into the eggs and muddying their color. When I had finished I used a second tortilla from the clay pan to soak up the salsa and beans left on the plate and this seemed to please the man who nodded his approval. He had only had a few bites of the food in front of him, but he seemed satisfied nonetheless, and it was the young girl who returned to clear the table and she looked at me and smiled a shy smile and I tipped my hat in return. The old man spoke to her in Spanish and whatever he said caused her to giggle and blush and the old man smiled and seemed pleased with this outcome.

"What's the one cause?" I asked.

The man was still smiling and he nodded absentminded and looked down at where his food had been as if expecting to find it still there.

"Sir?" I said.

The man's face went serious again and he looked up at me and then reached toward me with his hands and I gave him one of mine and he held it there on top of the table.

"Did you see the vacas when you rode in?" he asked me.

"Yessir, I saw quite a few many head."

"This is how I am rich because this is how my grandfather was rich. You understand. The wars happen and different nations are drawn and undrawn and none of them own me because of these cows and the things they buy me. Do you know what money can buy?"

"Nossir," I replied. "I can honestly say I don't know much in that direction a'tall."

The man waved his hand back and forth in an exaggerated motion of sweeping, and I couldn't say if he was dismissing his own question or illustrating the vastness of the answer.

"Americans have their revolutions, Mexicans have begun theirs, the men fight for freedom and independence and honor and all of these things, but I am rich from animals. What do I care about such things? Do you know how men will be rich in the future?"

"If I did I imagine I'd be getting started on it myself."

"They will be rich from the land," he said.

"No offense, señor, but that ain't exactly news. Plenty of folks been getting rich off the land for longer than you or your granddaddy been around."

"Yes, yes. Men have long fought for dirt and been rewarded by it," he waved his hand again. "But now they want what is under the dirt. They want to bleed the earth and harvest the black blood in its veins. And they will. And they'll do it on land that belonged to my ancestors and even my cattle will not change their minds."

"So you aim to have Grimes and them boys fight the oilmen?"

The old man laughed and coughed and smiled and regarded me as if I were a caricature of a child repeating phrases meant to amuse. He closed his eyes and held a napkin to his mouth and coughed vicious and then was still. When he spoke again it was quieter.

"Grimes cannot fight the oilmen, no more than the leaves can fight the changing of the seasons. It is a nasty business, progress. But it is a business. This rebellion Grimes believes in will never come to pass."

"Then how come you back him?" I asked.

"How many people were killed in this town, Perry Springs?"

"A good many."

The man nodded.

"And do you believe this was the first?" he asked. "How many towns do you think Grimes has gone to? How many towns sit atop rivers of oil?"

"So you just want the land? Why kill for it? Why not buy it? Seems you got plenty of dinero."

"How much would a man pay for land?" he asked.

"Whatever price is fair, I guess."

"What price is fair for land where outlaws and murderers run loose?"

"You're trying to drive the price down," I said.

"Not trying," Grimes said from the doorway into the hall. "Succeeding. Abe just bought up almost ninety percent of the deeds in Perry Springs at half the price they cost last week."

Grimes knocked his fist on the wood table in victory.

"Caleb," he said. "I see you've met Señor Abel Guerrero. Abe, this young fella is Caleb Bentley."

Grimes removed his hat and placed it on a hook near the doorway, then raised his head high and looked down at me.

"This," he said, "is the man who saved my life."

He pulled a chair from the table without being asked and Señor Guerrero nodded as he sat.

"Abe here is gonna buy the land, and he and those oil boys can go on and make money come up from the ground or fall from the sky or whatever suits their fancy."

"And you'll have a chunk of the country to grow your new world."

Grimes smiled and gave one long nod.

"Still a smart boy," he said. "Now tell me, how come it is you're setting here in the first place?"

I looked to the old man, who looked to me, both of us wondering what I was going to say.

"You see them señoritas out yonder? I was trying to get lost and have one show me the way home, if you get my meaning."

"Does this mean you're not still enchanted by my daughter?" Grimes asked.

"To tell the truth, it ain't my enchantment that's the problem. She don't want nothing to do with me, and I ain't much for begging."

Grimes leaned back and considered the news and then smiled again.

"Well, she's always been a tough one to break. Probably for the best. When we ride out, Sophia's gonna stay with Abe here."

I watched the two men exchange looks; their meaning I could not place.

"Alright then," Grimes said. "Go on down to the barracks with the other boys and we'll send some girls down shortly to call y'all up for supper."

"All that out there's for us?" I asked.

"Sí, señor, I hope you're hungry."

I rose and looked again at the old man.

"The leaves don't have to fight," I told him.

"Qué?"

"The seasons change, but it's always the same. The leaves come back around the next year. I hear what you're saying about progress, Señor Guerrero, and I know the world out there might look a good bit different than when our granddaddies were young in it, but things have a way of coming back. Triumphs and mistakes alike."

The old man considered this.

"Do you know the one cause?" he asked.

"I know what yours is, but that don't mean it's everybody's."

I tipped my cap and walked back out into the yard and to my horse and rode down to the barracks and left the two men to discuss their plans of progress.

26

They departed on the morning of the fourth day. Randall rode Storm with Charlotte behind him. Tad rode Mara, and the child sat atop Pumpkin. They moved south across the eastern ridge of the Guadalupe Mountains, passing in and out of arbutus trees and stands of evergreen sumac. The boys foraged for prickly pear pads, and Charlotte continued her thinning of the rabbit population. Randall mostly slept.

There were no roads to speak of and each morning they would look out at the Chihuahuan Desert never-ending and at night they would camp at the furthest point their eyes had seen. It was a process unbroken until they reached the low hills overlooking the town of Boracho.

Boracho was one in a long line of settlements and trading posts along the western route of the Texas frontier. Kent, Plateau, Wild Horse, Van Horn, Allamoore, and many others were lined along the road, which ran east to west, with the Guadalupe Mountains to the north and the Davis Mountains to the south.

The buildings were mostly still made of wood, but some brick and steel manors stood along the main street. The overcast skies gave the noon a weary look. The desert passage had left tired the animals and their riders and all were anxious and ready to stop for a good night's sleep. Randall was back in Mara's saddle and felt almost a man again. Charlotte had attended to his bandages each night and again in the mornings and had kept him well fed with rabbit and cactus and pinto beans. He stared into the valley at the town below and saw what may have been a parade of some sorts. Through his spyglass there were many figures gathered at one end of the main thoroughfare and he saw what he thought to be children being hoisted upon the shoulders of men.

The closer they came to the town the more unsettled things appeared. What had looked like a parade was revealed to be an angry mob with ill intent. There were indeed children riding on the shoulders of their fathers, but from their mount they threw rocks into glass windows and shouted down at people on the streets.

Randall stopped his party in an alley a couple of blocks from the chaos.

"I don't know what this is, but it's not good," he said.

"Horses need food and water. We could do with a little ourselves after coming through that damn desert," Tad said.

"The boy's right," Charlotte said. "Maybe we can find supplies without getting mixed up in whatever is going on out there."

Randall sat his horse and thought.

Two young people, a boy and a girl holding hands, came running down the side street and into the alley.

"Hey," Randall called as they passed. "What the hell is happening?"

The boy stopped. He looked confused.

"You ain't heard?" he asked and the girl pulled at his arm. "They hung Antonio Rodríguez over in Rocksprings. The Mexicans are up in arms. Say they're gonna burn the place down."

"Who's Antonio Rodríguez?"

"Sorry, mister, me and Callie are gettin' while it's good. I suggest you do the same. Half the damn town is Mexican. More coming up every day trying to get clear of the fighting down there. This ain't no place to be."

The couple fled and soon more people dashed past Randall and toward the hills.

"Alright, Tad, you and the child take the horses back toward the east side of town. Find a trough if you can. Charlotte and I will try to grab some provisions and meet you out there. We'll have to head east a while. Any further south and we'll only be getting closer to the border and the mess that comes with it."

He held Charlotte's hand and they stayed low against buildings, ducking in and out of doorways and windows to see if there was a mercantile untouched by the rioting. Fires had begun across the town and the air collected the smoke and the shouting and the day sounded of war. Randall's breathing was labored and he held his hand against his stomach as they moved.

"There." Charlotte pointed, and he could see a café on the far side of the street that had seemingly been passed up by the mob.

They ran, still crouched, across the street, their heads swiveling in all directions, and burst through the door of the café, quickly shutting it behind them.

"We need food. We have money," Randall said hurriedly as he turned to the woman behind the counter. She was a young, dark-haired girl and she stared at Randall with fear beset in every corner of her face.

"She's Mexican," Charlotte said. "That's why they didn't stop."

"It's okay, it's okay," Randall told the girl, reaching toward her. "We're not going to hurt you."

The girl screamed and ran past the two of them and out the door.

They looked at one another, then raced behind the counter and through the curtains to the back of the café, where the food was stored. They began grabbing things from the shelves, and were readying their escape when they heard the door open out front.

Randall put his finger to his lips and Charlotte nodded and they stood frozen in the supply room. The footsteps and hushed Spanish voices grew closer.

Charlotte pointed up. A ladder ran from the corner of the room and disappeared into a hole in the ceiling. They climbed.

Charlotte was the first into what was an attic of sorts. It was a small hideaway with one window and barely enough room for two people to sit comfortably. Charlotte pressed herself against the window as Randall crawled up from the hole.

"Ay!" a voice called just as Randall pulled himself into the crawl space. Men flooded the supply room and scrambled toward the ladder.

"Window, now!" Randall said.

Charlotte yanked at the bottom of the pane but it wouldn't open. The first man poked his head through the hole and Randall kicked him in the face with his boot.

"Move," he cried, and Charlotte stepped aside as Randall crashed through the window and rolled out onto the pitched roof. She watched as he slid down the shingles and then disappeared over the edge. She cracked the skull of the next man through the hole and then climbed through the window and stutter-stepped to the edge and looked down.

Randall was slowly lifting himself from the dirt. He held his arms across his stomach and bent forward in pain. She heard movement near the window behind her. She jumped.

She bent her knees and braced for the landing and when she hit the ground her left foot twisted over onto her ankle and she screamed but kept moving. She hooked Randall's arm and the two of them hobbled into an alleyway with none of the food they'd come for.

They made for the edge of town and were relieved to see Tad and the child standing with the horses near the back corner of a blacksmith and saddlery shop. As they approached, Tad did not look at them but rather at something on the other side of the building and then he put his hands into the air and nudged the other boy that he might do the same.

"Stop," Randall whispered, and he and Charlotte pulled up short just feet from the two boys.

Around the corner they could hear men shouting directions. Soon a man appeared and began to tie Tad's hands behind his back. The child looked at the man and then behind the building at Randall and Charlotte. Randall shook his head and put his finger to lips.

"Alive," the child said and pointed.

The man paused and raised his head toward the two of them. He let the rope fall and reached for his gun. Randall was faster. He drew and shot the man in the shoulder and then in the chest. Tad hit the dirt and the child crouched down and tapped him on the head.

"Alive."

Charlotte and Randall turned the corner with guns blazing and saw two of the men fall and a third running back into town to find more strength in numbers.

"Let's go, *now*," Charlotte said, and within seconds they were mounted and driving the horses at full sprint down the road headed east.

A mile or more from town they crested a rise in the road and looked back and there saw the thing they hoped most to avoid. Dust rose and spread from the road and crawled into the hazy sky heading toward them with a group of mounted men under it all.

"We don't have the horses to outrun them," Tad said.

"You don't know that," Randall told him.

"The hell I don't. Wasn't exactly a nice rest they got back there."

"Follow me," Charlotte said. "We can lose them in the canyons if we get off the road. They'll probably quit the chase by the end of the day."

"If they don't?"

"If they don't, we'll head through the mountains and into Fort Davis. There'll be army there. But they won't go that far anyway."

"How do you know?" Randall asked.

"It's going to snow," Charlotte said, looking up. She put her horse down a slope covered in sotol and its razor leaves and Tad followed with the child at his back.

"You coming?" she asked as Randall sat his horse in the middle of the road and watched the riders grow nearer.

"You all go on ahead. I'll meet you in the mountains above Fort Davis."

"What?"

"They'll follow my tracks, and it'll make it harder to know that you left off. Mara can make it."

Before she could protest, Charlotte watched him turn the big Arabian in a full circle in the road and take off down the other side of the hill.

"Let's go," she told the boys, giving one last look in the direction he'd gone.

* * *

So this is courage, Randall thought, the wind combing back his hair as he held his hat over his sore and aching stomach to keep it from flying away. Mara breathed steady from her nostrils and kept an impressive pace for nearly eight miles before slowing. Even at a curtailed gallop Randall still believed he was putting distance between himself and the men hunting him. His only hope was that they had continued along the road and not seen where his companions had abandoned it.

The first water crossing he came to was a tributary of the northern Pecos and without hesitating he put Mara into the current three feet deep and rode alongside the river's offshoot to cover his tracks. The water narrowed and eventually gave out near the northern base of the Davis Mountains. He put the horse onto the banks and led her across rocks and avoided the sand until the ground turned to grass and he gave her back her head and together they ascended switchbacks and game trails leading into the mountain pass.

An hour into the climb he stopped and dismounted and looked back toward the water and he waited there until near nightfall and no one appeared. As the last of the day's light faded into the growing darkness he felt the first snowflake of winter on his face.

27

The barracks were just that. Long, empty hallway-like structures of cut linden, roofed with tin, and by the time I arrived the air was steeped in the smell of cologne and musk as the men excitedly talked among themselves about the pending fiesta.

Other men began to arrive and stable their horses and they ranged from musicians to businessmen to the young ranch hands Señor Guerrero permitted to attend. A group of fresh-faced young men passed by with their chins out and chests flared. They removed their hats and used the palms of their hands to slick down their hair before covering it again.

"It's their clothes that gives them away," a man named Averitt whispered to me. "It sure as hell ain't their pride."

The girls came down and each took two men about their arms and they led us back up the hill and to the courtyard, where we sat and were served a feast of goat and chicken and peppered peas. Tequila was poured and consumed and poured again and Jimmy made it a point to loudly announce his disdain for "Mexican bathwater," and he drank only from the whiskey bottle he'd acquired in Perry Springs.

The sun began to set and the light turned red the sky and the paper lanterns marked the courtyard with the colors of a day made dusk and when the band played it was to the tune of celebration. The men drank away the massacre as I was sure they had done before. Some flirted and danced, but many simply drank and me among them.

Sophia's fingertips found my arm briefly as she passed by and when she did not look back I followed her and we drifted to one of many fires and stood alongside the young vaqueros and their slicked hair.

"You see now," she said, looking into the fire.

Her hair was pinned back with colorful birds, and obsidian earrings shone black against her skin. She wore a long black skirt and a ruffled white blouse. When the soft gusts of the coming winter wind crossed through the courtyard, her well-ridden boots emerged from the flowing skirt and she was both the symbol and reality of beautiful strength.

"I do," I told her.

"Will you stay?"

"No."

"When will you go?" she asked.

"When you come with me."

She did not answer for a long time and instead we stood and listened to the boys goad and harass one another about sexual things they knew nothing of but hoped to someday.

"You must go to the mountains and wait for the snow," she said.

"What? No. I'm getting out of here, tonight. You coming with me?"

"We'll be caught."

"No we won't."

"And then you'll get killed."

"Not if we don't get caught. Listen, Grimes has done promised you to that old man. They're gonna make you stay here and be part of his little harem—do God knows what."

"I know."

"You know?"

"Do you think it will be easier to slip away from a band of outlaws or one old man?"

I sighed.

"Alright," I said.

She looked around.

"You must go with the Lobos. Go to the village in the mountains. Let time pass. When the first snows come, we will meet in the hills above Perry Springs."

"How will I find you?"

"When the time comes," she said, ignoring my question, "tell them you are a hunter."

Then she turned and was gone and the vaqueros laughed and maybe it was at me.

From the darkness of the yard I watched Mr. Guerrero sit his wheelchair under the porch lanterns. Men approached to pay their respects, and after a handshake and a few short words the bull of a woman from earlier chased them off with a glare. She stood like a twisted guardian angel behind his chair, scowling at the festivities until Grimes came and slipped a hand across her lower back and whispered into her ear and upon hearing his words her face turned to a mock and playful horror and then she giggled as she perhaps had as a young girl and Grimes smiled and took the handles of the wheelchair and leaned down to talk to the old man as he pushed him toward a group of men in fine suits and expensive boots.

* * *

I had never before tried tobacco, but that night I smoked. A young vaquero offered out a sack, and from it I pinched what I believed was a healthy amount between my thumb and fingers and, using my body to shield the wind, I sprinkled it into paper and rolled.

The young doctor passed by and I offered a seat, which he took. I also offered a share of my smoke, which he declined, but in good time he produced his own cigarette and we sat, the two of us, and watched the flickering lights and the burning wood and the music drifted across the yard and out into the places unseen and carried with it fragrance of a regret not yet known.

"You don't like it here," he said and was not asking.

I did not speak.

"I don't like it here," he continued. "I believe, or I did, in the cause. I believed in Grimes's words."

"And his actions?" I asked, raising an eyebrow.

"They are . . . murderous."

"And yet you stay."

"And yet I stay."

For a time we did not speak and when that time came to an end, the young doctor tossed the last of his paper into the fire.

"It is murderous men who shape empires. Alexander, Caesar, George Washington, even Lincoln had to be willing to spill the blood of a nation so it might heal stronger. But Grimes is not well, it's true. He is a sick man and his sickness lies in the mind. For this I have no procedure. There is no bone to set nor wound to tend. I am afraid his wound, whatever it may be, was suffered long ago and cannot be so easily mended."

I nodded.

"Maybe," I said. "Or maybe it ain't no wound a'tall. Maybe some men just choose to be how they are and that's the way of it."

"Maybe," the doctor conceded. "But that has not been my experience. I believe even the most evil man could have been good, had things only turned more in his favor."

I thought of my brother.

"In any case," he continued, "I came here to save lives, not take them."

He paused and pulled from his pocket another cigarette.

"I could have practiced medicine anywhere, you see. I came here and I did not like what I saw, nor do I like what I see now: the killing, the kidnapping."

He emancipated a charred stick from the fire and used its glowing end to light his smoke before condemning it again and watching for a while as it was consumed by the flame.

"Let me ask you, Doc. What happened to the girl's mother?"

"It's difficult to explain."

"Try."

"Señor Guerrero did not approve of his daughter's choice of husband. Some Mexican gambler from a border town down south." The man pulled on his cigarette. "So, as sort of an insurance policy on their arrangement, he let Grimes have her."

"Guerrero is Sophia's grandfather?"

The doctor nodded.

"Anyway, for some reason—maybe the daily dose of laudanum he gave her—the woman fell in love with Grimes. Problem was, Grimes never cared about the woman in the first place. His eyes were on her daughter the whole time."

"Sophia?"

"That's right. So one day the woman takes a mysterious fever, not like anything I've ever seen. The next day she's dead. Of course, now he has to wait for the old man to die too. No way is Guerrero going to let Grimes marry Sophia. He'd send an army stop him."

"But he's leaving her here. Why would he do that?" I asked.

"He knows the old man will protect her. Being his blood and all. Then, once he dies, or maybe once Grimes gets his little mountain utopia set up, Grimes will come back for her."

We both paused to ponder the strange ways in which the world turns.

"There is a man I knew from my school days," the doctor said at last. "He is a Texas Ranger. I have his address in San Antonio."

I stopped him there.

"Sounds like one hell of a mutiny of the open seas," I said, raising my brow.

"Can I count on you, Caleb, when the time comes?"

"I don't know what you've got planned, and to be honest, I don't give two shits."

"If you love the girl, this is the only way to be with her."

"You got some sand even telling me all this," I snapped, "and it damn well better not end up getting me killed. Now get the hell away from here and don't ever speak to me again."

"Well then," he said, rising and flustered. "I'll leave you to it."

"I think it's best you do."

"I hope I can at least count on your discretion in this matter," he said in a hushed tone.

"Go on, Doc," I told him and looked back to the fire.

28

The first of the snow had turned to mud and Randall followed the tracks through the Davis Mountains. He found his party alive and well and watering at a stock tank near a sheep trail. For a time they were able to manage the mountains in the light snow, but soon it was too deep and falling too heavy and with Fort Davis still a day's ride, they needed shelter. They sat their horses atop a rise in the earth and looked out. The blizzard, fostered by the winds that had come down from the northwest, was the first of the season and though they'd seen it coming for well on two hours they passed neither town nor dwelling and they huddled together the four of them and the horses and looked down into the valley, where smoke rose up from a lone chimney.

They held their hats on their heads so as to not lose them in the gusts and they squinted in the cold and hollered to one another even though they were feet apart.

"Must be a hard man to set up in this country," Randall said.

"Must be a goddamn fool," Charlotte replied.

"Don't much matter which it is," Tad told them. "We got to see about getting outta this storm."

"Alive," the child said.

"Yea, alive would be good, Pumpkin," Tad said, nodding.

"You name that boy Pumpkin?" Randall asked him.

"I reckoned he oughta have one."

"Pumpkin?"

"It's as good a name as any, and we sure as hell know he likes it enough."

"You named him after your horse?"

"Nossir, I didn't. I named the horse after a pumpkin, like how Miss Ashby used to put out on the porch during the harvest season."

"So?"

"Well, I guess I'm trying to say that must be what the boy's named after too. Not the horse."

"But you got two Pumpkins, so how are they gonna know which one you're talking to?"

"I'd imagine the horse will know it's his name when I'm saying it in relation to horse things."

"Horse things?"

"Yessir."

"And the boy?"

"He don't know nothing in the first place. What are you getting all worked up about?"

"I'm not the one getting worked up. I just asked a question."

"You asked a few of 'em," Tad said. "C'mon, lets get down out of this cold and see if this crazy fella has more charity than he does sense. Let's go, Pumpkin."

Both horse and child perked their ears.

* * *

They put the horses on the slick path and moved down the ridge and into the wet, white fields and the horses sank five inches with every step and the child held out his hand to gather the snow but each flake captured melted in his palm and the pain on his face spoke of a hypocrisy which he did not yet understand.

Tad leaned his head and opened his mouth and stuck out his tongue and let the snow fall onto it. The child did the same and all grief was forgiven.

No one came to the porch in greeting and there was no light burning from within, but they agreed the smoke from the chimney meant someone was inside.

Randall dismounted and walked up the wooden steps and knocked the snow and mud from his boot on the top of the last step and the door opened before he reached it.

"I expect y'all need a place to hole up until this shit storm blows over," the woman said. She wore a long nightgown and a fur coat over it and after she spoke she turned and went back inside and left the door open.

She stopped a few feet from the threshold and looked back.

"Are y'all simple or some other such shit keeps you from under-standing things? Hurry up before all the goddamn heat goes out of the goddamn house."

"The boy is," Tad said.

The woman stared at him.

"Well, that's just wonderful. What's your excuse?"

* * *

Randall took the horses around to the barn and was surprised to find a half-dozen pigs, several chickens, and two other horses already occupying the hay-covered grounds. The horses shared a single stable, and he walked his own mounts through the rest of the animals and tied them loosely to two posts near the back wall. There were sacks of feed, a shelf piled with home-canned pickles and okra, and a workbench littered with wood shavings. There were steel traps, jars of bait rub, and from the rafters hung tanned hides of spectac-ular variety. A collection of deer and elk antlers lay on top of one another near the water trough and Randall counted at least four gloves, each of a different pair, in various positions on the ground. A low fire burned in a makeshift pit cut from a steel drum and Randall added wood to it from the stack outside and the pigs followed him back and forth and back again hoping for food.

He raised up his shirt and examined his belly and the wound was red and pink and along the edges a dark blue but there was nothing seeping and the last of the blood had dried days before and he considered all of this to be proper and promising, though he could not say for sure.

He twisted from one side to the other and what hurt he felt was of a sore nature and not the sharp, painful type. And it was not lost on him the notion of his grandfather's deeds versus those of the native people who saved his life and at this thought he dropped his shirt back down and put on his coat and left the barn.

Inside the cabin the woman labored over a table as water boiled on the stove. The stove itself was iron and the design of the iron was elegant, as if this stove were meant to be in some great hall but had been lost to its purpose and instead wandered the desert and ended up here and could never go back. The base held up by clawed footing was adorned with swirling steel and the fleur-de-lis and from within the red-orange glow of the fire could be seen through the gap where the door met the frame. The top of the stove flared out and there was space for four pots or pans though the woman only bothered with one and had for some time as the other cast-iron rings were rusted over from neglect. The umbilical piping rose up to and through the ceiling and it had been the smoke from this stove which had led them there in the first place and Randall stood staring at it and the woman noticed and stared back at him in turn.

"Can I help you? Is there something wrong with the way I'm boiling this water?"

"No, ma'am, not at all. Thank you for the hospitality."

The woman scoffed.

"Hospitality," she repeated and scoffed again.

She turned back to the table and gathered up herbs and parsed them out into five piles and picked up each pile and placed it in the bottom of its own cup and then took the pot from the stove and poured hot water into the cups one by one and as she did so she leaned down to smell the steam as it rose up and with each cup she smelled she nodded and seemed satisfied.

"Get the crackers down from that shelf," she said without turning around, and Randall hesitated, which was not to the woman's liking and she told him so. "Never mind. I'll do it my goddamn self. You want anything done around here, I swear to Christ, you just have to do it your goddamn self."

"I'm sorry, ma'am, I wasn't sure which shelf," Randall stammered, and Charlotte smiled and seemed to be enjoying the interaction, while Tad appeared as nervous as Randall and Pumpkin studied the ceiling with his hands in his lap.

"*Sorry, ma'am*," the woman mocked him. "I give you shelter and make you tea and you can't even get the goddamn crackers. Well, I don't know what I expected from a man. My husband—may he rest in whatever hell was waiting for him—he was as useless as tits on a bull." She looked at Charlotte. "All men are, you know. Every man to ever walk this earth has been kept alive only by the patience and practicality of a woman."

"I can believe that," Charlotte said.

"Well, it's a matter of fact not belief. Belief's got nothing to do with it."

The woman put a cup in front of each of them and she stopped and stared at Pumpkin and he never took his eyes from the ceiling.

"When we first came out in eighteen and forty-three my husband, bless his ignorant heart, was going to strike it rich in the gold mines of California. 'Course, as you can goddamn well see, we didn't make it to California or nowheres close before he got hisself snakebit. Might've lived if it was only the one bite, but he was in such a hurry to get back to our camp to get the poison out, he stirred up another snake and this one got him a couple more times. Dumb sumbitch, my husband."

"And you didn't go back after that?" Randall asked and the woman looked at him with disgust.

"Go back, hell," she said. "All that was back east was more dumb men. No, I was wilder in my younger days and I figured I'd live on my own in the wild until a worthy man came along and swept me up. You all see how goddamn well that worked out."

"You didn't have no problems with Indians?" Tad asked.

The woman laughed.

"Indians," she said. "I almost married an Indian, after my husband died. A beautiful Mescalero boy. He was dark and hard with the most lovely black hair that hung down his back. Let me tell you, the bedroom activities were never dull with that one."

Tad choked on his tea.

"But unfortunately, he was also a man and worse than that, he was an Indian man and if you think men are simple in our world you should try the world of an Indian man. They hunt and smoke and hunt and smoke and tell stories and play grab-ass with one another. The women do all the work. I mean everything. They dress the animals, they cook and clean and set up and tear down anytime the village moves. They raise the children, they tan the hides, they farm the gardens, they make the tools and the pottery, and the whole thing was just too goddamn much. I mean, there's nobody ever accused me of shying away from no work. It ain't about that. It's about working for somebody else and not getting paid a wage—you understand what I'm saying? Anyhow. I sure do miss the pecker on that boy though. Black boys got big peckers too, I've heard. Is that right?"

Tad's mouth hung open, and Randall's eyes went wide.

"I couldn't say," Charlotte answered, hesitant.

"Couldn't say? What, are you with this one?" the woman asked and motioned to Randall. "Hell, I thought he was your boss or something. I didn't know you was with him. You need to train him up, honey. He couldn't even find the goddamn crackers."

* * *

That night Randall sat on the porch wrapped in an Indian blanket the woman had tossed at him and smoked his pipe. The storm had passed and the night was quiet and still and the chair under him creaked and the floor under it creaked as well and far across the plain a panther came down from the rocky hills and pawed at the fresh snow.

The moon shone bright and reflecting off the white fields it was brighter still. Randall watched his own smoke rise into the air and there it lingered for a moment and then moved on and joined up with the thick column from the chimney and together they drifted toward the moon, as if being called home.

The woman opened the door and stepped onto the porch and closed the door behind her and sat in the empty chair next to him without saying anything. Above them dark shapes passed through the moonlight, and Randall leaned forward to better see.

"Geese," the woman said. "I been wondering when they was gonna come. Head down to Mexico—and further, I reckon—about this time every year. 'Course they probably weren't counting on this goddamn storm."

"Probably not," he answered.

"Can't blame 'em. There ain't much in the world you can count on. Your black girl in there tells me you all are on some mission for vengeance. Says a couple of lowlifes killed your boy."

"She's not mine. She's a free woman."

"Well, whatever you want to call it. She'll never be free, though. None of 'em will. They may go back to the chains in time, or they may not, but they won't be free. Not here."

The old woman produced from her gown pocket a small sack and in it was the trimmings of an aromatic leaf and Randall watched as she pinched a dose and placed it unceremoniously into her mouth and began to chew.

"That's not tobacco," he said and the woman rolled her eyes.

"I guess you must be the smart one of the bunch," she said. "You want any hashish? I got an old Mexican fella who passes through from time to time and brings it for me. His wife up and died a few years back, and I think he wants to marry me. Or at least wants me to go down to Mexico and take care of his ass."

"No, thank you, ma'am."

"You sure are one polite sumbitch to be riding all this way looking for some folks to kill. The boy says you already had it out with some of them road-running sacks of shit."

Randall nodded.

"Well, I guess if that didn't turn you around, there ain't much that will."

"I guess."

"What's wrong with the little one?"

"Couldn't say. Found him in a town with no name and no people other than an old priest who looked about ready to die."

"So you just thought, I already got one child gonna be in danger, I might as well put another one there with him."

Randall shrugged. "I didn't want anyone coming with me to begin with. Now they've been here long enough it seems natural."

"Well, it ain't. If you and that woman wanna go get yourselves killed, then go right ahead, but you ought to leave them boys with me."

Randall leaned away from the woman and eyed her with great curiosity.

"Oh, don't look at me like that. I'm a mean old cuss, but I ain't heartless."

"If you aren't, you put on a good show of it."

"I imagine that's fair," she said. "I had me a boy once too. Me and my husband, back in Virginia. It's how come we were headed west in the first place. He died in the war and we couldn't set there in the house where we raised him, or even the state for that matter. We loaded up and went running from our sorrows, and it shouldn't taken no genius to see they was gonna follow along for the duration. And they did. The West ain't no different than the East, and as much as there ain't neither side gonna say it, the North ain't no damn different than the South. It's all just people in a pot and we're boiling in the summer and freezing in the winter and in between we hope to make some money and make some love and maybe raise a few babes to carry on after us. Funny how we do that. So scared of dying we think we can work our way around it all by living on through our children. But children die too. Some quicker than others."

She tucked her sack away delicately in its pocket and leaned back in her chair.

"I'm gonna go ahead and assume you ain't never killed a man, and save us the time of me asking or you lying," the woman told him. "Now these boys killed your son and that's a damnable offense, no doubt. But let me tell you a little secret, Mr. Dawson. There ain't nobody holding your son captive 'til you get your revenge. They ain't gonna let him go soon as some more bodies hit the ground. Do you understand what I'm saying?"

"Yes, ma'am, I believe I do."

"But you still think this is something you got to do? Is that it?"

"That's it."

"Makes you feel more like a man, does it?"

"Maybe so."

"Mm-hmm. Of all the species on God's brown earth, men are the dumbest and the race ain't even close."

"Maybe so."

"You leave them boys here. You know it's the right thing."

"I'll talk to them."

"You'll get 'em killed is what you'll do."

"I'll see about it."

"You goddamn well better. And let me tell you one more thing, before this green leaf puts me to sleep. Revenge isn't real. You can't buy coffee with it. It won't warm your bed at night. And killing only leads to more killing. You want my advice, you take that pretty one in there and y'all go on and get married and you have yourself another boy to make you forget about the first one. That might seem harsh, but I've lived too long and seen too much to tell it any other way but the way it is."

The woman stood and put her hand on his shoulder and he stared up at her face and it was as soft a look as he'd seen.

"You seem a good and decent man, sir. I've known very few, but the ones I knew all had the decency pulled out of 'em by the woes of the world. It didn't happen overnight, neither. It was a slow burn of a growing flame and eventually it ate up the humanity that made 'em decent in the first place."

Randall placed his hand atop hers and nodded and thanked her and said again he'd talk to the boys. When she opened the door a rush of warm air blew past him from inside the cabin and it was gone before she closed the door again.

29

We rode south into what looked like desert never ending and then there were mountains where before there was nothing, as if they'd been set down momentarily en route to a more deserving home. The weather came and it came fast and the mountains were gone again, blocked by a snow that blew sideways, moving east without regard for those who would not follow.

Marcus and Tom made the line, passing out coats taken from the dead in Perry Springs, and I took mine and looked past the bullet-sized holes in the fabric and knew that in the face of the storm there was warm or cold and nothing else.

When Shelby came for a coat there was not one given and he was told they were only for those who killed and he complained and said the girl had a coat and Tom asked if he was a woman. I tried to give him mine and he refused and there was a hate in his eyes and I understood why. I watched the fog of his breath fill the air around his face like a mask and then he was gone, pushing Bullet toward the front of the column.

The storm broke near the base of the Chisos, the desert behind us and the climb ahead and the sun setting soon.

The next morning we started into the mountains, where Grimes said dozens more men were waiting. A dry arroyo started wide at the base but turned narrow and the men dismounted one after the other and walked their horses over the slick rocks and thawing snow. Marcus took my reins in hand with his and led us, the two horses and me, and he no doubt harbored a guilt for drawing down on me.

We saddled up again on the shaded side of the mountain, where the path disappeared into a pine forest and the air was colder still and it spilled out onto a set of steep switchbacks leading up. I worked my jaw around with my mouth open to relieve the pressure in my head and slumped forward onto the horse holding tight the horn of the saddle lest I slide backward on the steep grade of the trail.

I watched the mules and wagons navigate the sloped trail, the wooden wheels somehow failing to crack and splinter against the rock, and I felt the eyes of mule deer ventured down to below the snow line to forage and now come upon this winding snake of men and beasts. The grackles screamed at us from their branches and named us intruders, their wings and chests becoming wide and puffed in their defiance. When we made no move to turn back, they for a moment relented but then flew yet to other trees to repeat the notion.

The gray clouds and the peaks above us hid the sun like a glowing treasure behind their backs, and we could see they would not let it go until morning. The trees swayed and shook and shed in the blistering of the wind, the cold lassoed to it like a stubborn cowboy. I pulled tighter my coat around me and sought to tuck my jaw downward and erase the length of my neck so that I might bury my face into the fabric like a turtle into its shell. Other men did the same and soon it was as though a band of coats and hats rode up the mountain pass with only dark, inset eyes to guide them.

Even with our small party the going was slow and laborious and it occurred to me the suffering and logistical difficulties if the army were to send men up this mountain. It was also not lost on me the proximity to the Rio Grande and how easily the Lobos could slip into Mexico if they were to receive any unwanted company.

We reached the main camp at day's end, and it looked more a proper village than the tent city I'd imagined. There were a handful of log cabins, a livery, and several bonfires burning throughout the clearing.

"What do you think?" Marcus asked, riding past me. "Home sweet home."

The Perry Springs women were taken to one of the cabins, and I was shown to a tent near the livery by one of the men from the mountain.

"I'm G.W.," he said and held out his hand. He looked a part of the mountain, covered in hides and hair and with a grizzled beard.

"Caleb," I said, and we shook.

"Grimes says you'll bunk with me. Says you like horses."

I nodded.

"I like women," he replied, disappearing into the tent. "But to each his own."

I looked out at all that was before me. The sun was sliding from the sky and threatening to go west forever. The clouds moved in the opposite direction, as if they'd had a falling out or just come to some different conclusion about things. I watched them go. I watched as the shadows of dusk arose from their graves and were given life by the fading light. Soon the world would be covered in darkness and the shadows would return to the feet of those things from which they were birthed, but here in this magic hour they were free to move and grow and exist on some balanced plane between light and dark.

* * *

The sun shone our first full day in the camp, and men set about tasks of all nature. Some worked on building shelters, others chopped wood, a small group gathered to argue over the best way to smoke meat. G.W. and me followed the savory smells to the middle of the camp.

A tanned and leathered old woman of not much physical stature sat on an overturned bucket with her legs spread. The front of her dress, discolored red, hung between her thighs, where her hands were fast at work plucking the feathers from a brown hen.

A man held position over a large cookfire where sat an iron grate full up with various cuts of beef.

"You got them steaks 'bout ready, Big John?" asked a slender man.

"They gettin' there. Good steak takes time, son."

"The hell it does. You overcook that meat, and Juanita ain't gonna stop at them birds."

The old woman spoke in Spanish, and the big man near the grill grunted.

"You just worry about your pollo, Abuela," he said. "Leave the real meat to me."

She glared at him.

"That's Abuela," G.W. said, leaning toward me. "She's been here longer than me. Folks say Grimes killed her son, and now she just follows him around. Like he's all she's got left of her boy or something."

"Seems strange," I said.

G.W. shrugged. "Them old Mexicans are a strange bunch."

"How long you imagine we'll stay up here?" I asked him.

"Hard to say. Once it starts snowing, it ain't likely to stop until spring. But that'll give us plenty of time to breed that fresh crop y'all brought in yesterday."

"The women?"

"Hell, yeah, the women. What? You still thinking about horses?"

"Have you done it before?"

"Not me. Last winter was the first, but there weren't as many girls, so it was mainly Grimes and a few of the boys who'd been here longest."

"And they had children?"

"Yessir. Got a whole nursery set up in one of the cabins," he said. "Can't wait to add mine to the bunch."

I nodded.

"One more question," I said. "Is there a cowboy up here goes by the name of Frank?"

The man shrugged his shoulders.

"Don't know any Frank," he said.

That night I went to the tobacco cart and took a small sack and filled it and wrote my estimate on the ledger and signed my name. I didn't know the day so I drew the shape of the moon with the pen and left it full and unshaded so that it might mirror the image staring down at me from the starry world of blackness and blaze.

In front of the tent I fed a small fire and watched it lay and rise with the wind, and the flames would swirl up and then die with each great gust and from the dead they rose time and again as a savior from the cold.

"Come on," G.W. said. "Time to howl."

I didn't know what he meant, but I followed, and dozens of men fell in with us, all moving toward a giant bonfire just outside of the camp.

Grimes stood pale and naked before the fire and the others looking up as if he were some monument to a bygone world. He raised his arms high to match the growing flames, and there he was, erect in the light of the moon and the stars and all these things burning. He took in such a breath and stood, mouth closed and eyes wide, and looked to each man in his own eyes and then turned upward toward the floor of the universe and let loose a guttural moan, and those before him stamping their feet into the rock and silt and sand.

He pointed at the men, and the all of them did commence with returning his cry. They howled and barked and screamed out until the false line between man and beast was overrun with savagery. Grimes smiled and held out his hand and the he-wolves quieted and he looked at them again.

"My sons," he said. "My brothers."

He bent down and squatted above the dirt and was slow in doing so. He moved his hands overtop the ground in long sweeping motions. He patted the soil, then plunged his hand beneath its surface and came up as if being brought forward by some wave, the earth falling through his fingers and down his arm.

"The moon rises full. A light for believers and nonbelievers alike. All turning to the night sky with straining necks and searching eyes. Not unlike those who came so long before us. Such creatures, these distant kindred of the first men, such frightened vessels of an assiduous evolution from which their own forebears were molded and shaped. And to the moon, whole and blood and immortal, they did turn. Panting, shrieking, snarling. And all of it some unknown edict of a strange need not met. This moon, this other world where spirits roamed or demons lurked. This glowing godhead, birthing a great light upon the darkness. This astronomical despot to which all the stars paid homage. This moon, and with it the madness of being, the species-altering desire to understand. And still the wolves howled.

"With revolutions came a straighter stance, but with each answer a swell of questions new. And with each path taken, a foundation poured atop a divergent future. The flow of knowledge compounding on itself, continually engineering an outcome no more likely to occur than another. And always some moon to stand against the midnight, to illuminate that not yet discovered. Men were drawn to power, to purpose, to the re-creation of self. A misstep not foreseen by the natural fibers of selection. Human domination of the earth brought forth a great many improbabilities.

"If the earth were to tell the story of men, it would need only a matter of minutes, perhaps even seconds, and there would be nothing left to say.

"All this, and then there is us. And what then is our purpose? What is our charge? The story of this country is still being written. Written by the land and the men who control it. Written by machines and the men who own them. Written by the bankers and lawyers and the politicians they install. But what's left for us, gentlemen? Where, in all the chaos of industry and greed, do we have our say? It will be here, brothers. It will be here that we lay the foundation of a new world. A world where voice is given to the voiceless. A world where our children's children will not be forced to carry the loads of some higher class upon their backs."

The men howled and yelled and began to shed their clothes until they were, to a man, as naked as their ancestors. I'd never seen the like.

I didn't join them. Instead, I crept away from the fire and back to the camp and thought of Sophia until I fell asleep.

I dreamt that night of a great black horse, a stallion coated so dark it shined even in the twilight, and no man could ride it as it was bound always to be free and with that freedom came all the knowledge and pain of this world and the worlds before. And in the dream I knew the horse. I knew its shape, there, the moon upon it, and each desire in its heart was also in mine. I could feel the battle everlasting between isolation and love, and in such fighting there are no victors save madness and uncertainty.

The horse reared and whinnied and stomped, its soul fracturing from within as the earth once did and perhaps will again. It raced down from atop a stretched mesa and into an endless and shadowed valley, and as it ran its muscles pressed against their skin in flexed masses of gluteus and vastus and femoral strength, and from its nostrils spewed breath heavy and salient upon the night air. And wherever the horse ran, I somehow followed, my own breathing labored and unworthy, until at last we stopped as one and stood in silence, looking out at the country before us with eyes undecided.

I felt my chest rise and fall and with the coursing of my new lifeblood there came both suffering and strength. The tissue beneath my skin tightened and I could feel some unseen aggravation which sought to magnify every awareness within my broadening bones. I shuddered and jerked and turned my head upward toward the infinity of the stars and my front two feet raised and kicked as I screamed for all things forgotten and all those left to come.

30

Randall awoke before the day and Charlotte and for a while he stood with his coffee and leaned against the frame of the door as if he were a picture and in the picture he watched them sleep and the old woman snored and the smallest child stirred and in the unsure daze of sleep he searched with his hand for something known only to him—a memory perhaps. His fingers found Charlotte's hair splayed black across the once-white pillow and his hand rested there and he moved no more.

Tad was the next to wake and sat up and looked about the cabin in confusion and at the bedrolls strewn across the wood floor and he blinked his eyes and found Randall and nodded and Randall nodded back. He poured the boy a cup and Tad pulled on his boots and coat and they walked together to the barn to see about the animals.

"Hell no, you ain't leaving us here with that crazy old bat," Tad protested. "She's meaner than any rattlesnake ever slithered cross the ground. She's liable to put Pumpkin in the barn if he goes to pitching one of his fits, and you know he will."

"I can't have the two of you getting hurt or killed if things go sideways. I can't have it happen to one or the other, for that matter."

"That ain't fair in no way or shape."

"Maybe not. But it's not meant to be."

The tears welled in Tad's eyes.

"Hey, c'mon now. We'll come back and collect you once all this business is taken care of. We shouldn't be but a few weeks—if that."

They began to fall.

"I killed one of 'em," he cried. "I shot him and shot his horse too."

"I know you did, son."

"I killed one of 'em, and now you won't let me come with you."

"We'll come back and get you."

"I don't want to go back. Can't you see? All he does is drink and beat on me. Can't you see?"

The boy cried and Randall took him into his arms and the boy pushed away and shook his head and Randall gathered him up again and Tad buried his head into the man's shoulder and wept.

"Can't you see?" Tad mumbled softly through short, broken breaths, and Randall held the back of his head and quieted him and beyond the barn the sun rose into the world and gave light to things so that they might be seen more clearly and whether they are or not is dependent on the seer and not the sun.

The woman made them breakfast. She cooked up fry bread the old way: a thick batter spread thinly over the bottom of an iron pan and put to the coals of the kitchen stove. The bottom of the mix would firm up into a crust and she'd distance the pan from the flames and let the loaf raise and bake and the whole house smelled of heartwood pine.

Randall leaned against the kitchen counter and watched her work. When the bread was done she slid it onto a plate and tossed thick chunks of bacon into the hot pan. The meat and fat sizzled and cracked and cooked down, and the grease popped and spit into the fire. She sang some old song in Spanish as she plated the bacon and walked out into the light of the morning and rapped the pan against a porch post and it rang out in the dull, smothered tones of some woebegone bell.

* * *

Randall and Charlotte rode away and Tad refused to say goodbye. The old woman stood on the porch with the child and neither waved, only watched as the two riders grew smaller against the country and smaller still and when they could no longer see them the woman turned to go inside and the boy stayed, staring at what, who could say.

* * *

Randall and Charlotte rode into Fort Davis as the snow thawed near midday and a young private with a thin mustache led them to his commander's cabin and stood outside the door and yelled there was a man and a nigger here to see him. Randall glared at him until he felt Charlotte's hand on his shoulder, pulling him away.

They entered the cabin and found it to be one large room. In the front, a bald man of stunted height and exaggerated plumpness sat behind a wooden desk scribbling mercilessly onto a pad. There were papers piled high around him and another young private at his side taking the sheets, folding each into letter size, and stuffing them into envelopes. In the right corner was a military-styled bunk with wounded men on each cot and a medic asleep on a stool. To the left of the makeshift hospital was a row of tables with even more papers and envelopes.

"If this is about the goddamn pigs, there's nothing I can do," the short officer said without looking up. "They're pigs, they root. I'd get rid of them, but the bacon would go bad before we could eat it and the last thing we need to do is waste bacon."

"It's not about pigs," Randall said. "It's about murderers."

The man stopped writing.

"Murderers?"

"Yessir."

"Who'd they murder?"

"My son."

"Goddamn."

"Yessir."

"Well, my condolences."

The man gave Randall a pitied look, then went back to his letters.

Randall did not move. Charlotte stood near the door.

The man looked up again, confused.

"Yes, can I do something for you?"

"I'd like to know if they've passed through this way."

"How would I know that?"

"I have a likeness. Perhaps your men, or maybe your scouts, could take a look."

The man stood. He was even shorter than he appeared while sitting.

"What's your name, friend?"

"Randall Dawson."

"Where's your spread, Mr. Dawson?"

"Sir?"

"Where do you live?"

"Longpine."

"Longpine."

"It's in Arizona."

"Arizona."

"That's right."

"Okay, Mr. Dawson from Longpine, Arizona. Do you know what's going on across the border?"

"A revolution of some sort is starting up."

"A revolution, that's right. And maybe you've seen some of the anti-American riots happening all across the state of Texas? There are Mexicans, Mr. Dawson, thousands of Mexicans in this state, and more coming every day. That is the concern of the United States Army, with all due respect, not finding a man who killed a boy in some godforsaken territory out west."

"Will you at least look at the poster?" Randall asked, pulling the paper from his pocket and unfolding it.

The officer glanced at it, shook his head, and handed it back. "Good day, Mr. Dawson."

Randall began to say something else but thought better of it and turned to leave.

"I seen that boy," a voice said.

It was so faint that Randall thought it could have come from the back of his mind, but he saw on Charlotte's face that she'd heard it too. They both turned to look in the corner of the room, where a man had risen halfway from his bunk.

"Lemme see it," the man said, softly.

Randall moved toward him.

"Hold on a goddamn minute," the rotund officer said. "That man is not under my command and is to be hanged for treason as soon as he is well enough to stand trial."

"If he hasn't stood trial, how do you know he's gonna hang?" Charlotte asked, still standing near the door.

The officer turned to face her.

"Because he's a goddamn traitor. That's how. Rode with the Lobos, which means he's as good as dead. The patrol that found him should have left him to die in the first place, instead of wasting our resources on an outlaw."

Randall handed the man the poster. There were bandages double-wrapped around his throat and a flap of skin from his ear to his neck was badly infected where it had been crudely sewn on.

"That's him," the man said, pulling at his own wrappings to make room for his voice. "That's the boy who did this to me."

31

The next morning the world turned dark again and the threatening skies lingered for three days, holding the mountains hostage but never producing rain or snow. On the fourth day they were silent no longer.

Hail and snow fell thick from the gray clouds, and two scouts returned to camp with news of meat. A herd of mule deer had been spotted moving through the basin and it was agreed a hunting party should be sent so that the food stores might be filled further.

"Marcus, take five men and bag as many as you can," Grimes ordered, and Marcus nodded.

Tell them you are a hunter. Sophia's words echoed in my mind.

"I'll go," I said, and perhaps Grimes saw the eagerness in my eyes.

"No, you stay here. I'm gonna need your help with the horses."

I kept my face steady but inside I panicked.

"Let the boy come down with us," Marcus said. "He's a good shot, and them horses ain't goin' nowheres."

Grimes waved his hand.

"Fine, go on. Just get down there before they move out."

Marcus called for three other men, none who'd rode with us from the Davis Mountains. G.W. was among them. We saddled up and rode into the blizzard.

We moved down the mountain on a different path than the one we'd taken up and soon we were in a canyon of black rock, the walls sloping up on both sides and dozens of creeks and streams shot out in every direction.

"That stuff keeps falling," Marcus said, looking up, "and this is all gonna be one big river 'fore too long."

"How far 'til the herd?" I asked.

"Few more miles through this canyon, then I imagine we'll fall right into 'em."

I nodded and looked for any chance to slip away but the canyon had me pinned and soon we'd be on the deer and I wondered if Sophia had already fled from her grandfather's hacienda. With the storm still hovering overhead it would be hard to track her no matter how quickly it was discovered she'd gone.

"When we get down there," Marcus said to us all, "the horses ain't gonna be able to run with 'em. So we gotta keep turning the herd."

We nodded.

"But don't go shooting off in the same direction as the rest of us are riding. Wait 'til they all turn, then shoot as many as you can and we'll work to turn 'em again."

We nodded and rode on and the goldenrods and bigtooth maples shivered in the snow and grabbed hold of the flakes before they hit the ground and piled them there as if protecting the earth, sacrificing themselves for some cause already lost in the blinding white of the storm.

The breath of the horses spilled from their nostrils as steam and when we emerged from the canyon they smelled the herd, perhaps also sensed the pending action, and their breath came quicker and mine did too.

The deer were in a field beyond a tree line marking the beginning of a sparse forest on the mountain's west side and Marcus and one of the men circled around to the far end of the valley to push them further from the trees.

I waited with the other two men who whispered to one another or maybe they spoke plainly only to have their words reduced to a whisper by the wind as it battered against the canyon walls and spilled out behind us into the frosted valley.

The herd dotted the field and the distance between lessened them to gray ants moving across spilled sugar as they foraged for the buds and twigs of woody plants. With the winter and the settling cold they would soon stop moving to conserve the energy needed to create life where there is only a shell. Their metabolisms would slow to a necessary crawl. They do what they must to survive, I thought. We all do.

I knew the hunt was on when the deer stopped moving. They looked up from their various positions and froze, as if they were part of the landscape and always had been. Save for the flicking of their tails they became statues, lifelike tributes to a world passed by and never to come again, left behind and stranded in this new time and place. A few lifted their chins and blew and waited and watched and blew again and then, as if a whip had been cracked upon them, they fled away from the woods and across the valley, the two riders charging hard behind them. They were silent in their stampede, crossing toward us as specters upon the snow. We readied ourselves but before they reached the mouth of the canyon they turned, leaning on some old-world instinct, and moved south along the mountain's base and we put our horses into a hard charge alongside. Marcus led the way on the outer edge of the field and forced the herd to double back on itself, and as it did the two men with me began to fire. The deer moved together as one and we picked them apart, the meshing of violence and grace told true by the blood spilled bright upon snow.

When the last of the deer slipped past our closing ranks, we dismounted and spread out across the killing field so that we might harvest the dead as do the reapers in dark stories told by the living.

We knelt over them like wraiths come to collect souls. I propped the first deer on her back, sliding two large rocks under her shoulders and another under her hips. I pulled the hunting knife from my boot and began behind the hind legs, making a short cut that ran to the pelvic bone and another shallow slit up to the jaw. With gloved hands I grabbed and tugged at the skin until it began to peel away and save the meat from being covered in fur. I flipped the knife and hooked the pelvic cut and drug upward, cutting through the muscle and pulling it up and away from the stomach and intestines. I flipped the knife again at the breast bone and sawed through so I could spread the ribs. Steam rose from the warm body of the dead animal and the snow around us melted and sunk and became a mix of mud and blood. I moved to the anus and cut another hole and tied it off with trimmed cord and hoped it didn't spill out. I cut the esophagus as far up as I could and used both hands to yank out the windpipe so as not to taint the meat. The entrails came free and fell down to her midsection and I cut away some of the connecting tissue near the backbone and the diaphragm and then rolled her onto one side and let them fall away and then did the same on the other side. I pulled loose the outliers and labored through the cutting of the pelvic bone and splayed apart the once great beast and drug her toward the pack horses as she drained.

I looked across the valley and saw each man bent before a carcass and each working diligently to save the meat and no one man was paying attention to another. I knelt again, quickly, and cut from the big doe several chunks of backstrap and shoved them into my satchel and packed it tight with snow and went back out to repeat the process. The others were finished around me and Marcus had stopped to count our bounty and I heard from within the forest the bawl of a wounded animal. The others looked up and paused and then turned back to their work. I walked out across the snow and found a blood trail. It was dark and mixed with green and brown and led into the woods. I followed it past the tree line and found the small fawn, its tongue lolling from its mouth, having collapsed into a pool of its own gutshot blood.

It was small, likely born late into the summer and thus not much chance to survive even without being hunted. Its eyes were closed and its chest heaved in unsteady breaths. Its ears twitched at my approach and its eyes opened and rolled forward and the pupil shrunk at the white light of the snow or perhaps some other white light unknown to all but the dead and dying. The fawn tried to rise but could not and instead raised only its head and again bawled and I stood watching. After a while I moved forward slowly and it let me and I put my hand on its side and felt it rise and fall as do the fortunes of all species and all worlds and all galaxies. I slipped my knife again from my boot and pressed it to the throat of the innocent and did what many had done before and will surely do again and I wondered if intention was heavy enough to outweigh all other causes and so too their effects. I emerged from the woods bloodied and the men watched me walk to my horse and I looked somehow changed to them and perhaps they would later recall this or perhaps they would let it drift by and be buried in the snow with the lives of the deer and the bears and the ancient men.

We drained and cleaned the last of the animals and loaded them onto the pack mules and they hung stacked and splayed atop one another bound by rope and we put our horses into the canyon draw and moved on from the valley. I counted almost one hour, then called to Marcus.

"I left my knife in the woods."

"We'll find you another one back at camp."

"Grimes gave it to me. For saving his life. It means a lot."

Marcus stopped our procession in the last of the snow and it fell silent around us as the winds had moved on with the bulk of the storm.

"Okay, go on and look for it but take G.W. with you."

"Yessir," I said. "We'll catch up."

"You better."

G.W. wore a homburg hat rather than the Stetson Boss worn by most of the men and rode a small horse that looked to be of Indian stock. He asked me as we rode if I had picked a girl yet from the captives, and I told him I had not.

"I can't wait to get me one," he said. "I reckon Grimes'll get the first pick, then Marcus and Tom, but I'll cut a man he tries get ahead of me after that. There's a purty redhead I got my eye on so don't go getting attached."

"You have my word," I told him.

"Cut a man good," he said again.

"So you don't mind that them girls are here against their own will?"

"What?" His face was one of genuine confusion.

"It ain't like they chose to come up here and have you put a baby in them," I said. "Just don't seem right."

"Oh, I see, you're one of Grimes's thinking boys."

Now it was my turn to be confused.

"Grimes likes to think about all kinds of stuff and whether he'll admit it or not, most of us are just hard cases looking to fight and fuck and not get arrested. He gets bored with that, goes and finds him a thinking boy or two so he can have somebody to talk with. You must be the latest."

I wasn't sure what to say, but G.W. continued anyway.

"I don't much care for learned men, or what they may believe is right and wrong," he said, and turned to stare at me with menacing eyes. "Nossir, I'm gonna get me what's between that little redhead's legs whether she wants to give it to me or not."

We crossed over the valley and into the woods and I dismounted near the dead fawn and began to search the ground, using my gloves to clear away snow and pine needles. G.W. sat his horse and picked at the tattered edges of his coat and when that held no further appeal he sighed and climbed down.

"It's either here or it ain't," he said, hands on his hips.

"Go a little faster with you helping me look," I said, and he rolled his eyes and crouched down and swept his hand haphazardly over the ground.

"Your redhead—she got freckles?" I asked, inching closer to him.

"Never known one not to," he said.

"I knew one back in Longpine who didn't."

"Well, this one does."

"That's good," I said and shoved the blade into his throat and out the other side and there it stuck with him clawing at it and staggering about on his hands and knees. I left him, sputtering and choking on his own blood, and took both the horses deeper into the forest.

32

Randall and Charlotte rode through the pastures and dry grasslands beneath the mountains. Their horses moved across the empty plains heading south, crossing over thawed snow turned mud and blue-green desert ferns sprouting from the earth. They spotted a lone bobcat perched in a tract of beargrass, watching them through animal eyes oscillating from predator to prey as if unsure of its place in the world.

They passed through the upper regions of northeast Presidio County and circumvented the sharp plateaus and broad cuestas of the Trans-Pecos highlands. Eventually the land arched and sloped into the Marathon Basin of Brewster County and they followed ephemeral streams southward, toward the border.

They made camp on the third night in a rock canyon which provided shelter from the wind as it pushed the twilight clouds across the sky, dressing and then undressing the stars. The two of them lay on opposite sides of the fire. The only sounds were the occasional popping of the wood as it burned or the far-off cry of coyotes as they pursued the movements of shadows in the moonlight.

"Are you sure you want to do this," she asked, and he could see her face through the flames as they quivered and leapt from the dry post oak.

"No," he replied.

"But we're going anyway."

"It doesn't seem right to turn back now."

"I miss them boys."

"I do too," he said. "But it's best this way."

"I know."

"Come here," he told her, and she did.

* * *

The night's clouds turned into the day's rain and the two riders found the going both slow and cold. They put the horses toward the elevated table-lands to the east and took shelter under a bedrock overhang and held each other and didn't speak. Below them a herd of pronghorn antelope passed by on the far-reaching plains, unimpeded by the wet weather.

The storm passed, but Randall still saw the weary and burdensome look on Charlotte's face.

"We'll be okay," he assured her.

"Spoken like a true jackass," she replied.

"We aren't going to fight them over the brothers," he continued. "We're going to buy them."

"Buy them?"

"For a group like the Lobos, if what we heard in Fort Davis is to be believed, money is more valuable than a couple of men. We'll buy the brothers, then we'll take them back to Longpine to hang."

"Back to Longpine," Charlotte repeated.

"That's right."

"Back to your wife."

* * *

The rains left the desert foothills ripe with the smell of creosote and ocotillo. The plants drank in the morning sunlight, releasing their compounds into the air, and Randall wondered how a world so magnificent in its nature could also be devoid of empathy and awareness.

Even the creosote itself, in its survival, killed those once-living plants around it, stealing from them the life-giving water when it fell. If awareness came to such flora, he thought, what then would the process of nature look to for guidance? Awareness, he thought, is meant to promote righteousness and civility. To do evil or violence is to cast aside such awareness, such evolved cognizance as man has been given, and revert to a nature not our own. There are but two natures, one is man's—human nature—and the other is nature itself from which we have separated ourselves. And though he believed these things, Randall began to pity himself, and his naivety of the world.

33

The storm moved on, the snow melting, and the atmosphere seemed covered in a gray haze. No sun, no clouds, and the only thing left was a cold wind. Sophia rode my Missouri, and I rode the dead man's horse.

She'd found me in a rock quarry north of the Chisos. She held her pistol to her breast and when she saw me she noted the blood on my hands and nodded, and we set out to the north at hard ride with hopes of outpacing those who were sure to follow.

We rode up through the desert toward the Horse Head Hills and past the frozen agrito berries, which fell as they thawed and dotted the ground with red. We rode through the night, twice spelling the horses at stock tanks near the roadway. The sky was dark and starless. The hills before us were embellished by the blackness and we rode through each pass expecting always the next until the dawn cowed away the night, unraveling its hold on the earth and bringing forth an end to our slow stumblings.

Sophia led us into a canyon and under an overcast sky she picked up an all-but-hidden game trail twisting out of a draw and finding the road again five miles north. At midday we rode through the forgotten dreams of a long-deserted township. Two rows of rotted wood and broken adobe structures ran perpendicular and crossed near an old well with neither rope nor bucket. Most of the buildings were in the throes of collapse and had been for some time. The entire town seemed to be leaning, as if it were too exhausted to stand but too proud to fall, and in the grayscale of the day it appeared even more unsure of its place among the living.

Three dogs came out from one of the abandoned clay houses and trotted alongside us for a while and then stopped, all three of them, and stood in the middle of the road as if they'd been stayed by some invisible command. I twisted in the saddle and looked back and they matched my stare for a while and then turned and plodded back off the street, their ribs pressing into their skin with each breath.

"What is this place?" I asked her.

"Nothing, now."

"Well, what'd it used to be?"

"A Mexican village."

"This ain't Mexico."

"Not anymore."

The sun appeared just in time to set and we watched it and then rode on. The stars shone for a while but were replaced by the moon and in the absence of clouds, the new light helped outline the mesas and horizontal strata. We rode toward the dark shapes and found a path up and took it and the horses shied and stamped and we urged them on up traprock switchbacks and false summits until finally the trail spilled out onto the tableland.

Coyotes unhappy with our being there yelled out and the horses didn't much care for that either and I threw a handful of rocks into the night and told the predators to move on and I told them they could have it all back tomorrow.

We sat together and held one another and looked out over the low plain we'd crossed and watched for movement but all we saw was the still silence of the world. We slept on and off and rose before the sun and Sophia made a fire just big enough to boil coffee and I fed the horses and went through the supplies she'd stolen and matched a day to each scoop of oats, and I marked lines on the sack of beans and I didn't bother looking at the dried meat.

From the nothingness of night came the false shapes of the dawn and every bush in the lowlands became a man or beast and only once the sun had topped the plateau did they turn back to their true form.

The Mexican village was ten miles to the west and we could see the shadow being lifted as the sun moved higher still and from where we sat drinking coffee the buildings did not look broken and the town was not filled with ghosts.

I thought I saw movement on the plain and reasoned it was one of the dogs from the village, but when I looked again there was nothing there save whatever lay hidden in the brush.

I took my coffee cup and tapped it against Sophia's in a celebratory gesture, and she shook her head and smiled and stood to saddle her horse. I shrugged, looked once more for the dog, then tossed the grounds from my cup over the ridge and watched them fall.

We rode into a creek and followed it north against the soft current, and the horses weren't pleased with the cold water. They turned their heads and walked sideways and tried to come out onto either bank but we kept them to the middle until we were satisfied our tracks had been gone long enough.

"Tom will still track us," she said.

"I know."

We doubled back and out a different side and split up and came back together and the whole time leaving some tracks while covering others. It was a practice in patience, and a frightful one at that, to stay closer to those hunting you rather than to ride wide open in one direction.

We slept little and less and drank cold coffee and the more we rode the more this thing began to chew on me.

I thought of the boy and my brother and all the others. If I didn't stop the thought it would go back forever to the beginning of time and take me with it over the graveyards of old. Death hung in the air around me and I had begun to believe it always would. I thought of Grimes and his ghosts and how only the innocent ones haunted him. And so it chewed on me until we came upon familiar country and I looked to the west and then at Sophia.

"Do you believe bad men deserve to die?" I asked her, and she looked at me concerned.

"Some men are worse than others," she said.

I nodded.

"That old Mexican's ranch is yonder, up against them sierras."

"Guerrero?" she asked, then nodded in confirmation.

"Well."

"You mean to kill him?"

"He's your grandfather."

She nodded.

I looked again toward the darkening mountains. The sun flagged below the horizon but its luster remained as a memory upon the land and turned the sky all manner of violet and red. And there, under the day's amaranthine recollection, I pressed my lips to Sophia's and hoped that in her kiss I would find some answer. When we pulled free from one another, each seemingly unwilling to let the other go, she told me of the *agua escondida* above the ranch and said she would wait there with the horses.

My worry over my soul, which I couldn't say if I believed in or not, was a worry fettered to my own destiny. After my conversation with Señor Guerrero I had decided I had no authority to judge or intervene and yet I found myself now changed in heart, believing myself some servant of the world, believing that if I were to kill an evil man, then the world might be a better place upon my doing so.

We take these liberties, as Grimes had warned again, as if they were given by God and of course they are not. But Grimes and I differed in our supposition of God, to the point where my own judgment was my own judgment and if my soul were to face a tribunal it would be only what I myself could conjure in the way of morality.

All of this, and still the Dawson boy remained. My crime, for which moral acuity was unnecessary, layered the far reaches of my mind and thus could not help but affect and even direct my future actions. Grimes, Guerrero, and every evil man in a world full of them, might die by my hand and yet never could I heal the scar of guilt and culpability from my life or any I might thereafter seek to lead. I thought these things, and more, as I crept slowly into the big house with my hunting knife at my side.

34

Thunder came up from beneath the ground, unsettling the earth and the things upon it, stirring a mixed flock of redpolls and warblers from a copse of palo verdes. Mara stamped and blew, nervous below him.

"We best get off the road," Charlie said, turning Storm toward a honey mesquite thicket.

Randall followed and they both dismounted and watched the road. Carved through the foothills from the gravel and sand the road snaked in and out of the brush and disappeared over a low rise. From over the rise dust began to swell up into the air and the rumbling of the ground intensified. Randall and Charlie looked at one another and back to the road as the riders began topping the hill and then descending toward them.

Randall counted at least twenty and he watched the column of mounted men as it turned in unison off the road, fanning out and encircling the low-growing mesquite. He patted Mara's neck to calm her and squinted up into the eastern morning, which shone through from the backs of the riders and gave them a shadowlike appearance.

"Hello, there," he said, addressing the nearest man.

"Howdy." The answer came from a different direction and Randall and Charlie turned as the man who'd spoken put his horse forward in front of them.

"What can we do for you?" Randall asked.

The man smiled and for a long time said nothing. The birds began to return to the underbrush, though not as close as they'd once been.

"We're looking for somebody. A couple of somebodies," the man said, turning in his horse and staring out at the country ahead of him as if perhaps his quarry was watching from afar. "You all ain't seen a little Mexican gal cross your path? She'd be riding with a boy about her age, goes by the name Crawford. Real name's Bentley—Caleb Bentley."

Randall and Charlie exchanged knowing glances and the man leaned back in his saddle.

"Y'all know the boy?" he asked.

Randall nodded. "He killed my son, back in Longpine, Arizona. We've been hunting him."

"Well, hell. Killed one of ours too. Left him for the bears. Nasty business."

"I'm sorry to hear that," Randall said.

The man waved off his apology and looked again to where the road met the northern horizon.

"So, I'm guessing that makes you Randall Dawson?" he asked.

"Yessir, that's right. The boys confessed, then?"

The man nodded.

"Let me ask you, Mr. Dawson. You got somebody up the road yonder waiting to get the drop on me and my boys?"

Randall looked confused. The man waited.

"No, huh?" he said. "That's good."

The man whistled and, from some place Randall did not see, a rider appeared in the road and he nudged an angry boy up before him.

"Serrano found this here young man trailing you. You wouldn't happen to know him, would you?"

Randall nodded, "Yessir, he belongs to us."

"I don't belong to nobody," Tad shouted, and the man called Serrano gave him a boot to the back, causing the boy to fall on his hands in the dirt.

"We left him back near Fort Davis. He must've followed us . . . again," Randall said. "He didn't mean any harm."

"I'm sure he didn't," the man said and smiled again and eyed the boy. "How old are you, son?"

Tad pushed himself to his feet and knocked the dust from his breeches.

"Old enough to go where I please without being harassed by folks," he said.

The man's smile grew and he laughed a boisterous laugh and the men around him followed suit.

"I like his fire," the man said to Randall as he leaned over to smooth the mane on his palomino.

"Alright then," the man said, slapping his thigh as if some predetermined timer had expired in his head, and he and the rest of the riders filed back into the road. "Rest assured, Mr. Dawson, I will kill Caleb Bentley and avenge your son. You all have nothing to worry about on that front.

"Let's go, boys," the man called, then motioned to Serrano. "Put the kid on a real horse, we can use his animal to carry water."

"Pumpkin is a real horse," Tad protested, "and I ain't goin' nowhere with y'all."

"Wait," Randall called, and the man turned his horse. "The boy is with us."

"The boy *was* with you," the man said. "Now he's with me. I'll make a fine man out of him."

"No offense intended, sir, but I can't let you take him."

The motion along the road stopped and all eyes turned to the two men as they faced one another. Charlie rested her hands on her pistols.

"Mr. Dawson"—the man was still smiling—"I think you've misunderstood the situation here. Not only am I allowing you to go on living, I'm also going to kill the man you've come all this way to see die. In my view, you are in a great debt to me. Therefore, it is quite rude of you to make demands. Additionally, I have two dozen men to your one woman."

Randall looked into the faces of the hardened men around him. He looked at Tad who shook his head and then at Charlie, her eyes calculating the angles.

"It's your choice, Mr. Dawson," the man said. "But either way I'm leaving with the boy."

The man sat his horse, staring down at Randall, his arms crossed. The sun reached higher into the sky, locked in its never-ending quest to stay atop the world if only for a moment. The tar-like smell of creosote drifted across the plain on the back of a soft breeze. The algarita and Apache plumes bowed their heads in deference. But for the breathing of horses and men, the land lay silent.

The birds gave the first sign of the coming encounter. They again fled the stability of the bushes and swirled up, squawking, into the open disquiet. Hooves pounded the road, drawing near at a quickening pace.

"Mr. Dawson"—the man's smile was gone—"you expecting friends?"

"I swear to you, I am not."

"Army?" the man called to Serrano.

"Rangers," he answered back.

"Rangers," the man said, slowly. "Alright, boys, this is it."

The men dismounted and stood in defensive positions near their horses.

"Mr. Dawson, if you truly had nothing to do with this, I suggest you and your woman slip away before the shooting starts," the man said. "But if this is your doing, know that I'll kill you both dead—and the boy too."

"I'm not leaving without him," Randall replied.

The approaching riders wore hats and badges and carried an assortment of long rifles and Colts. They formed a single line across the road and into either side of the brush.

"Lawrence Grimes," one of the Rangers called. "Your day's done come."

"I'm not sure about all that, Hargrove," the man answered.

"Sanford?" Randall shouted.

The Ranger rode forward with his pistol pointed at the sky.

"Randall?" he asked. "My God. I got your letter. These the boys killed Harry?"

Grimes looked to Randall, then to the Ranger, then back again.

"You're the first to die, Dawson," he growled. "You understand that?"

"It wasn't me," Randall answered, stammering. "He's my cousin, but I didn't know they were coming."

"The first to die," Grimes repeated.

"Alright now," the Ranger called out. "This doesn't have to go bad. We just want Grimes and Marcus Freeman—and the Bentley brothers, who killed my cousin's boy. The rest of you just throw down your guns and ride on from here."

The Rangers inched their horses forward. The Lobos stayed on the ground. Randall and Charlie crouched near the mesquite, looking back and forth between Tad and the closing horsemen.

Tad's eyes were wide and darting, he was covered in dirt and looked as if he hadn't eaten for days. Serrano had partially shielded the boy with his horse and was paying him no mind as the greater threat was in front of them. Tad studied the knife tucked into the back of Serrano's breeches. Randall saw it happen in slow motion—the boy yanked the knife out, and as the man turned, Tad plunged the blade into his chest.

"No!" Randall cried out, and the man fell to his knees, then slumped forward as if in prayer.

One of the Lobos fired at Tad and Randall didn't wait to see if the boy was hit. He fired back and killed the man and one of the Rangers shouted, "Hold," but it was too late. The sound of gunshots peppered the air around them. Randall tried to find Grimes but he had disappeared and all the men looked the same except for Charlie. She stood strong and dark and beautiful, a pistol in each hand, firing methodically and without hesitation at one target and then the next. The Rangers charged into the fray like the cavalries of old and the scene descended into an indiscernible amalgam of smoke and dust and bullets.

Bodies fell and piled upon the dirt with no favoritism to the righteous or the wicked or the disenfranchised. Randall fired and ducked and fired again. The lawyer turned rancher turned lost soul absorbed the madness of the moment, his skin burning with a frightened adrenaline that was mirrored by the blistering iron barrels from which he administered some untouched, aching rage.

Bullets flew past his head and shells fell at his feet and when his rounds were spent he reloaded, searing his hands on the hot steel. The providence of his life fell away before him and only when there was no one to fire back did he realize he was screaming.

35

A man can feel his death if not see it and in such a feeling is a grasping. Regret of some one elusive thing, or more, and all of it nameless save the memories, and even the memories taste bitter and unfulfilled, and the outer is stripped away and inside is only ego and fear and an encompassing desire for more. More time. More life. More choices.

Our choice had been made and with it we felt heavy the inexorable but unhurried beauty of impending loss. And into its imminence we awoke from a restless few hours of troubled sleep and took hold of one another in a way both foreign and natural.

We lay panting in the grass and I had heard on awful authority the sensitivity of a woman in these moments but in Sophia I found only an unadorned sense of desperation. She rolled atop me and grabbed my face in her hand and kissed me and more and it was as if these little deaths might somehow prepare us more intimately for the finality of life, though the more our passion grew the less was I ready to say goodbye to any of it.

Strange that the urgencies of fleeting creatures and the sincerity therein are all set about in a world infinite, a world timeless. And when those imperatives are acted upon, satisfactory or not, the world continues its revelations, man his revolutions, and God His indifference to each.

We held each other that night, too scared to speak, too frightened even to move, as if one shift, one single imbalance, would provoke an early sunrise and cut short what little time we had together.

The stars bore out from the darkness, glowing indentations to remind us of all we don't know. There are moments over the course of a life wherein that life is forever altered. I'd seen such moments. I'd felt my very lifeblood adjusting to some new flow. And there, under the quilted twilight of the desert, the feeling came once more. We needed one another, that girl and me. To what end, I couldn't say, but if I was ever to find redemption, it would be by her side.

* * *

The winter had stayed wet. It snowed and when the snow broke it broke hard and the rain and sleet fell violently, as if the land and those upon it had called down the wrath of an angry God and the two of us, Sophia and me, burrowed into a hillside and into one another and into our minds, where we hoped to find strength enough to see us through, though we knew not how or how long that would be.

And so it was that we found ourselves in that strange but familiar tale in which men often linger. The matter of our past having not been left there but rather following, in both the literal and metaphysical sense, and our future thus an uncertainty dependent upon both the present and the trailing past but also the changing circumstances of the future itself, which can never be assured but only guessed at with a vague confidence by those bold enough to do the guessing.

I was not bold alone. I could not say if Sophia took anything of worth from my being beside her, but I drew from her bravery the way a rancher draws water from a well and for that I counted myself fortunate even in these the most dire of situations.

The next morning it seemed as if the world had reset some mystic clock and the red sky turned to dark, crawling clouds and for yet another day we could see the rain fall in sheets ahead of us and there was nowhere to go but into it. We reached the Pecos and it spilling over its banks and there was no way across or around and whatever distance we'd put between us and those following was sure to evaporate before the flooded waters and we looked to one another in a solemn and knowing way and headed for high ground to make our stand.

On a knoll overlooking the river we maneuvered the horses under an unlikely bur oak and climbed down and watched as the rain beat down and the cold made us shiver. I asked Sophia if there was room to the north but she said the river bent north and west and would cut us off and the only way was south, which would take us closer to those in pursuit and should we not slip by them before they made the river we would be pinned against it and outnumbered. She assured me they would be carrying fresh horses and would ride us down if it came to that and even if we shot our way out there would likely be another party trailing behind.

"I always figured I'd die in the rain," I told her, and there was no response as she looked up into it as if maybe she could see beyond the clouds.

Lightning fractured the sky and kissed the horizon and the world from one end to the other was covered in dark and whatever dominion the sun once held had been ceded and this was the storm I had seen coming for what seemed like my entire life.

We waited and the horses with us and none in our party were too pleased and the longer we waited under the tree the more we figured it would end up being lightning that did us in.

I saw the first rider reach the river just after what should've been noon, though the gray sky made time seem void. I nudged Sophia's shoulder and we watched the man to the south as he dismounted and walked the mud flats of the flooded river and he bent to the ground on occasion as if search-ing for something and then he stood for a long while and stared at the rushing water and the shore beyond. Finally he swung himself back into the saddle and turned his horse south and west and disappeared into the storm.

I recognized the horse and enough of the tall stiff man atop it but didn't say anything. Instead I held on to some notion that I could be wrong—a notion Sophia quickly scattered to the wind.

"Indian Tom," she said, and I nodded.

"Reckon he found tracks?" I asked. "That river's still coming up. Could've washed them out."

"He found them," she answered, and my heart sunk over again.

An hour later four horsemen topped the last ridge before the river and stopped and sat their mounts for a while and I could pick out Tom but the others remained unknown at such a distance and I looked upon them as faceless angels of death.

"If there's only four, we got a chance," I said and as I spoke three more riders appeared on the ridge and joined the others and they all started down the hill toward the river, then turned north and put us directly in their path.

At the base of the knoll they all stopped again and I heard Marcus call out through the rain.

"Let Miss Sophia come on down to us and you can ride on. You got Lieutenant Grimes's word on that."

"Grimes down there?" I answered.

"Nossir, he ain't."

"Well, I guess I'll have to settle for killing y'all instead."

"All seven of us, huh?" a voice asked, and I grimaced at the sound and Sophia looked at me wide-eyed.

"He send you after me or did you volunteer?"

"Volunteered," Shelby answered.

"That's what I was afraid of."

I crawled out from under the tree and laid on my elbows and stared down the hill at the riders and my own brother among them. I thought of what awaited on the other side and tried to make it pleasant but it was not and there was no time to change any of it. The men separated the horses in either direction around the hill and Sophia kissed me so hard I tasted blood but I thought maybe it was just the taste of what was to come.

I gave Sophia the pistol and boosted her into the tree and our look lingered before I tore away and put myself on the sweet end of the rifle.

The first face I saw was the man Averitt, the only one not smart enough to dismount, and he looked more terrified than me as his horse trudged up the slope. I did not bother asking forgiveness.

The rifle cracked backward and so too did the man's head and then all things were set in motion at once. The horse bolted from under the dead man and crashed through underbrush atop the hill and a shot fired to my left. I levered another bullet as I spun and fired and the man fell. I heard Sophia shoot and saw another man dead near the tree.

When I turned back I saw Shelby and there was no time for either of us to think as a rifle fired from nearby and I felt the bullet punch my right shoulder and twist me down to the ground. Shelby froze as I fell and Marcus advanced on me and Sophia's pistol was still firing and I tried to scramble for my gun but Marcus was on me and I closed my eyes and pictured Sophia the way she'd looked in my arms that morning and the gun sounded and I felt nothing as Marcus's limp body fell into the grass next to me.

"Goddamn it," Shelby said, as I used my left arm to pull myself up and look at the smoking pistol in his hand. "Goddamn it all, Caleb."

He didn't look at me, but instead looked back down the hill and took off his hat and wiped the rain and wet hair from his face.

"Y'all get the hell out of here. Now," he said without turning toward me. I looked for Sophia and found her face in the tree and two men lay lifeless below her. Her eyes were searching and suddenly they widened and she screamed and I thought it was the sight of my wound but I heard my brother make a strained noise like a man trying to lift something too heavy to carry and I turned back to see him fall at Tom's feet.

Sophia screamed again and dry-fired her empty pistol and the big Indian smiled at the metallic clicks and wiped his blade across his chest. I pushed myself up onto my feet, my arm dangling beneath the blood-soaked shirt.

"Stay back," I told Sophia, but she did not and so the two of us stood together, unarmed in front of the giant man and he ran his tongue along the dull end of the blade and laughed and moved forward.

We both came to meet him and found he was faster than any man that size should be. In one motion he parried my flailing left, caught Sophia with a forearm that took her off her feet and then dodged my next punch while driving out with his knife and opening a thick gash above the right side of my chest.

The pain sent me to one knee and he flew toward me and I rolled away and behind him Sophia still lay motionless on the ground. Again Tom advanced and again I rolled away. I scrambled backward, moving in a fit of kicks and tumbles. He looked down at the knife in his hand and flipped it handle up and I tried to move again but couldn't avoid the spinning blade completely and it burrowed into the back of my thigh. I cried out and reached for the wound but couldn't grip the handle and my blood flowed into the pine needles and the grass and mixed with rain to feed the trees and the earth. I lay dying with my face in the wet ground and with much effort I pushed onto my back, my leg careful to not drive the knife in further and there I looked up at the sky and found the rain gone and in its place was only a dreary fog. I could hear Tom walking toward me but he stopped short and then yelled something which was drowned out by my rifle firing in Sophia's hands. Tom staggered backward and looked at the hole in his stomach and felt behind him for a tree that was not there. He dropped, almost graceful, into a sitting position and hunched forward over his wound. Sophia walked toward him, another hollow point in the chamber, and fired and his entire body jerked and his arms flew up as if in surrender but he was already dead and we left him there, his empty eyes staring up at blackness.

"Caleb," my brother said, and I drug myself across the earth and by his side.

"You look awful," he said, and I coughed up a laugh and it hurt something fierce.

I pulled open his shirt where it was stained red near his heart and I looked at the wound and knew he should already be gone. His face was pale and covered in sweat and his head was laid off to the side and he was staring at something in a world I couldn't see.

"Does this mean we're still brothers?" I asked him.

"I'm not sure we ever was," he said, and in his voice was a calmness I'd never known from him or me or the rest of the wide world we'd been born into.

"I'm not sure you're wrong. Shelby, they send anyone else?"

He shook his head.

"You sure?"

He shook it again.

"You gonna watch me die?" he asked.

"I suspect so, but I ain't happy about it."

"Figured you would."

"Watch you?"

"Be happy about it."

"Well, I ain't."

"Alright then," he said and my brother began to cry and who could say if his tears were falling because his life was ending or because it had never begun and I felt a sadness not just for my brother or me but for the nature of the world and the people in it, all those come before and the ones coming after. The sadness told me every man sets forth with questions in his heart and no matter his ways or his wanderings he dies without answers and the questions pass on to the next first heartbeat, and for thousands of years these unmet longings of man have covered the world in a morose mask and behind it any answers stay hidden and the secrets of the soul are no closer to my revealing them than they were to my father and his father before him and all the fathers back to a time unknown.

"Tom told me," he said, his eyes fading, "there's some tribes who dress up in bright colors for funerals."

"Alright," I told him. "You don't need to talk."

"So maybe they ain't all scared like you thought. Maybe dying ain't all that bad."

"Just hush now."

"I'm still scared, though."

He whimpered and breathed in hard and then out and then in hard and then out and then nothing and whatever he was looking at I hoped it was pretty.

Sophia knelt beside us, the notorious Bentley brothers, dead and dying. She looked over my wounds.

"I have to pull it out," she said, and I nodded and she grasped the knife handle and yanked and I hollered to hell and somewhere a thousand miles away in the Mexican mountains a lone wolf turned his yellow eyes to the daylight moon and howled.

36

The two men sat their horses and looked down into the valley and watched the road and pulled their coat collars up over the back of their necks. They crossed their gloved hands over the pommels of their saddles and waited, their eyes looking south for any sign. The sun was bright and the day cold and dry and they looked to one another and then back to the road and each nudged his horse and the animals stepped forward across the plain.

They dismounted and one of the men knelt and picked up a stick and stayed kneeling. He used the stick to move dirt and mud and he made note of each spent cartridge and poked at the dried blood and nodded his head.

"I ain't never seen such a mess in all my life. I truly have not."

"Well, what do you reckon?"

"What do I reckon? It's a goddamn flat-out mess, that's what. You had the rancher come in, according to him, with his nigger woman, and they was setting the road about here, facing south. Grimes and his outfit was moving up from down near the border. Seems it was at least twenty of 'em. The rancher says our boys come in from the east and that's when all hell broke loose."

"You think he's telling it true?"

"I can't see no advantage he'd have in lying."

"Where is he now?"

"He's with the woman up in Sutton County. She took some bullets."

"And Sanford's his brother?"

"Cousin, I believe."

"But he didn't know the rancher was down here?"

"Not so far as I can tell. Way I understand it, Sanford got word from some doctor who'd been riding with the Lobos for a spell. I believe that's what he and the rest of our boys were doing down here. 'Course we can't exactly ask him."

"Or any of our other boys."

"Or any of 'em."

"What about the outlaws? You reckon any got away?"

"Rancher says he ain't sure. I ain't seen no blood trails leading off."

"What about the doctor?"

"Damned if I know."

"Want we should ride around them foothills a little more."

"Yeah, we'd better."

The two men set off from the road. "Hell, I thought we weren't supposed to mess with the Lobos. On account of Guerrero?"

"You ain't heard? The old man's dead. We won't be seeing any more money coming in from him. That's the only reason the captain let Sanford come down here in the first place. No Guerrero, no protection for the Lobos."

"Well, I'll be damned."

"So will he, if there's any sort of God a'tall."

"And the rancher didn't catch any bullets?"

"Not so far as I could see. Luckiest sumbuck there ever was, I'd say."

"Why the hell was he here in the first place?"

"Looking for some men who killed his son back in the territories."

"His son?"

"Yessir."

"That's awful business."

"It ain't no good, that's for certain."

"These outlaws the ones that done it?"

"Couldn't say."

"What's the rancher say?"

"Says he don't know. Says it don't matter. He's headed home once the woman heals."

"Will she heal?"

"Can't say that neither."

"What about the boy the rancher had with him—one called Tadpole—that another son?"

"Well, he says it is."

"But you say it ain't?"

"I got word back to his people in Longpine. They say the rancher only had one son to begin with. The one that got killed."

"This one got killed too. Son or not."

"Yessir."

"And now the rancher's headed home."

"Yessir."

"Probably for the best."

"Would've been best if he never left in the first place."

"Think we still would've had this mess?"

"Maybe. A man can't think about things like that. A choice here, a choice there, maybe things would've been different—that ain't how it works."

"How does it work?"

"Some other way."

37

The sun finally shone and the river waned and gave back the lands it had swallowed and Sophia put us and the horses into it and I held onto her waist and my life as the water rose up around us. East of the Pecos we rode hard and switched horses and rode hard again. Our clothes were wet with river and blood and we shivered in the cold morning and recited the names of shrubs and trees in English and Spanish.

We rode away from Terrell County and into Crockett. We rode past *rancheros* and *llanuras desérticas* and *estanques poco profundos*. As the sun climbed higher and the earth warmed we passed cattle shaded up under alder and cottonwoods and willows and they lifted their heads to watch us and flicked their tails and then we were gone and perhaps they wondered if we were ever there and perhaps I wondered the same.

We switched horses again and it was all I could do to stay in the saddle and Sophia had to ride behind me and get her arms around me lest I lean too far in one direction. One of the horses broke loose and she let him go and he trotted into a winter pasture and turned to look at us and I thought maybe he'd wanted us to follow or to call out or to care.

We rode alongside barbed-wire ranches and passed by men and women mending fences and they stood when they saw us coming and made a cross over their hearts when we were gone. Somewhere in the great swath of Texas cattle country a rider came blistering up the trail behind us and Sophia turned the horse and pointed the pistol toward the man from under my armpit.

"No dispare! No dispare!" the man called. "Agua! No dispare!"

He pulled up in the middle of the dusted road and reined his horse so hard it came up on its back legs and holding on with one hand he used the other to toss a canteen at us and Sophia reached around to snatch it from the air and then the man set off back the way he came and at the same fevered pace.

I drank the water and the drinking hurt more than the thirst. I teetered on the edge of consciousness and sanity and from the ride itself I can recall only moments, as if they happened all in a single day, but surely they did not.

My mother told me that with pain comes learning and by the time we reached the many small tributaries of the Concho River I could take no more lessons in language or hurting and I begged Sophia to find a spot of sun near the water and let this be the end.

"Please," I begged, but she would not stop and when my eyes fought to close she grabbed my face and shook it and urged the horse onward.

We rode into the sunset and then through it and into the world of night and if the days ran together then so too did the darkness. And in the long night there were stars born and stars that died, and the rest of the sky was somewhere in between and the burning wood before us whistled and popped and sent red-orange sparks winking into air.

Sophia cleaned my wounds as best she could and allowed herself only a grimace and then we were back in the saddle and moving on and the horses around us were ridden by ghosts.

In the dead of night we rode into a small town in Sutton County. My head sagged about on her back and the world beyond seemed not but a vision into some place I had come from long ago. We rode down the main street and in the alleyways there were dark shapes and shadows of shapes and if they were real or not I couldn't say. Lanterns hung from rafting overtop the wooden planks of the drag and each flame blurred to a dancing orb in the night as we passed.

A man drunk and still drinking staggered out of a saloon and took stock of us, then turned and stuck his hand out to steady himself against the air and disappeared back through the doors.

There was a wooden sign hanging by two thin chains and it swung and creaked even in the calm night. In navy letters with a white backing was painted Arnold Cobb—Doctor. The building behind the sign was two stories and there was no light in the windows and the door was latched. Sophia all but drug me up the front steps and laid me against the wall and pounded the door with the side of her fist. The doctor was a long time answering and when he did he was heavy with sleep, but he ushered us in and helped her carry me through the parlor and into a room where he quickly lit a multitude of lanterns which gave birth to flickering shadows across every wall.

"Save him," Sophia demanded, and the doctor did not pause to answer her. He cut away the cloth around my wounds and then cut more and by the end I may have been near naked and he asked that Sophia light a fire in the stove and she did and the room warmed quickly and the doctor still in his nightwear pressed against my stomach and my chest and looked into my eyes and asked me questions I can't remember answering.

"Much blood has been lost," he said finally, and Sophia snapped that it did not take a doctor to know such a thing.

"The bullet passed through clean and the wound does not appear infected. He will not need to lose the arm. However, the cuts are much worse."

"Save him," she said again.

"I will try," he replied. "But I cannot guarantee his life. Or his leg."

* * *

My father put his finger to his lips to hush us, though we were already silent. The three of us were crouched and motionless in a thicket of palmetto, which grew in the river bottoms below the rim country. Two deer, a doe and her lanky offspring, moved quietly across the first fallen leaves of autumn.

"Let's shoot 'em," Shelby whispered.

"Wait," our father replied.

Shelby fidgeted impatiently, and my father scowled him into submission.

The deer stepped lightly and the doe was uneasy, twisting her neck and looking behind them more often than she picked at the acorns on the ground.

"Just wait."

Within minutes both the doe and her baby were at full alert and staring toward a creek bed in the distance. The bigger deer bolted and the small one followed and Shelby was on the verge of complaint when a buck stepped out from the opposite direction and stood, staring after his own kind.

My father slowly turned his head and nodded at Shelby and my brother raised the rifle to his shoulder.

"Hey, big fella!" my father yelled and the buck lifted his head and turned broadside and Shelby fired and there was blood and fur and the deer leapt into the air and landed on the run, crashing through the underbrush back toward the creek.

"Goddamnit," my father said, rising from his crouch and reaching for his flask.

"I hit him," Shelby said.

"You hit him, alright," my father shook his head and slapped his son in the back of the skull. "Looked like you gutshot the sumbitch."

Shelby's shoulders sagged. He rubbed his head and looked at the ground.

"Might as well go see," I said and pulled my brother away from our father who found a dead stump upon which to sit and drink.

There were tears in Shelby's eyes and I told him it was okay and he told me to shut up. We found the blood and it stank of rot and Shelby cussed and threw the gun down. I looked back out at our father who sat shaking his head and holding the flask to the sky as if in offering.

"We can track him," I told Shelby, but he just walked away and walked past our father who said something to him I could not hear and I waited there a while and finally followed them both home.

The next morning I woke before my brother and crept into the kitchen and began to pack a lunch of fruit and leftover sweet rolls. It was only after I was finished and on my way out that I noticed the coffeepot on the stove. I felt it with my hand and yanked it back quickly. The front door was open and the morning air seeped in through the screen. I stepped out onto the porch and my mother sat rocking in her chair and when she smiled at me it was as if she'd been waiting for my arrival.

I stood in the doorway.

"Momma."

"Mornin', baby," she said.

"Mornin'."

"You headed somewhere?"

"Down in the bottoms."

"By yourself?"

"Yes, ma'am."

"What you gonna do?"

"Track that old buck Shelby shot yesterday evening."

"Shelby know?"

I shook my head.

"Your daddy?"

"I ain't seen him since he went into town last night."

"That makes two of us."

"What are you doing up?"

My mother stared wistful at the tall pines and the junipers squatting beneath them and the rolling forest of the rim country in the early light and waved her hand about her in response.

"Just watching the morning."

"What's it doing?"

She laughed and motioned me over and I went and stood awkwardly at her side. Once she had been the strength upon which I'd built my trust for the world and now she was some small, sad thing and I hated to be around her. I hated to feel the frailty with which she held me, the limpness. I hated her for lying to me with her kindness and good nature when the world was neither. And most of all I hated her for not being as angry as I was. She was leaving, and no one cared as much as me. She should have cared. If not for herself, then for me. She should have cared about leaving me.

She wrapped her wire arm around my waist and softly leaned her head into my side.

"You'll have to take care of them," she told me. "But I suspect you already know that."

I stayed silent.

"You're too much like me, and your brother is too much like your father, and I don't know why but that's the way of it. And that means you're the one it'll all fall on."

"What if I can't do it?"

"Look after them?"

"Live without you," I said and fought back the embarrassing tears of a little boy unwilling to let go of his mother.

"You can live without me," she said. "You can live without anyone or anything if you have to. As long as there's mornings, you can live."

* * *

I found the blood trail and followed it for a mile. Down into the dry creek bed filled with pine cones and up the other side and along a ridge and into a gulch that bled out into the Piñon Canyon. I lost the blood and backtracked and found it again and turned east and kept going and moved through a tract of Spanish alamos with a doleful look to them. The trail thinned out and I walked a hundred yards in each direction and saw nothing. I set down with my back against a hard pine and looked at the sun and saw it was close to noon. I ate the sweet roll and not the fruit.

As I rose to leave I saw him. The buck was in front of me, lying in a twisted mesquite thicket. There were forty yards between us and as I moved toward him I kicked over the freshly fallen leaves and looked beneath and found the blood I'd missed earlier. I stood over him and he made no attempt to rise. There was dark blood covering his stomach and the ground and he had mesquite thorns strewn about his torn fur. The smell was rancid and unrelenting and I swallowed my throat so as to not add to the mess before me.

The meat was long ruined, I knew, but the deer was still alive. The sky around me began to darken and I felt a gun in my hand and could not remember it being there before and across the thicket stood my mother and my father and they smiled at me and my mother waved and I strained my eyes to see them through the growing gray of the world.

"You'll have to take care of them," she said, and as she did my father raised a pistol to his own head and fired and his legs went from under him like collapsing tent poles.

"You'll have to take care of them," she said again, still smiling, and I looked down at my feet and the deer was gone and it was my brother, covered in blood and looking up at me, his tongue falling out of his mouth like a dying animal. His eyes unable to focus. He made a bawling noise that grew louder over time and I dropped the gun and covered my ears and it was louder still and I could feel my throat tightening and I scratched at it as if to open it from the outside to let the air pass.

In a swelling panic I sucked in hard and my body shot up from the bed and Sophia rushed to me and put her arms around me and whispered to me in Spanish.

"Es solo un sueño, mi amor. Shhhh, es solo un sueño."

38

The same Ranger he'd first spoken with returned and this time there was another man with him. They asked after Charlie's health and he told them what the doctor said and they nodded and asked how he was holding up and he said, "Alright."

"We were able to find the Arabian and bring her back. Got her tied out front. Couldn't find no others."

Randall nodded.

"We went through the bodies—thought you should know. Neither of the Bentley brothers were there."

The stove kept the room warm. Randall stared at the fog on the window.

"You ought not try taking the law into your own hands, friend," the new man said.

Randall looked up at him and nodded again.

"Your cousin's dead."

"I know."

"So's all his men."

"I know that too."

"Well."

"You know about those outlaws, the Lobos?" Randall asked.

"Yessir, we been onto 'em for a while."

"A while?"

"Yessir."

"And Sanford was going down there for what? To arrest 'em?"

"Something like that."

"The one who called himself Grimes," Randall said, "is he behind all this?"

"Far as we can tell. Him and an old Mexican named Guerrero."

"Guerrero?"

"Yessir."

"Where's he?"

"Got found with his throat cut some weeks back."

"Murdered?"

"I don't imagine he cut it himself. Servant woman found him at the dining table, bled out."

"Who did it?"

"Couldn't say. Maybe an enemy, maybe Grimes himself. Either way, the Lobos are finished."

"I doubt it."

"What's that?"

"I doubt they're finished."

"Why's that?"

"My grandfather came out west and my father after him. They fought outlaws and Indians and their own government to try and civilize this part of the world. And for what? It's not the world that needs taming, gentlemen, it's us. It's men who bring savagery to the land. Oh, yes, nature has its violence, but that violence is purposeful and necessary. So what purpose is the violence of men? The Lobos are finished—maybe—but others will take their place. The gap of violence will always be filled."

"Well, I'm sure you're right about that. It's a sad thing, but I'm sure you're right."

"And what choice do we have? What part must we play as men when the wolves are at the doorstep and it is kill or be killed?"

"You do what you gotta do, I imagine," the Ranger said.

"Yes, yes, I suppose you do."

"We put the boy on a train to Tucson. Got a man at the station who can carry him up the rest of the way."

"His body."

"What's that?"

"You put his body on a train," Randall said.

"Sure. Well, listen, a lot of good fellas died out there. And we're sorry for your losses and wish the best for your . . . for your woman here. Seeing as how there ain't much else, you probably won't be hearing from us."

Randall nodded.

The men placed their hats back on their heads, synchronized, and left the room and Randall did not watch them go. He looked at Charlotte and it was like she was sleeping peacefully and he imagined that she was but it did no good.

* * *

There was always a candle and it was always burning and they must have changed it, the nurse or the doctor, but he couldn't remember ever seeing it replaced and so it became some supernatural fixture which was ever present and he likened it to the feeling of death in the room, which was also ever present and unchanging.

Charlotte had not been conscious for days and the doctor said it might be that she never would wake and said so in a way that suggested he needed the bed free, and Randall said he would pay good money and that if he suspected the doctor was slacking in his care, he would put a bullet in his head and then go call on his family and do the same.

By the light of the candle Randall read aloud from *The Picture of Dorian Gray* and he drank coffee by the pint and stayed awake longer than a man should and still there was no change. He sent the nurse away and brushed Charlotte's hair himself and bathed her and rubbed her feet and when he could put it off no more he wrote a letter to Tad's father and told of the boy's fate and in the writing he said Tad was brave beyond his years and killed many outlaws before he fell. He wept when the letter was finished and wept other times for no reason and at first he prayed and then thought of praying and then ultimately lost the will to speak with God.

He decided that no matter Charlotte's fate he was done with this quest and would return to Arizona as soon as she healed. He'd said as much to the Rangers who came asking after him and they seemed to agree this was a fine idea.

There were many nights in the dark hospital when Randall woke and saw a man's face in the candlelight and then it was gone and his heart raced and the candle burned.

One day, nearly three weeks after his arrival, he heard a mass of footsteps as they thundered down the hall.

"He's done killed ol' Hollis," someone shouted and the footsteps passed back the way they'd come. Soon after there were gunshots and men hollering and then everything fell silent again. Randall latched the door and stood with his guns drawn and sweat on his forehead.

The next morning he asked the doctor what had transpired, but before the doctor could answer Charlotte stirred from her infinite sleep and her eyes opened and she turned to Randall.

"The boy," she said, and Randall shook his head and she closed her eyes long and opened them again.

"You get them brothers?" she asked, and again Randall shook his head and she grimaced and he fell to his knees at her side.

"Please, don't worry about that or anything else."

"I died," she said, and he told her no and that she was just in a coma, and she insisted and said she knew she'd died because her brother and father had been there in the place she'd gone to, and Randall relented.

"Well, good," he told her. "Glad you got that part out of the way. You'll have to tell me about it sometime."

"I'll tell you now," she said.

"You need to rest now."

"There were colors you can't say. Colors that give you feeling and emotion and they were everywhere."

"Dream colors," he told her but she waved off his words with her hand and the gesture was frail enough that he didn't argue and she continued to speak.

"Not a dream. Not anything. Just colors and I went into them."

"Into the colors."

She nodded.

"I went into them and I *was* them and my family was all there, back in East Texas and the humidity hung so thick in the air you could drown from breathing. The loblolly pines and the great big shade oaks and honeysuckle growing up over everything and giving the whole world a sweet smell like the ones from when you're a child, and I could see it and smell it and it all stretched out before me and was never ending. It was like I was there for the first time and yet I recognized everything and it put me at ease, like waking up from a troubled sleep and realizing it was only a dream.

"I saw my sister and my brother and myself by Caney Creek and we were hiding, the three of us, from Daddy, but not in a frightened way, it's just that we didn't want the day to be done. There was always a somber finality to coming home in the evenings and knowing it would be another night and another day of chores before those magical hours when we were free to be only children. And in a child's mind there is no tomorrow and no yesterday and no waiting to live, there's only living. We lose that. Somewhere along the way such a notion as to live gets overshadowed by other things and in these things we bury ourselves and bury our will to live and who can say if this is right or wrong. And when I died I found myself giggling beneath the edge of the creek bed, crouched and secret in a moment shared and wanting to live forever and I blew with the wind and the colors of the dusk into my own hair and then I opened my eyes."

* * *

The next day a letter came for Randall and the man at the door who was not the doctor smiled and was cheery and such a manner was off-putting to Randall and did not seem to belong in this new world he had created within the four walls of Charlotte's room. But he took the letter in kind and thanked the man and shut the door when he left.

The letter was from Joanna and bore bad news as letters usually do.

His mother had taken the flu and it had weakened her and soon the pneumonia was on her and it was only a few days after that she died.

Joanna had called for a doctor from Albuquerque and when he came it was found that he had studied medicine under Joanna's father and though he was unable to save Randall's mother, he was heading back to Philadelphia soon and Joanna would be going with him and they intended to marry. She wrote these things and more and told him Roscoe was still in charge at the ranch and he seemed to be doing a good job, though she admitted her ability to measure was questionable at best. She told him the winter was hard and getting harder and she had heard of the great shootout and was happy he was not injured or killed. She told him Tadpole's father had not been seen on the ranch in two weeks and most believe he had gone to California. She told him the doctor's name was Jeffrey.

He read her words and gave no reaction. He called for a pen and ink and wrote a simple response.

> *Dear Joanna,*
>
> *Tad's body is being brought to the ranch. Have Roscoe see that he has a proper burial next to Harry's grave. There is a widow near Fort Davis named Cole. She has a young boy in need of proper care. I have written to her so that you may have the boy sent to your new home in Philadelphia. I know you will do right by him. You were always an excellent mother.*
>
> *Best wishes,*
> *Randall*

In the early morning hours he sat in a small chair by the small window and watched the empty street. Men would come before the dawn and shovel the street free of manure and do their best to fill in ruts after storms and he watched these men closely as they worked and he named them in his mind or at least assigned to them their own discernible acknowledgment and from this he began to know them in the way a sleeping man knows the travelers of his dreams. But Randall was not asleep.

He seldom slept and when he did it was fitful and he saw always the mountains behind him to the east and the rim country of his youth and the red rock and canyon lands to the north and the desert to the south and Arizona was not some welcomed image come to comfort but rather a vision upon a vision of death and things to come. And always he was flying and always the pine trees stood burned and bare and in that manner appeared as whole forests full of sickly creatures, stoic giants from some time unheard now stripped and starved and huddled together to face a fate they did not expect. And in his dreams he flew down past the naked limbs of the trees, dead where they stood, zombies unmoving, and he flew lower still to where the golden manzanita, once called ghosts of the flame, had begun to grow and flower after the unseen fire. And he flew downward into the ash and soil and darkness and there he became a seed and waited for the rain and thirsted for it and longed for it as his skin dried and cracked and bled under the earth. He smelled it. The storm coming down from the northwest and darkening the skies over the tablelands and off-loading the weight of water into the gusts of wind, which scattered it about the goldenrod and mesquite, and he fought the roots of his enemies and his friends for the nourishing rain as it seeped in all around him. He drank it deeply and without pause, as if in some feverish state of unrest, and he felt it course through him and make him strong and he emerged suddenly and violently from the ground and opened his eyes.

* * *

Charlotte was awake long enough to drink and he tried to have her eat but the pain was too great and so he watched her wither and shrink before him and become something she was not yet had always been. He loved her deeply, this he knew. And soon she could not speak other than to ask for water or the bedpan and he would take her hand in his and hold it as gently as the clouds in the night sky and he would tell her stories of his childhood and stories of his successes and failures and admitted there were more of the latter.

He told her of the innocence of young love, and the naivety. He told her of the joys of being a father, and the terror. But mostly he told her how much he loved her. She was a long time dying and Randall refused to leave or turn away and he placed every loss of his life into the bed with her and watched as the guilt and pain of all that had befallen him was slowly hardened around him and if Charlotte had become unrecognizable so too had he. His thoughts. His soul.

On the morning she took her last breath, he sat by the window.

"Shall I tell you of the world outside?"

"No," her voice was a whisper. "Quit talking and let me die."

"It's a gray day. The grass is turned to winter pasture. The roads are mud and the ladies are holding their skirts as they walk."

"God, it's happening—you're really gonna talk me to death."

"I don't know the day of the week, but I think it must be Sunday, the way the people are dressed. There's some birds gathering on the top of the mercantile. Goldfinches, headed south for winter, I'd imagine. I can't hear him, but there's a man picking a banjo near the post office. He's sitting on an apple box. I couldn't say for sure, but it looks like it's a sad song, the way he's singing it. There's a coach out front of the hotel. Probably that theater troupe folks have been talking about. Maybe we'll go see them perform, once you're feeling better."

"Don't be angry," she said, and he did not turn to watch her go.

39

Doctor Cobb called it an unlikely outcome. Sophia called it a miracle. I couldn't say who was right or why, but I didn't lose my leg and barring some unforeseen infection or heavy fever, I would live.

I had been so ready to die that this news seemed almost too late. I didn't even smile.

"Oh yes, by all means," said the doctor, throwing his hands up. "I bring cowboys back from the dead every day. No need to thank me, and certainly don't be too happy about all this."

"I apologize, doc. I guess I didn't plan this far ahead."

He rolled his eyes and left the room and as soon as the door was shut Sophia climbed into the bed and kissed me and the jostling of the mattress made me wince and she stopped and said sorry but then started up again.

I lifted my good arm and put my hand on her shoulder to steady us both.

"Anybody come asking after us?"

She shook her head.

"Any posters?"

"No. I looked at many of the buildings and saw nothing."

"What about the law? Doctor probably had to tell somebody something."

"He says he did not. But if the sheriff comes I will tell him you are a Mexican bandit and I am here to arrest you and take you back to Mexico to hang." She grinned.

"I'm serious," I told her. "We can't stay here. We gotta keep moving."

"The doctor Cobb says it will be a week until you can move. Probably longer until you can use your leg again."

"They'll be here in a week. They won't stop hunting us. Ain't that what you're always telling me?"

Her smile faded.

"Give me two days," I said. "Then we gotta get."

She nodded.

"Three days," she insisted.

The first two days passed with little excitement. The pain in my leg seemed worse than it had before, though my chest and shoulder were healing nicely. I tried to stand and fell and caught myself on the bed and cussed and told Sophia I didn't need to be able to walk, just to sit a saddle.

We heard other patients coming in and out for various illnesses and medicines and the doctor seemed preoccupied with a woman down the hall. Sophia didn't know much but said the man Finch who helped the doctor had let slip that a very rich man had paid a large sum of money for the doctor to look after her. He didn't say whether she was young or old or sick or dying.

On the morning of the third day I was able to put enough pressure on the leg to stand, but walking was still a mighty challenge and even so I told Sophia to saddle the horses.

The doctor had thrown up his hands a second time when we told him of our lack of money but we offered a horse as payment and he accepted and when he left the room Sophia cursed him in Spanish and said that in her country doctors would help you no matter if you could pay or not and I reminded her this was not her country.

Sophia had gone to the stables where our horses were being kept. She would saddle two, trade one for food and supplies, and give the last one to the doctor. My only task while she did all of this was to put on my shirt and hat, as she had already helped me pull on my pants and boots. I was midway through the grueling process when the door opened and a man dressed like a caricature of a cowboy entered the room.

He wore brown canvas pants with black boots and silver spurs. His shirt was a striped hickory and his vest hung open over his ribs. His hat was black felt with a tall crown and a strip of brown leather hung around the crown and was studded with copper coins. A gun belt hung loose at his waist.

"You Caleb Bentley?"

"Who?" I asked, grimacing as I tried to swing my leg over the side of the bed.

"Just stay put now," the man warned, and he touched the heel of his pistol. "I'm Hollis Hayes, and I'm taking you in."

"Listen, bud, I'm not Caleb whoever you said. And I'm about to call the sheriff."

The man stood. The sunlight shone through the window and the thin white curtains and cut across his lower half. His upper body was shrouded in shadow.

"My wife's about to be back and whatever game you're playing at, it's gonna sure enough scare the devil right out of her."

The man slowly pulled a folded paper from his pocket and studied it. He smiled.

"Just so you know, Bentley, it was the doctor who gave you up. Funny thing, don't you think? A man would save a life just to turn around and give it up."

"Sir, I honestly don't know—"

"Save it, son. You can either let me put these chains on you, or I can kill you where you sit."

"Would you at least let a prisoner get his shirt buttoned?"

"Well, seeing as you ain't got nowhere, or no way, to run. You go on and take your time."

The man pulled a pouch of tobacco from his vest and buried some in the deep pocket he'd dug over time between his teeth and the inside of his cheek.

"You're gonna have to help me stand and walk," I told him and as he moved toward me I readied myself for the coming fight. But there was no fight to be had.

The man tilted his head down to spit juice onto the floor and instead he grunted and the dark liquid spilled from his lips and ran down his chin. He held both hands to his heart, where the knife in his back had come out, and looked at it and looked at me and never has a face seemed more puzzled.

"Let's go," Sophia said and she lifted me and I moaned but we moved as one out of the room and down the hallway and my breaths were short and painful and she told me everything was going to be alright.

Outside I used my good leg to spring up toward the horse and Sophia helped push me the rest of the way into the saddle. Three other men entered the doctor's office as Sophia mounted her horse. I leaned over and gritted my teeth and snatched the reins of the third horse.

"That is the doctor Cobb's horse," she said.

"Not anymore, darling."

"There's that sumbitch, yonder," someone shouted from the porch.

We rode wide open down the thoroughfare as shots rang out behind us.

40

Randall paid for the body to be sent by train to Chicago, to her sister. When it was done he walked into a bar without reading the name and sat on a stool and ordered whiskey. The barkeep nodded and poured and Randall drank and ordered again. He drank and stared past the barkeep at the mirror along the back wall. He stared at himself or what, if any, was left.

"What do you see?" asked a Hispanic man who appeared to be Randall's age.

"I don't know."

"You don't know what you see? Or you don't know how to describe it?"

"I don't know. Both, I guess."

"In all things men look and see only themselves," the man said. "It is their ego that blocks the view, but men do not know or care; and so they believe then that the world is of their own making, when of course this is not true. It is only the fool who believes the world can be made or unmade by his hand. The world is of itself and nothing else, and it will be as it is and as it always was. There is no changing for the world, only for the man. And when the man is changed in his heart so too is he changed in his eyes and, perhaps, the world appears different than before. I think, sometimes, this is a good thing. But other times a man sees only the shadows of the world, and this is a hard man to reason with because for him there is nothing worth seeking that has not already been sought and captured and corrupted. It has always been this way. So if you are looking into this mirror and do not know what it is you see, then perhaps you are a changed man."

Randall's laugh was short and unamused.

"I just see dark hair ready to turn gray, like my father's."

The man shook his head.

"When men look to their ancestors for a comparison, they have already erred," he said. "There can be no comparison as we are one and the same with the ghosts of the earth."

"I'm not the same as my father."

"Of course you are. You are the same as your father and my father and all of the fathers back to the first," the man told him. "They acted as they must act, and we act the same. Even if the actions are different."

"If the actions are different, we're not the same."

"Here we must disagree. Here I must tell you the world your father grew up in was different from the one we are in. Do you agree?"

"Times have changed, sure."

"Right. So, if our fathers were in this different world, or different time, as you call it, what then is there to compare?"

"How they handled certain things," Randall said and motioned to the bartender.

"Things of a different time?" the man asked.

"I guess. But not everything changes."

"Why?"

"Why what?" Randall asked and emptied his glass and called again for more.

"Why does not everything change?"

"You still have to eat. You still have to drink."

"You still have to die?" the man asked.

"Yes, death," Randall answered, thinking of Charlotte as he assumed he always would with no ending. "Death doesn't change."

"Ah, but it does," the stranger countered.

"All men die."

"This is true. But in the ancient world did they not die differently? Did they not go to their graves believing in gods who rode the sun into the sky, gods who set storms upon the sea? Did those who first lived in these lands not go to their graves believing white men to be gods reborn of iron?"

"Sure, but they still died."

"So they did," the man nodded. "And they lived, and we live and we will die, and all in a different time and place that is changed but the same, and so to compare is a practice in lying."

"You say a lot of words, señor, to say nothing at all."

The man smiled. "If your father eats an apple when he is but a boy, and then you eat an apple from the same tree at the same age, are you the same as your father?" he asked Randall.

"Well," Randall sighed, "in that particularly narrow situation, I guess I am."

"But you do not know why he ate the apple."

"I imagine because he was hungry."

"You imagine," the man said. "And to imagine is to lie."

"Well, if that's the way you see it."

"There is only one way to see it. To see it another way is to imagine, and here we find ourselves at the same ending."

"So if you can never say for sure why somebody did something, then every action outside of yourself would be a lie," Randall said.

Again the man nodded. "This is what I believe, yes."

"That's a hell of a way to see things."

"That is not how I see things. But it is the way they are."

"Even dying?" Randall asked.

"Yes."

"So no man ever died?"

The man shook his head. "As you said, all men die."

"You're not making any sense," Randall told him. "And I'm only getting drunker from here."

The man shrugged and held up his fingers and the bartender came and poured two more glasses and Randall caught his wrist and asked that he leave the bottle and he did.

Randall drank and looked at the man.

"If I was to tell you every person I loved, young and old, was dead, what would you say?"

The man thought for a moment and answered, "I would say a prayer for them and also for you."

"But would you believe they're dead?" Randall asked.

"I would believe they are dead, yes," the man said. "But I would still believe death is a lie. Lies exist all around us, my friend. Just because they are not true, does not mean they do not exist. Do you understand?"

Randall placed a dollar bill on the bar and turned the bottle upward. "I'm starting to," he said.

"Salud," the man replied, raising his glass.

* * *

Ten days later Randall sat alone at a dark wood table in a café in Alamogordo. The steam rose from his coffee and touched the cold window and left there a soft fog and he watched it fade. Outside the glass his horse was tied and blanketed and the flurries of snow were beginning to fall from the gray sky. Beyond the town, some twenty miles to the south, the Organ Mountains sat swollen on the horizon in shades of blue and black. The snow fell thicker.

He was headed home, but what that meant he could not say. No more letters had come from the ranch. He'd passed again through the valley where the old woman had sheltered them from the blizzard, and there he found the homestead emptied and abandoned. Perhaps Joanna had been able to arrange transport for the boy. Perhaps she had not.

Randall read in the newspaper of the growing violence in Mexico. He read of the rich Republicans meeting in secret in Hoboken, New Jersey, likely deciding how to become richer. More money, more land, more power. The manifest destiny of country imagined by greed and founded in blood. Forever the blood will flow, he thought. Forever.

He had once clung to the notion that it would be men like him, educated men, who would change this country. Like the philosophers of old, he would teach thought and reason and compassion. Now he was barren of such hopes. Not because he couldn't teach these things, but because no one would listen. None would learn because none cared to.

His family had stolen this land, as had all the other families since the first men came to these shores. They had exalted things like independence and freedom but had intended it only for themselves—the freedom to take what they wanted, the independence to never answer for their crimes. Oh, but we will answer, we will answer in time, all of us. Ill-gotten spoils, he thought, sipping his coffee. We will answer with every child born to violence and every man prone to hate. We will answer with this American disease of independence. Men should not be free. All types of men—the greedy, the lazy, the privileged few—prey on the minority. The minority being those men who are both honorable and empathetic and willing to sacrifice for the greater good.

By his second cup, there was no God, no one to look after the sick and dying children—no more than there is anyone to look after a flock of birds or herd of lost sheep. If a man wants justice he need not turn to God or the law. He need not appeal to the courts or the hearts of men, rather in his own hands he holds the measure of vengeance. In his own being does he find the executioner of truth.

Randall thought all these things and more. He paid for his coffee with what little coin he had left and rode out into the snow.

"Merry Christmas!" the girl called after him, and he did not turn back.

* * *

Men returned are more often men changed, and so it went with Randall. He woke in a darkness outside the Gila Forest, having the day prior traversed the cavernous passes of the White Mountain Reservation. He rolled onto his side and lay covered in his serape atop the frozen ground. Without rising, he used a bowed branch to revive the fire. It smoldered and hissed and grew with no urgency and Randall watched it and flexed his toes. He could feel the cold around him. He poked again at the fire and drew himself up and sat cross-legged and hunched and blew on the coals through cupped hands.

On the other side of the fire, Mara snorted and her hot breath exploded into the icy atmosphere and hung there in a tuft of smoke before disappearing into some woebegone ether. She cocked her head and whinnied and looked off into the dark morning.

Randall heard the man from a great distance. He crashed through the underbrush and stumbled up the ridge toward the growing fire. Randall slowly moved his right arm behind him and felt for his gun belt.

"Friend coming in," the man called as he approached. "Starving, freezing friend coming in. Don't shoot."

Randall didn't answer.

The man brushed past Mara without taking his eyes off the fire and he didn't slow until he was almost on top of the flame.

"Howdy," he managed as he turned and shifted and tried to warm himself over the small fire. "You wouldn't happen to have any food would you, friend?"

Randall let go of his pistol and tossed the stranger a sack of jerky.

The man ate savagely, stuffing handfuls of meat into his mouth. Each bite was bigger than the last and he chewed with his mouth open and Randall watched the shadows dance across his face as food fell into his tobacco-stained beard.

At last the man sat across the fire from Randall, his knees inches from the fire. Randall continued to study his face.

"Where's your wife?" Randall asked the man.

"Say again?"

"Your wife, Geanie, where is she?"

"Who the hell are you?" the man said. "How do you know about Geanie?"

"I don't know about Geanie. That's why I'm asking. Where is she? Where are the girls?"

"I don't know what you're talking about."

"Yes, you do."

"I don't have to tell you a goddamn thing."

The man looked to either side of him and then turned to look behind. He stared at Mara and tilted his head.

"I know that horse," he said, turning back to Randall and the fire. "You're the old boy riding with the nigger."

Randall didn't answer.

"Well, where's your woman?" the man asked, laughing. "Where's them boys?"

He took another piece of jerky and bit off a hunk. "The way I see it," he said, still chewing, "I just did what I had to do."

"What'd you do?"

The man grinned. "Fella in Las Cruces made me an offer for the girls, so I took it. I don't even know if they were mine in the first place. 'Course Geanie didn't take too well to that, and one night I woke up with a knife to my throat, so, like I say, I did what I had to do."

Randall nodded. "You're the lowest kind of animal to ever breathe," he told the man. "You know that, don't you?"

The man stopped chewing. "To hell with you, fancy boy. How about I kill you where you sit and take that fancy horse of yours?"

"You gambled that money away, didn't you?" Randall asked, sliding his right hand behind his back. "The money you got for selling your own daughters."

"That ain't none of your goddamn concern," the man said, rising from the ground.

"Maybe," Randall answered. "Or maybe I'm making it my concern. Maybe I'm making this whole morally hollow world my concern."

The man opened his mouth but the words never came. Instead, Randall whipped his arm forward and fired and the bullet burrowed into the man's chest and there it stayed as Randall kicked dirt over the coals and mounted up.

The light began to break through the trees and he sat atop the big Arabian and stared out at the rim country to the west and then down at the body before him. He pulled tight his gun belt, lowered his hat, and turned back east, riding into the rising sun.

If the world was full of monsters, he would destroy them. He would have vengeance and blood and more. He would become all the things he'd always hated and thus grow to hate himself, and in that hate he would find the only the solace left to him. He would let it fester and rot until every trace of his humanity became consumed by blackness. If the world was full of monsters, he would become one.

41

The horses weaved through the thorn-covered ceanothus and blunt-tipped lobes of the apache plume and the high desert reached out ahead of us, laying certain a path into the morning and we followed it at a trot. The sun grew curious, as it does, about the happenings to the west and moved toward the empty plain to look closer upon it and by the time it was overhead we had reached the hills outside of Austin.

We moved east until we met the sloping Colorado River and continued east alongside it. We stopped on the outskirts of town, where oak trees grew unfettered and shaded the country and those who traveled it. We pulled the last potato from the sack and cut it into chunky strips and fried it in the cast-iron pan over a small fire. There was no salt, but we ate just fine and watered the horses and ourselves in the calm river.

Ahead was the vast Brazos Valley and the rivers coming up from the gulf like a reaching hand, cutting tributaries into the land and nourishing the farm fields and timber tracts alike. Here was the beginning of a landscape unseen by me or many of those born in the rugged, rocky dirt hills of the West. As my wounds healed so too did my soul, and with Sophia at my side I gave no thought nor concern to such things as heaven or hell or gathering storms. I wanted to be where she was, and she was here, and this was now, and all else was of little regard.

We came to the Brazos three days later and in the distance the light from the sun played tricks upon the water's surface and we rode toward it in a way both desperate and relieved, and we rode the horses down into the river and sat and patted their necks as they dipped their heads to drink. The water came up to our knees and I leaned to my good side and scooped water into my hand and drank and repeated the process many times over while Sophia did the same. Small pines grew along the eastern bank and gave good cover and a vantage of the way we'd come. We put the horses across and out and into the trees and left them saddled, and Sophia made a fire over which to cook supper. I walked back to the river we'd crossed and looked out at the country we'd left behind.

I filled our canteens in the shallow water and stretched my shoulder and fought the urge to itch at the wounds. I knelt and removed my hat and cupped my hands and splashed the river onto my face. I stayed hunched over in the small rocks for a time uncertain and there in the soft, understanding flow of the water I watched my reflection shimmer and stretch and reform again. I saw the world and everything in it turned upside down and wondered at a life in such a place and wondered if when we die we simply grow gills.

Sophia had piled pine needles against a charred log burned in some long-ago fire and she bade me sit and rest, and I did. She brought me pan-fried strips of backstrap and when I had eaten them all she brought me more. The meat was tender and filling and soon I was asleep against the log without having untied my bedroll.

I dreamt that night of my brother and in the dream we were walking, the two of us, down a dirt road, and the road was laid out across prairie land and rolling hills and it would disappear over a rise and then pick back up closer yet to the horizon. Shelby said it looked like a great rope laid across the land by God, and I told him it was built by men. We walked the road and came in time to a single horse grazing in a field of oats and ryegrass and we stopped to watch her.

She was an American saddlebred, all brown with a slightly darker mane and then lighter near the feet. She stirred a bit and walked slowly toward us with her head down and only then did I see Shelby was carrying his saddle and I couldn't remember him having it before. He worked the straps under the horse's belly and then found the stirrup and swung himself up. I knew I couldn't go with him but I wasn't sure why and he looked down and tipped his hat and said mine would be along shortly and then he rode away. I called to him and said I didn't have a saddle, but he wouldn't turn back.

I awoke and Sophia had curled herself beside me and slept with her head on the left side of my chest and she'd doused the fire and covered us both with blankets. I couldn't tell the hour but it was dark still and I could see in the moonlight the outline of the horses where they were tied. I heard no sounds save the crickets and cicadas and an owl who'd taken to a tree near the water and there stood guard over the river world. I kissed Sophia's head and closed my eyes and thought of the Dawson boy and him leveling the pistol and when I bore down on him it was Shelby's face at that age and he was frightened and our mother was sick and death comes for young and old alike.

* * *

The following morning we were intimate for the first time since I'd been wounded. After, we lay on the blanket in the wet grass and watched as the sun woke the rest of the world from its slumber. Shadows became country and Sophia's dark hair fell across my chest with her head on my shoulder and I took it in my hand and felt of it, and she asked what I was thinking.

"I'm thinking about this," I told her and motioned out to the thick grass just outside our pine grove and the banks of the Brazos beyond to the blue water and great hills dotted with green and then finally the horizon as it held up the clouds bleeding into the purple sky.

"And what do you think about this?" she asked.

"Nothing's ever been more perfect."

"He will not stop looking for us."

"He might," I said.

"He will not."

"Well, then I'll kill him when he gets here."

She scoffed, "You cannot kill a demon. They do not die."

"He ain't no demon. He's just a man gone wrong."

"And you?"

"What about me?"

"What kind of man are you?" she asked.

"I'm the kind who won't ever leave you. Who won't ever pick up another gun unless I have to. I say we go out to the logging camps, change our names, settle down like a real family might, and never give another thought to all these things left wild."

42

THREE YEARS LATER

East Texas was as green a place as Randall had ever seen. The hills were masked by pine and sweet gum and oak, the lowlands full of dwarf palmetto and club moss, and the two of them, Randall and Mara, never went more than half a day without coming upon a river or creek or some tributary thereof.

Randall rode through Mount Selman, Jacksonville, and Rusk, following the Neches River and the logging camps that had sprung up alongside it. His face was dry and it itched in the spots where his beard had been thickest. He scratched his chin and looked at his own hand before him. It was rough, pitted, and calloused over. The dirt under his nails seemed as natural an occurrence as sunrise, and the aches in his back and legs from riding would leave him unwhole were they to disappear.

Two years he'd spent in the saddle, trekking east from the rim country into New Mexico along Apache Creek. He'd seen Santa Fe and Taos and ventured north into Colorado, then east again through Oklahoma and Arkansas. His reputation as a bounty hunter grew, in part due to his never staying still, but also because of his famed standoff with Harvey Dwyer.

Dwyer and his outfit, a few Appalachian boys who called themselves the "Hang Gang," had romped through Tennessee and Arkansas lynching black men, and even a few black women. They holed up in the Ozarks with federal men closing in. A lot of the locals took up the cause and saw fit to protect Harvey's Hang Gang by spreading misinformation, disabling motor cars, and in general causing chaos in the hills.

Randall saw it all in the Tulsa paper. He had been reading about Agua Prieta, how it was captured and recaptured, and how *el revolución* was still in full swing. He'd thought about going back to the desert to fight, but there was no solace in killing soldiers—soldiers were only doing what they were told. He wanted the men who were deciding their wrongs—men like Dwyer.

So he rode east from Tulsa and into the Ozark Mountains and while the federal boys scrambled to control the locals and obtain warrants in each county, Randall pushed past them and caught Dwyer and his men just outside a place called Eureka Springs.

There were six of them by a creek and Randall could see only one awake. He shot that man first. The rest were no trouble, Randall mounted and firing from each hand. It was over in seconds.

He'd been in tighter spots riding alongside dozens of lawmen in Oklahoma, chasing down Elmer McCurdy after his failed train robbery in 1911. Still, the story of "Dead" Randall Dawson spread. People bought him drinks, patted his back, shook his hand. They're all weak, he thought, like I was.

In three years he'd seen mighty country and killed unmighty men. Sometimes, from the corner of his eye, he'd think he saw them, faces from the past—the boy, the Bentleys, his beautiful Charlotte. But in truth his past was falling away quickly and now, looking at his own hand, he recognized nothing of the man who'd come west all those years ago.

Randall sat Mara near the base of a mulberry tree in full bloom and the limbs above him hung low, weighted down with the fresh fruit of spring. He reached up and picked a handful of berries and ate them and Mara took a step and he reached up again. When he'd eaten his fill his mouth was stained and so too his hands, and when he looked down at them he saw only blood.

* * *

He awoke under the tree, Mara tied loosely to its trunk. Cows huddled nearby, paying no more mind than the occasional glance. They fed on the scutch grass and tall fescue and Randall sat awhile and watched them. He looked at his map and added the days between himself and the gulf, and when he reached it, he thought, what then?

He pulled from his satchel some parchment and a pen and wrote quickly, before he could change his mind.

> Dear Joanna,
>
> I am glad to hear the child is doing well. It was good of you to take him. I have sold the ranch and all it comprises. My man, Mr. Landrum, will oversee the details. He will be in contact shortly. I have put all the money in your name. I am sorry I could not do more.
>
> Randall

He folded the paper and tucked it away and the cattle began to stir behind him. He put a hand on his gun heel and turned to see two farm boys atop sad-looking mounts, come to collect the cows.

They stopped when they saw him.

"Mister, this here's private property," the older of the two boys said.

Randall took him to be in his teenage years. He slowly held his hands up.

"I don't mean any trouble, boys," he said. "I was just passing through. If it's alright with you all, I'll be on my way."

The younger boy leaned over on his horse and whispered to his brother, then they both stared back at Randall.

"Is that Mara?" the older boy called, and Randall turned to look at his own horse and then back at the boys. "Are you 'Dead' Randall Dawson?"

"I am," Randall answered, which set both boys off into a frenzy of hoots and hollers.

"I'll be damned," the older one finally said, breathing heavy. "Randall Dawson is right here on the Neches River. Hell, he's right here on our farm."

The younger boy shook his head in amazement.

"You a-huntin' somebody?" he asked Randall.

"Yeah, I suppose I am."

Again the boys were beside themselves.

"Who is it? What'd he do?" they asked excitedly.

"Didn't keep a promise," Randall answered. "An important promise he made to himself and his son."

The boys exchanged glances, then shrugged.

"You been after him long?"

"A few years now."

"Dadgum," the younger boy said.

"Would you mind, Mr. Dawson, signing your name onto something for us? Daddy ain't gonna believe this."

Randall bent down to his satchel to look for the fountain pen while the boys argued over what to have autographed. He pulled and put to the side some papers, a few cans of beans and a tied bag of peppered beef. When at last he emerged with the pen, he found the boys staring at him.

"You after Mr. Crawford?" the older boy asked, confused.

"What's that now?" Randall replied.

The boy pointed to the fading and fragile poster, torn near the edges, creased and covered in time.

Randall's breath caught in his throat. "You know that man?" he asked.

"Sure, that's Mr. Crawford. He worked the camp down in Alto for a bit. Used to come up on trade days with his wife. Real pretty thing."

Randall steadied himself.

"He still there?"

The boy shook his head, and Randall felt his heart sink.

"Think he caught on with an outfit down in Angelina County," the boy said. "You can just follow the river on down and be there in a day or two, I imagine."

Randall shoved his things back into the satchel and unlooped Mara from the mulberry tree and mounted up.

"Thank you, boys," he called, riding hard through the pasture, the cows crying in protest as he raced by them.

"Wait," one of the boys called after him. "What about signing your name?"

He felt Mara's strength beneath him, carrying him through the fields and forests. He stopped to give her food and water and rest but took none of these things for himself. He was a man long lost having finally remembered his purpose and he survived on that purpose alone.

"We found him, Harry," he said aloud.

43

I paid for the horse with my own money, and because of that I called her my own, and I named her Gracie. Together we rode out to the big lake near Manning and rode the dirt trails around it. Sophia's aunt from Piedras Negras had come up a month past and was waiting on the baby like everyone else, and at the kitchen table she'd smiled with her coffee in one hand and a cigarette in the other and I'd told her Sophia was sleeping.

I was riding just to ride. Watching the morning. Squirrels ran along the trail with all the urgency of life and death and then froze solid for a heartbeat and quit the path, fleeing into the woods with some new destination in mind, or maybe an old one, just a new way of getting there. The trees reminded me of my childhood in the rim country, but that was a place from long ago—a place purposely forgotten, buried and rebuilt upon.

I traced the west side of the water and sat Gracie near a low bluff and watched the sunlight turn the surface of the lake to diamonds. The azalea was in bloom and the honeysuckle made sweet the thick air, and I could've sat forever.

The timber work was hard and that's what I liked most about it. It was hard and honest and at the end of the day I was exhausted and happy. I used the name Crawford, like Shelby had said, and no one looked twice.

I suspected I wasn't the only man in the logging camps trying to hide. It was difficult in the beginning. The camps would move and the conditions were raw and unforgiving and I didn't like leaving Sophia in the scum and squalor of the tent towns near the work sites. My hands bled from the saws and axes and the felling of trees was only a portion of the job. We hoisted and loaded logs and drove mules and horses and worked some in the river, everything flowing south to Beaumont.

In less than three years' time we'd cleared more tracts than had been cut in a hundred years. The logging industry was booming and a permanent town was set up in Angelina County near the Manning sawmill. Mr. Manning, some old boy out of Monroe, Louisiana, had built one of the first steam-powered sawmills in East Texas back in the '80s, and the Carter-Kelly Lumber Company took it over a few years back and moved all us hands down into the deep pines. Once the railroad connected through to Huntington there was more work than we knew what to do with. More than seven hundred people settled in Manning, with a post office and a schoolhouse and everything me and Sophia could want.

We built a two-room cabin between the mill and the lake on a little parcel I leased from Mr. Crain. There was a living room and a kitchen in the front, separated by a piped stove, and a bedroom in back. Sophia didn't have to sleep in a timber tent, and I came home to a warm house with a sturdy roof.

Some nights I woke shaking and sweating and Sophia would hold me and whisper to me and the ghosts would dissipate and she'd hold her hand over my heart.

She had saved me—if not my soul, then certainly my life. And now there would be a new life to shape and shelter, and perhaps we could right the wrongs visited upon us as children. The building and rebuilding of the world hinges on our ability to correct our mistakes rather than continue them, passing them down as heirlooms or birthrights so that each generation may be as tainted and broken as the last.

The light leapt through the trees and danced across the pine needles, led by the slow swaying of the wind. A crane swooped past and settled into an effortless gliding just above the water. I heard something moving down the ridge and dismounted and squatted and watched a velveted buck cautiously drink from a narrow stream.

He raised his head and looked across the water and then behind him and then drank for a short while before checking the world again. After he'd had his fill he climbed back up the sloping bank and paused at the sight of Gracie and me. I stayed squatted. We looked at one another and I could see him breathing, heavy and uncertain. I was foreign to him. Some two-footed god come to kill, as all gods do. And it occurred to me nature's obsession with death—the frailty with which most all animals view their own life, and why not? They have no concept of life, no awareness. They know only death, and death is always coming.

It's a terrifying thought, that when we close our eyes there's nothing waiting, and after working so hard on being human it turns out we're just that—and that means goodbye. But we don't think of it that way—we can't—and somehow the mystery of the world was solved at least once, on that day when our minds and souls and all our gods got together and said we wouldn't think of it, lest we be driven mad by the knowledge of our thought.

The buck stiffened, looking past me into the road, then bounded away through the pines. Gracie shook her head as a rider approached. He rode a great white Arabian at a slow walk. I held up my hand and he tipped his cap and put the big horse off the trail in my direction. As he approached, I felt something familiar wash over me, the way an old man's mind might remember a dream he once had and call it real. And what are dreams if not memories of something, lived or desired, broken or whole.

I had touched my dream, pressed upon it with my lips and held it in my arms. This thing I believed could never happen then did, and in the end there were no storms or dark skies or moments of panic. Only a fleeting thought of wanting to stay in this dream a while longer, a wish to not be woken.

The man came closer and I breathed in the air around me and looked up through the canopy of limbs and squinted my eyes at the sun.

"Sophia," I said.

EPILOGUE

The boy sat away from the other men at the bar. He held open a dime novel and studied it with the intensity of a doctor midsurgery. There was nervous and excited talk about the revolution near the border. Some men had taken to carrying stools to the river and watching the fighting as if it were theater. Others worried for their ranches and their horses and their cattle. None seemed to worry for the future of Mexico.

There was talk of growing unrest in Europe, talk of weather, drought or floods or both, and talk of women—always women. The boy paid no mind to any of it. He just sat and read and waved away the bartender each time the man approached.

"You doing alright, Thomas?" a man called to him.

The boy nodded.

"Kid lost his father to a horse kick," the man explained to his companions. "Momma ran off with some card dealer. Shame, too, Thomas is a bright boy. Also been a dead aim since he was ten. I saw him shoot nine cans with six bullets."

"The hell you did," one of the men said and the argument ensued and devolved and life carried on as it often does.

An old man, shadowed by a dark coat, finished his beer and rose from the corner of the room. He had an air about him that the other men found discomforting. He walked with a limp and there were scars about his hands and face and his boots landed heavy before him and to the end of the bar, where the boy was perched upon his stool. The old man ran his hand through his beard, then slicked back his thinning hair.

"Son," he said, smiling at the boy. "Have you ever heard the story of Lightning?"

ACKNOWLEDGMENTS

I would like to thank everyone in the Blackstone Publishing family, including Josh Stanton, Rick Bleiweiss, Josie Woodbridge, Jeff Yamaguchi, Lauren Maturo, Greg Boguslawski, Megan Wahrenbrock, and Mandy Earles. You all helped make this book better than it would've been anywhere else.

Tremendous thanks to my agent, Mark Gottlieb, and the entire team at Trident Media Group. Mark, you were the first person to read the book, and the person most responsible for making sure this story was able to be told. I am forever in your debt.

To my incredibly talented editor, Peggy Hageman, thank you for understanding what I wanted the book to be and helping me take it there. You are a joy to work with.

Thank you to Michael Krohn. Your attention to detail is unmatched, and this book is so incredibly fortunate to have had your touch.

To Kathryn English, thank you for designing a book cover so perfectly commiserate with the world these characters have to live in. I will treasure your work, always.

Thank you to Coy and Dorinda Wade. Without you I wouldn't be me.

Thank you to Luke Calhoun, my best friend and brother. I'll see you at the Astrodome.

Thanks to Stacy Faison for being such a wonderfully cool person, and a great friend.

Thank you to Jimmy and Kathy Strassner for all the SBNOL moments you've given me.

Thank you to Julie and Andrew Landrum for being free spirits for life.

Thanks to family: the Cains, the Hassells, the Ricks, the Stephensons, and Nina Wade.

And to friends: the Byler family, the Cobb family, the Havard family, Denise Hoepfner, Dr. Derrick Holland, Jenny Klein, the Powell family, and the Stone family.

To David and Cheryl Calhoun, thank you for letting me be a part of your family.

Thank you to Trent and Nickie Ashby for your kindness and generosity.

Thanks to Roy Knight and Scott Riling, two of the best men I know, for your guidance and friendship.

Thank you to Dr. Eric Wiedmann of South Austin Medical Clinic for all you've done for me and the Austin community.

Thanks to Becka Oliver, Michael Noll, and everyone at the Writers' League of Texas.

Thank you to the Austin writing community: Owen, Felix, and Seth at One Page Salon; Sam and Spencer at Chicon Street Poets; Oscar, Tom, Janet, May, and so many other talented folks who took me in and made me feel like I belonged.

Thank you to Joe Lansdale for telling me to put my ass in a chair and write every day.

Thanks to those who are gone but left a lasting impression: Professor Perry Carter, James Edward Wade, Terry Lamon, and John Mitchell.

Thank you to Betty the Bullet, our trusted travel trailer, for all the miles and all the memories.

Thank you to Bronn and Paris. We miss you always.

And thank you to Jordan, my life partner and greatest love. You made me do this, and I can never thank you or love you enough.